THE POSSESSORS

**WILDSIDE PRESS BOOKS
BY JOHN CHRISTOPHER**

The Little People
The Possessors
The Twenty-Second Century
A Wrinkle in the Skin
The Year of the Comet

THE POSSESSORS
JOHN CHRISTOPHER

COSMOS BOOKS
An Imprint of Wildside Press
New Jersey • New York • California • Ohio

THE POSSESSORS

First Cosmos Books edition: December, 2000

ISBN: 1-58715-237-1

The Possessors had a long memory, but not long enough to encompass their origins. At one time, it seemed likely, they had had a separate life, but for aeons which were now uncountable their life had been bound up with the—to them— evanescent lives of the Possessed. Without them, they could not act or think, but through them they were the masters of this cold world. They raised cities above the ice, spun on strange sailing craft across the vast deserts of snow, conquered at last the chill cloudy skies. All this they did, living in the bodies of the Possessed, at once united with them and remote from their brutishness. It was not that they despised their hosts who were their slaves; in a way, and insofar as the term had any meaning in their experience, they were fond of them. When the disaster came, they would have saved them if they could.

With a longer warning, it might have been possible. Already their rockets had reached the planet's two moons, had probed toward the three other worlds that made up the family of this sun. A century would have been enough, even fifty years. But the facts were clear, the extrapolation certain. In less than ten years their sun would explode, turn nova, increase in size until the planet's very orbit lay inside its flame and fury. There was no way of saving the Possessed from their fate.

For themselves, though, there was a chance; or rather for the spores which were their children. A small chance, but a chance. The metal arks were built by the patient dextrous hands of the Possessed, set up on launching sites, prepared and made ready. And in due course they watched, Possessors and Possessed, as fire broke out beneath them, lifting them, forcing them up into the pale windy skies. Already it was warmer, and the sun's heat had begun to melt the planet's crust of ice. The Possessors knew that the end was not far off.

But the spores, in their steel cocoons, were safe for the moment in the cold deeps of space. Most, in the end, would perish. Perhaps all would. But some might survive. Somewhere, in the unimaginable future, on some inconceivably distant world, the Possessors might live again.

There was neither time nor distance nor sentience: merely life, suspended. As, over thousands of years, their fates took them, they were unaware of death. It was almost always the same—the effortless fall through the mesh of a new solar system, faster and faster until the ship, already melting, plunged into the sun. This end, as the Possessors had known, was the one the probabilities overwhelmingly favored.

But the ships had been launched in their hundreds, and there was a chance that some might fare better. Three did. Three were caught in the lesser gravitational fields of planets, and plunged into air, not flame. And when they did, the automatic control worked as the Possessors had planned. Long before the metal of the capsule began to glow with friction from the atmosphere, the spores were ejected. And floated down, like bubbles.

One was a world of water, another of fiery scorching desert. The bubbles survived a little longer in the first than the second, but in either case not long. The third world was less homogeneous than the other two.

They drifted down through the thickening air to many different places. Some landed in water, some in desert heat. They fell in jungle and on grassland, among rocks and on fertile meadows. The results were the same. One dropped in front of a child, brown, naked, sitting on his haunches and playing with a primitive wooden toy. The child watched, stretched a hand out, drew back and whimpered as the balloon, before his eyes, burst and dissolved into nothingness. Hours later, only one spore survived.

It lay where it had fallen, in a crevice high up on a mountain. There was snow all around, and fresh snow seeping out of a steely sky. As time passed, the snow buried the spore. It lay there, protected, insentient but alive, throughout the winter.

The spring and summer brought a thaw. Ice and snow were melted, to flow in small bright rivulets down the mountainside. But not all the snow melted. The glaciers were advancing again, slowly, barely perceptibly, moving forward in another stage of their age-long dance. Winters were a little colder, summers a shade less warm. Year by year, the snow piled thicker, heavier, on the buried spore. The pressure did it no harm. It lay in its cold protective prison, mindlessly waiting.

And in time the glaciers retreated again. The snow blanket thinned, taking one decade with the next. There were stresses and strains, the shift and crunch of pressures that had been stabilized and now once more were unequal. Ice cracked, snow began to slide. After long long years of stasis, suddenly there was motion.

I

There were two intermediate stations on the way up to Nidenhaut, where the rack-and-pinion railway came to a halt at a covered-in station festooned with icicles. They had crossed the snow line a few hundred yards beyond the second stop; in half an hour they had climbed two thousand feet from the valley floor, itself a thousand feet above sea level. Douglas Poole hefted his bag down onto the platform, and carried it out past the barrier. Sunlight, reflected from snow, dazzled him. He was blinking and could not, at first, see much of the person who addressed him.

"Mr. Poole, is it? George Hamilton."

The voice had the clipped assurance of an ex-R.A.F. accent. A hand was extended, and he took it. The grip was firm. As his eyes grew accustomed to the light, he saw that the rest of the appearance fitted: a lean large-boned man, with some puffiness about the face and a bristling mustache, black flecked with white. He was wearing ski pants, a blue anorak, and a black astrakhan hat squarely on his head.

"Yes," he said, "I'm Poole. I didn't expect to be met, though. I didn't say which train I would be coming on."

"Most people who take the morning flight to Geneva wind up on this one. Actually, I wasn't meeting you specifically. There's some stuff on board for us—meat and veg. It'll take them a quarter of an hour to unload it. Feel like a noggin while we wait?"

Douglas hesitated for a moment. When he had looked at his watch, as the train was pulling into the station, the time had been ten minutes short of four o'clock. After all, though, he was on holiday.

"That'll be fine," he said.

Hamilton led the way past a Volkswagen Minibus, with chained wheels and a dented offside wing, to the Buffet de la Gare. Douglas had a glimpse of Nidenhaut itself, a single street with wooden buildings on either side, shops, a couple of hotels. The mountain slope stretched away above it to a summit sharp and white against blue sky. They went up steps, and turned right onto a terrace set out with tables and chairs, the tables topped with umbrellas advertising Campari and Pepsi-Cola. It jutted over the railway line, and looked across the valley to the southern peaks. Douglas recognized the serrated crest of the Dent du Midi.

"You drink beer?" Douglas nodded. Hamilton spoke to a waiter, too fast for Douglas's halting French to follow him. "Not a bad view, this."

"Very impressive."

"They drive you bloody mad at times, these mountains, but it's pretty fine, really. What sort of flight did you have?"

"Uneventful."

"The best kind. I stick to train and boat. I'm scared of the other stuff. You're staying a fortnight with us, that right?"

"Yes."

"I never know. Mandy keeps the lists. Have you done much skiing?"

"Practically none. A couple of weeks during my National Service. We were stationed in Austria. Nothing since then."

"We've got some nice easy slopes for you. And some other beginners so you won't get shown up too badly. It's a good crowd in at the moment. You'll like them."

He said politely, "I'm sure I will."

The drinks were brought out. There was a slight breeze coming down off the snow, but it was hot in the sun. The beer was welcome. It was very pale in color, but surprisingly full-bodied.

"They make a strong beer in these parts," he said.

Hamilton grinned. "It's better with a shot of cognac, don't you think? A bit thin on its own."

"Well," he said, "thanks for the warning."

"We like to turn the thing into a sort of family party, up at the chalet," Hamilton said. "With only a few guests, and pretty well isolated, one more or less has to. I'll tell you whom you'll be meeting. The Deepings, to start with. He's in business —something to do with textiles. They've got a couple of boys with them, but they're no trouble."

Douglas shook his head. "I don't mind children."

"Nor do I, provided they behave themselves. Anyway, the Deepings are only staying a couple more days. Then we have the Graingers. He's a surgeon, plastic type. Puts on new noses, lifts the sagging breast. Remarkably cheerful with it. And she's a sweetie. The other two are sisters. A Mrs. Winchmore, and a Miss Blackstone. But the Mrs. is a widow. Very pleasant, on the quiet side. The younger one's got plenty of life, though. A good crew, all round."

"Yes."

Hamilton finished his drink, and exhaled heavily. "As I

say, we run this show for coziness. It works, most of the time."

"I'm sure it does, Mr. Hamilton."

"George. George and Mandy." His smile was at once cheerful and peremptory. "We insist on that."

"Of course. I'm Douglas."

He was inwardly dubious about this crash-program approach to familiarity, and wondered for a moment if the whole thing had not been a mistake. He had accepted the need, the urgent need, for a break, but he could have chosen something else. A cruise, perhaps, on a large ship where one could get away from people if one wanted to. But he was here. He would have to make the best of it.

"Right," Hamilton said. "They should have the stuff off by now. We'll take off, if you're ready."

The speed with which Hamilton drove the Minibus with chains over the snow-packed road would not, Douglas felt, do his tires any good. It did not do much for his own peace of mind, either. Once out of the village, the road—track, rather —followed a shoulder of the mountain, nowhere very wide and in places alarmingly narrow. The drop was on Hamilton's side. Douglas had occasional startling glimpses past him of the valley floor, the Rhone a tiny rivulet wandering through minuscule fields. The car rocked, and he put his hand on the corner of his seat to steady himself.

"You're all right on the way up," Hamilton said cheerfully, "as long as you take it steady all the way. It's going down that's tricky. Chap went over the edge, the year before we took over. They fished him and the car out of a gully, about eight hundred feet below. Identification a bit difficult in both cases."

"How long have you been here?"

"Three years." He took a hand off the wheel to slap his chest. "And the old lungs have been clear for two. I used to whistle like a flute."

The road curved sharply, and at the same time narrowed dramatically. There was a rock overhang on the right, some snow-covered marker posts on the left; after that, a sickening emptiness. Douglas felt the rear of the car break away as the back tires lost adhesion. Only for a moment. Hamilton corrected expertly and confidently. But he had not, Douglas felt with some resentment, come on holiday to Switzerland in order to be scared out of his wits.

"Can't you take it steady at a slightly slower speed?" he asked.

Hamilton did not reply at once. He was revving the car even harder up a steeper stretch of road. He said, when he had eased off, "You've got to have a run at that one. Otherwise you can get stuck, even with chains. That corner back there is a bloody nuisance altogether. There was a landslip eighteen months ago which it took a week to dig out. Cost us a packet."

"So there are some disadvantages to living in the Alps."

The road began to level out, and Hamilton slackened speed.

"Plenty," he said. "We're nearly there now."

They swung around another corner, and Douglas saw the house. It was built high up in a bowl that some geological cataclysm, long ago, had scooped out of the mountainside. The road they were on zig-zagged up to it. There was no sign of a road beyond.

"You're at the end of the line, then?" Douglas said.

"In winter, we are. In summer they drive cattle higher up. There are a couple of herdsmen's huts, and a weekend chalet. All shut up now, of course."

It was a typical Swiss chalet, built in wood, with a wide terrace balcony on the first floor and smaller individual balconies on the two floors above. There were a couple of outhouses to one side, and a vast pile of cut logs stacked between them and the chalet. Smoke drifted up from a couple of the

14

chimneys, dark against the white hillside which framed the house. The place had a solid, reassuringly comfortable look. On an easy slope, about a hundred yards from the chalet, four people were skiing. Douglas was relieved to see that they were making a poor job of it.

The car rattled to a halt in front of the chalet, and he saw that the main entrance was to one side and higher up. The part immediately in front of them was by way of being a basement—the house had been built on a slope. As he got out of the Minibus, a door opened, and a man came out, gaunt-looking, in his sixties, wearing a blue apron.

"Peter," Hamilton said. He pronounced the name in the German fashion. "Look after Mr. Poole's luggage." He turned to Douglas. "Come in, and we'll see about getting you warmed up."

They went up stone steps, snow-covered but sanded. The front door was at the top, a heavy wooden affair, with narrow double-glazed windows on either side. It gave onto a tiny lobby, and a second equally massive door. Hamilton pushed it open, and motioned Douglas to go in. The hall was dim, but warm and smelling pleasantly of spices. Hamilton followed him.

"Mandy!" he called. "New arrival. Come and check him in."

By the time they went in for supper, he had got the hang of the house and knew a little of the people in it. His own room was one of three on the first level (taking the main entrance as ground level) and was a pleasant, simply furnished chamber, pine-paneled and with paintings of mountains on the walls. It had a washbasin, a radiator, and double-glazed French windows leading to one of the balconies he had seen from below. The view from it was impressive. The house looked southwest and across the valley to the peaks opposite. Hamilton had identified two of them for him as Grammont and the Cornettes de Bise. Looking right, one saw the lake, still and blue and distant. He had watched one of the steamers crawling toward Geneva.

On the ground floor, immediately to the right of the entrance lobby, there was a small room which was a combination smoking room and bar. Beyond that were the salon and the dining room, both with access to the veranda. They were furnished simply, but in good taste. In the dining room there was a long black oak refectory table, around which the Hamiltons seated themselves and their guests. Hamilton took the head of the table nearest to the salon, and his wife faced him at the other end. Douglas sat between the two married ladies, Ruth Deeping and Elizabeth Grainger. The former was redheaded and seemed excitable, with a thin face prematurely lined—he judged her to be in her late thirties—and showing signs of strain, but attractive when she smiled. Elizabeth Grainger, the surgeon's wife, was that rare thing, a genuine beauty. She was dark, rather above average height, her features lovely in themselves and well proportioned. She carried herself with grace, and with the assurance of a woman who has never doubted her looks, nor their impression on others. She did not say much, but spoke in a clear, confident voice.

Immediately opposite him were Leonard Deeping, and Jane Winchmore, the widow. Deeping was in his middle forties, a stocky jowling man with grizzled hair set in a careful wave, and a natty taste in dress. He had changed into a dark blue-check suit and wore a red silk waistcoat under it. Although he lived and carried on his business in London, he had a pronounced north-country accent—Lancashire probably. A bit dull, Douglas thought, and a bit of a trickster.

Jane Winchmore had been widowed early—she could scarcely be thirty. Her best feature was her hair, which was thick silky gold, cut short, but she had the kind of features that went well with it: high Slavonic cheekbones, a generous mouth. When she smiled, he saw that she had excellent teeth. She did not smile much, though. She gave the impression of listening to another conversation, watching another scene.

Her sister, sitting between Deeping and Hamilton, was altogether different, both in appearance and manner. She was slighter, very dark, reminding him of pictures of Princess Margaret. She had quite striking blue eyes, which she used to effect. She was a good deal younger than her sister, much the youngest present, and she chattered continually. Deeping and Hamilton competed amiably for her attention. She showed every sign of enjoying this, but Douglas noticed that once or twice she glanced covertly in his direction. A girl, he decided, who would be reluctant to accept that one could have too much of a good thing.

The final member of the party was Selby Grainger, the surgeon. He sat at Mandy Hamilton's right hand. He seemed slight in comparison with his statuesque wife, but was fractionally taller than she was. He had a lean, mobile, somewhat delicate face. He was about Deeping's age, but his manner was younger, volatile. He used his hands when he talked; they were finer, more delicate, than one would have expected a surgeon's hands to be. But a plastic surgeon, Douglas remembered; not the same need for brute strength, presumably. He was intelligent, extrovert, a man with charm, who knew how to use it.

The meal, which apparently had been cooked by Mandy Hamilton herself, was served by the little French Swiss girl, Marie, who, with the elderly Peter, constituted the domestic staff. It was wholesome, without being outstanding: a thick vegetable soup, followed by a pot roast, and a blueberry pie with ice cream. Mandy had been something of a surprise. He had not expected someone so distinctly British as Hamilton to have an American wife. She was a few years younger than he was, a woman who had been good-looking but whose features had coarsened. Her voice, though, was low, warm, pleasantly accented.

Coffee was served in the salon, a large room, pine-paneled like the rest, well supplied with easy chairs. The doors to the veranda were closed, the curtains drawn against the night. There was a baby grand piano in one corner, a radio in the other. There was also a television aerial plug but, Douglas was pleased to notice, no television set. He waited until the others had taken what were presumably their usual seats, and found himself a chair on the outskirts of the group. Hamilton, who had been out seeing to something, came back soon after Marie had brought the coffee in, and sat by him.

"Grub to your liking?" he asked.

"Very much so."

The confirmation was taken for granted. Hamilton nodded.

"Best cook I've ever met. She's wasted here. What do you feel like doing this evening?"

"Nothing in particular."

"Not much in the way of night-spottery in these parts, of course, but there is a place in the village where you can drink and dance. What they call dancing nowadays. Reason I mention it is, I don't generally go down myself, but the old bus is at the disposal of guests who want to."

Douglas remembered the drive up, and that in daylight.

"I don't think so. Thanks all the same."

"The Graingers will be going down, and Diana with them. I didn't know whether you wanted to make up a four."

He had a moment of extreme resentment. He could scarcely refuse to provide an escort for the girl, and he felt that Hamilton, knowing this, was forcing the issue unwarrantably. There was a limit, surely, to treating one's guests as members of the family. He said, with some stiffness, "In that case, of course, I'll be delighted."

"Only if you were keen yourself," Hamilton said. "If you did go, I doubt if you'd see the girl for more than ten minutes after you got down to the village. She's gathered in at least two local boy friends already."

Hamilton was grinning. Douglas said, with relief, "Then I'll . . ."

"Forget it. Now, if you're staying up here . . . Jane prefers a quiet read. The Deepings play bridge, and Mandy and I have been making up a four with them. She'd be glad to drop out if you feel like playing—all sorts of things that need doing, you know."

"I think I would prefer to read, too. Tonight, anyway."

"Fair enough," Hamilton said cheerfully. "Want anything with that coffee?"

"I wouldn't mind a brandy."

"Coming up."

When the Graingers and Diana had gone, a table was set up for bridge. Douglas was conscious of being left with Jane Winchmore. He had brought a book down, but could hardly start reading until she was similarly occupied. She probably felt the same way. They found themselves talking, a little awkwardly.

She had lived, it appeared, in Oxfordshire until her husband died, and had since sold the place and been living in hotels. Her sister had talked her into this holiday. Diana had favored St. Moritz, and they had compromised on Nidenhaut. She had been recommended to the Hamiltons by friends of a friend.

"I saw their advertisement," Douglas said, "in one of the weeklies. I wanted a break, but I'm not very good at being abroad, so the idea of an English place appealed."

"Yes." There was a pause, awkwardness returning. "What do you do at home, Mr. Poole?"

"I'm a solicitor," he told her. "We have a practice in Winchester. Poole, Stephens and Willoughby, but the placing is misleading. The first Poole was my uncle."

"And you like the law?"

"I suppose so. I haven't given myself much chance to think about it. I joined the firm direct from school, and I've been with it ever since." He hesitated. "I'm contented, I would say."

The answer, he reflected, was true enough. He had liked his work, and his work had been a refuge. Until lately, at least. And the fact that it did not help him as much as it had once done was no indictment of his occupation. It would have been the same with any.

Shortly afterward she excused herself, pleading tiredness, and he was able to settle down with his book. A pleasant woman, he thought, and a sensible one, not least in bringing a graceful end to a pointless conversation. Though her excuse might well be valid: she did look tired. He hoped, with detached sympathy, that she would sleep well, that she was not a fellow victim of the long empty hours of night.

When he awoke, he glanced at his watch, and saw by the luminous dial that it was a little before three. He was wide awake and knew, from past experience, that hours of wakefulness lay ahead. He snapped on the bedside light. The room was all around him, different in its details, but the same lonely cell he had left behind. The oil painting of the Matterhorn, seen for the first time the previous afternoon, was already agonizingly familiar.

It was warm, stuffy almost, with the windows closed and the radiator full on. He put on his dressing gown, opened the French windows, and stepped out onto the small balcony. There was no wind, but it was sharply, bitterly cold. The moon was absent from the sky, but starlight glimmered brightly on the snow. He almost thought he could see the slopes of the mountains on the other side of the valley, but that was probably a trick of vision. Far down and to the right, he did see something, a cluster of lights. A village, probably, but where? On the shore of the lake, perhaps. He would identify it in the morning.

It was too cold to stay out; he went in, closing the windows behind him. His bookmark, he saw with some concern, was not far from the end of the book. He had a couple of others with him, but he had better be careful until he knew what sort of reading supply there was locally. He had thought of bringing more books, but the idea had seemed a weakness, like taking one's umbrella when one has been assured the day will be fine. And most desperately wants to believe it.

He got back into bed, and picked up the book from the bedside table.

It was about six when he drifted off to sleep. He awoke muzzily when tea was brought to him at eight o'clock, and woke again at quarter past nine to find it cold and milk-scummed beside him. Breakfast, he remembered, was served until nine thirty, except by arrangement. He did not feel much like eating, but he was anxious to conform to the domestic arrangements, particularly when the staff was so small. He washed quickly, combed his hair, and went down in his dressing gown. Jane Winchmore was the only person at the dining table.

He said, "Good morning. I said I would see you at breakfast, but it's been a close-run thing."

She smiled. "The others are all out doing healthy invigorating things in the snow. I'm afraid I'm lazy. And I've got into the habit of dawdling over meals."

Mandy Hamilton came in, and asked him if he would have porridge, corn flakes, or fruit juice, and if bacon and eggs would do to follow. He realized suddenly that he was hungry, very hungry, and asked for porridge.

Jane Winchmore brought out a cigarette. "Do you mind? I can go into the salon."

"No, please stay." He felt for his lighter, and tapped the empty pocket of his dressing gown. "I'm afraid I can't offer you a light."

"It's all right. I have one."

She lit it clumsily; he had an impression that she had not been smoking for very long.

He said, "Do the Hamiltons have any kind of library, do you know? I doubt if I've brought enough books with me."

"Over there."

She pointed through the connecting door to the salon. There was quite a large bookcase against one wall. He had been sitting opposite it the night before, but by some quirk it had failed to register.

He laughed. "I must be going blind."

She said, "A mixed bag, of course. But if you run short, I've got a few in my room. Only novels, I'm afraid."

"I don't despise novels. Though I prefer biographies."

"Yes," she said, considering, "I would have thought you might."

She excused herself when his bacon and eggs arrived. He had a large meal, finishing off with several pieces of toast and marmalade, and went up to dress and shave with a pleasant sense of fullness. When he came down again, he met Hamilton at the foot of the stairs, in ski kit, with a weird balaclava-type hat, his face glowing from physical exertion.

"You've made it, then!" he said. "Good boy. Had your breakfast?"

"Yes, thanks."

"Jolly good. Then we'll get cracking."

Hamilton fitted him up, and took him outside. He said, "Don't want to waste a morning like this." It was perfect, in fact, without even the scattered clouds of the previous day.

Blue and white, both dazzling in their brightness, and the smudged green of fields very far below. "The glass isn't too promising."

"Bad weather on the way? It looks settled."

Hamilton shrugged. "We could do with a bit more snow. It's thinner this year than I've known it."

He gave Douglas some elementary tuition, and left him to get on with things, coming back from time to time to point out his mistakes and offer cheer. The cheer was badly needed; in the afternoon he was still trying baby runs down the small saucerlike depression just in front of the house, and still falling over half the time. After an hour of this second stint he gave it up, had a bath and changed, and settled down on the veranda to sun-bathe and watch the others.

Hamilton had taken the Graingers and Diana down to the village that morning, from where they could get onto one of the *pistes* provided with a ski lift. The Deepings and Jane had preferred to make their falls in relative seclusion, near the chalet, but they were still, he saw, a great deal better than he was. And the Deeping children were coming on well. They were boys of eight and ten, Andy and Stephen, the former small, quick, deft and talkative, the older boy quieter and more withdrawn in manner, physically bigger beyond what one would have expected from the two-year difference, dark and coarse-grained where the other was finely blond. At one point, following an argument, Douglas saw the younger boy trip his brother, and they fell scuffling in the snow. The fact that Ruth Deeping, having missed the beginning of the incident, rounded immediately on the elder, confirmed an impression he had formed that she was biased in favor of her second son. As one who had himself been an unfavored son against a favored daughter, Douglas sympathized with Stephen.

Over tea, he found himself trapped by Leonard Deeping, who asked him interminable questions about his work, where he lived, and so on, and did not seem at all troubled by the shortness of Douglas's replies. His voice was slow, carefully articulated, the consciously solid accent of the blunt reliable northerner. When he tired of quizzing Douglas, he turned to himself, apparently an even more engrossing subject. He was handling the London end of a Lancashire textile firm, but Douglas had a feeling that there might be more to it than that. At any rate, he was open about the fact that he had done very well over the past few years. He was thinking of retiring early; somewhere with a low tax rate. He thought of the Isle of Man, being from that part of the world, but his wife would prefer something warmer. Jersey, perhaps. Douglas let it wash over him, and stared across the valley at the distant snowy peaks. Cloud was building up around them, white and fluffy still, but very thick. The bad weather Hamilton had said was forecast, presumably.

Helping himself to a buttered scone, Deeping said, "They look after you all right, George and Mandy. It's a waste of money, I reckon, to go to one of those big places, especially with kids. You're paying for lounges and writing rooms and orchestras, and all sorts of stuff you don't use. No sense in throwing money away."

"No."

"Like schooling. I could well have afforded to pay for both lads, but they ought to get scholarships to a decent Grammar. With coaching, they ought—I don't mind paying for that. And Ruth wouldn't stand for them being away at school."

She was sitting at the far end of the veranda. The two boys were beside her, but Andy nearer to her, leaning against her legs.

Deeping said, "The Graingers have got a couple, too, you know. Boy and a girl. At boarding schools." He shook his head. "No, I can't see Ruth standing for it."

"Isn't it term time for your boys?" Douglas asked.

Deeping grinned and winked. "Educational tour. Well, isn't it? I know their headmaster. We should have come out in the Christmas holidays, but there was a spot of business on that couldn't wait. And it paid for the holiday, I might say."

"Good for you," Douglas said politely, and Deeping accepted the tribute with a nod.

Hamilton took the Minibus down to pick up the party from the village just before six. By that time, clouds had gathered on this side of the valley, and a bitterly cold wind had risen. The landscape turned grim and forbidding in the deepening twilight. But it was cheerful inside, with the curtains drawn and logs burning on the open fire in the salon. Deeping was there, but quiet, poring over the City page of the *Daily Telegraph* which Hamilton had brought up on his earlier trip. Jane Winchmore, like himself, was reading a book. Ruth Deeping was supervising baths for the children. Douglas felt pleasantly tired and at ease. With any luck, he thought, he would sleep well that night.

The others returning from Nidenhaut brought the news that snow had begun to fall. Grainger went up to the fire, rubbing his hands. "Warm in here, at least." He straightened up, and looked at Douglas, smiling. "What sort of a day have you had?"

"Rise and fall. Equally balanced, but plenty of them."

He grinned. "Yes, it's a bad stage. Very damaging to the ego. Nothing like alcohol as balm for the spiritual bruises. Don't I hear George opening things up next door?" He glanced at his wife. "How about it, sweetheart?"

She shook her head slowly; not from any reluctance, Douglas felt, but because all her physical motions were slow and graceful. She said, "I'm going up to bathe and change."

"Diana, Jane? Time for a quick one."

The younger woman looked as though she would not have

minded being persuaded, but her sister refused for both of them and carried her off. Grainger shrugged at Douglas.

"Well, that leaves us." He paid no attention to Deeping, who was still immersed in the Closing Prices. "I trust I can talk you into it."

In the next room, Hamilton was behind the bar and had already set himself up a large whisky and soda. Pouring drinks for the others, he said, "Taking the bus down tonight, Selby?"

The curtains were not drawn here. Grainger glanced out of the window; snow was falling thickly and whirling about in the wind. He lifted his drink.

"Cheers. Not unless that lot clears up pretty smartly."

"You'll be lucky," Hamilton told him. "Have a look at the glass. It's setting in dirty."

"Have to be the dicepot, in that case." Grainger yawned. "I can forgo the dancing very well. I've had as much exercise as I want today."

By the time supper was over, the wind was howling around the chalet, and Hamilton reported that snow was beginning to drift against the front door. There could be no question of going down to Nidenhaut; while the storm lasted, they were isolated here. The thought was not an unpleasant one. They were warm and sheltered, well supplied with food and drink. The noise of the wind only emphasized their comfort.

The Deepings suggested bridge again, and Mandy Hamilton and Jane made up the four. Douglas was cajoled by Grainger into playing Liar Dice, a game he had not encountered before. He had intended to withdraw at a fairly early hour and go to bed, but his tentative attempt, when the bridge school ended at half past ten, was firmly overruled by Grainger.

"Can't break things up at this stage, Douglas. Not after winning the last kitty."

They stopped playing a little before one, and then only through Elizabeth Grainger's insistence. In his room, Douglas reflected that he had enjoyed the evening, had drunk a lot of whisky but not, he thought, too much, and was entirely ready for bed. Fatigue returned, an engulfing wave. He pulled off his clothes, and draped them not very tidily across the chair. The wind screamed outside and from time to time rattled at his windows; but ineffectually, feebly almost. It was not going to keep him awake. He put on his pajamas, climbed into bed, and fell asleep almost right away.

It was not the wind that woke him, either. He was conscious of being awake for some time before he was aware of the steady, deeper roar of the gale outside. He looked at his watch. Half past four. Six hours back it would only be half past ten. Nothing like bedtime for the wife of a British Board of Trade official in New York. What would she be doing? Dancing? The theater? Dining late? And with whom—Robert, or some unknown? An American. Perhaps a Latin American. She had said once, in a joke, that South American men fascinated her. But the jokes, along with everything else, had gone bitter with keeping. Smiling, perhaps, her eyes closing slightly. He turned over restlessly in the bed. The barriers were down again, the past in spate.

2

After she had washed, and brushed her hair, and cleaned her teeth, Mandy Hamilton knelt beside the bed and said her prayers. It was the one religious observance that remained. The nearest church in which she could worship with any meaning was at Montreux, and the journey down there, difficult enough under any circumstances, was out of the question when they had guests in the house.

Her devotions took their usual form. An Our Father, and then a prayer to God to care for those she had known in her life and, in her poor way, loved. The children first, the unvarying pang. At one time she had attempted to see them in her mind as they would be in reality, but she no longer tried to do that. They changed so much at that age, and so quickly. Johnny, who had been five, would be thirteen, the girls young women. So she prayed for them as they had been when she had seen them for the last time: Johnny in his little blue suit, face flushed, blond hair untidy, Lois and Annette in their yellow frocks with the red pockets, brown hair neatly pigtailed, eyes puzzled and unsure. Oh God, she thought, let them be happy.

And John, bitterly hurt for all that armor of complacency —let the hurt be all gone, forgotten. Let him be happy with the new wife, whose face she had seen once in a magazine, oval, thin-lipped, quite pretty. His women always had to be a credit to him. Let the children love her and, please God, let her love them. She prayed for her mother, in the Florida sun, and for her dead father. For all the dead: her two brothers, killed in the war, for Grandfather and Grandmother Hardy. Remembering them, she remembered so many things. The house at Cape Cod, the long summers of sailing and swimming, the toboggan winters, the days of knowing one was safe, and being told that one was beautiful.

The wind, shaking the house, disturbed her reverie. She said the second Our Father, and got into bed. Curled up, she thought of George, of his surprise at finding she said her prayers before bed, of his delight and tenderness. A long time ago, but he was fond of her, and she of him. She hoped he would not stay up too late playing dice. He tired himself without realizing it.

She slept soundly, undisturbed by George when he came to bed, and awoke at six thirty. She lay in the dark, listening to the wind which was still raging outside and to her husband's heavy breathing beside her. This, always, was the hard time, the moment which might have turned to misery if she let it. Above her head, far off and faint, she heard the jingling of Marie's alarm clock. She pressed the switch of her bedside light, but nothing happened. A fuse gone, probably. She pushed the bedclothes back, swung her feet out of bed, and fumbled in the dark in the cabinet. The bottle was in its place, and the glass beside it. She poured out, guessing the amount, and clipped the top back. Then she drank the raw gin quickly, feeling its heat in her throat, the glow in her stomach. Anxiety receded. She had had her usual tot, and there was still some in the glass. But that had not been deliberate, she argued with herself; she just had not been able to see how much she was pouring. She drank the rest and felt better, much better.

Footsteps pattered outside, and there was Marie's voice, whispering.

"Madame?"

Mandy went to the door, and opened it.

"Yes?"

"The light will not work, madame."

"I know. You've got a torch, haven't you?"

"I can't find it."

She sighed with exasperation. The girl was reasonably intelligent and a willing worker, but had an incorrigibly scatterbrained streak. She went to her dressing-table drawer, found her own torch, and brought it to the door.

"Take this, and use it to look for yours. And tell Peter to go down and check the fuses."

When Marie had gone, she found her bedroom slippers and dressing gown. She sat on the edge of the bed. There was not much she could do until she had a light of some kind. She sat there for what seemed quite a long time, listening to the storm, before she reached for the bottle. She was careful as she poured the gin into the glass. Just a little . . . but perhaps rather more than that. She had scarcely poured any. She replaced the top again, and pushed the bottle firmly to the back of the cabinet. She took the drink in sips, rationing herself. Only when she heard Marie returning did she tip the rest back in a gulp.

Marie said, "Your torch, madame."

"Where was yours?"

"Under the bed."

"Did you tell Peter?"

"Yes, madame. He has gone down to see to the fuses."

"Get dressed, then. I'll see you downstairs."

There was a sound from the bed, as George turned over. He said drowsily, "What is it? Anything wrong?"

"Only the fuses. Go to sleep."

He did not answer her, was probably asleep already. So as not to disturb him again, she took her clothes to the bathroom, stood the torch on its end so that some light was reflected from the ceiling, and had her bath quickly. She dressed in the weird half-light, and made her way down to the kitchen. Marie had set her torch up also, and was looking helpless.

"The lamp," Mandy said. "Get one of the lamps out, and light it. You can't do anything like that."

Going down the last flight of stairs, to the basement, she felt a little lightheaded. She would be better after coffee, and she decided she would have some toast this morning, too. Getting up without lights, and with a storm raging outside, required some allowances to be made.

She called to Peter, from the foot of the stairs, "Haven't you found it yet?"

"No." He turned toward her, the light from the torch lighting up the wrinkles of his face, the harsh line of jaw. "It is not here. I have checked the main fuse also. The line must be broken, somewhere outside."

"My God, that's all we needed."

"There was a noise in the night. Avalanche, I think."

"It didn't wake me. Look, get all the lamps out of store, and get them lit. We have plenty of kerosene, don't we? Marie can take one up to each room when she takes the tea, and we can put the rest where they will do the most good." She listened briefly. "It's still blowing hard. We won't have any power till the weather clears. Even if it's a minor break, they won't fix it in this. Plenty of wood inside?"

"Yes." He nodded. "I will see to all that."

31

Marie had a kerosene lamp burning in the kitchen, which made things look a little better. The solid-fuel cooker was made up ready for lighting; she put a match to the paper and heard the comforting roar of combustion. She glanced at the kitchen clock. Five after seven. They would have their cups of tea by eight o'clock, their breakfasts, if they wanted them, by half past.

It meant a long wait for her own coffee and toast. She thought of going to the bar for a small tot and then, putting the thought behind her, got down to the work that needed to be done.

As she had guessed they would, they found the whole business rather exciting. The Graingers, as usual, were the first down of the guests, and they joined George who had already started on his bacon and eggs. He greeted them, and said, "You won't get much skiing done this morning. Or this afternoon, by the look of things. Not at the village, anyway. Even if it clears, I doubt we'll get the bus through."

"A day of relaxation will do me very well," Grainger said. He looked at George's plate. "Breakfast! That was what worried me. I thought you cooked by electricity?"

"We have a solid-fuel stove as a stand-by," Mandy said.

"You're a wonderful woman!" He waltzed exuberantly toward her, planted a cheerful kiss on her cheek. "Good old Mandy."

She accepted the tribute, smiling. She had seen enough of Grainger, during the five days he had been at the chalet, to have formed a view of him: not a lecher, but a man distinctly light with women. The chasteness of this particular salutation was a tribute to her years, not to her virtue.

She said, "The toast may be a little variegated. We've had to improvise a toasting fork."

"Toast made on an open fire!" Grainger said. "Can I come and make my own?"

32

Mandy shook her head. "You'd get in Marie's way, and we can't afford confusion this morning."

"And the light from a paraffin lamp," Grainger went on. "I haven't seen one since I was a boy. They used to have them in the gardener's cottage. I used to make toast there in front of the fire. They had a fork Kendall had made himself from thick copper wire. I used to sit on the hearthrug. It was one of those made of bits of rag—all different colors, in patterns."

Elizabeth Grainger said, "The old nostalgia is working overtime this morning."

George started to butter his toast. "I know just what he means," he said, "rag hearthrug and all. But it wasn't the gardener's cottage. *I* lived in it, with my old gran. And those lamps, quite frankly, were a bloody nuisance—trimming the wicks was one of my jobs."

He was smiling and, she saw, watching the Graingers. It was one of his tricks. He enjoyed seeing if he could produce a reaction; embarrassment he found particularly amusing. She felt herself, as always, warming to it. It was on just such an occasion that he had first stood out to her as a person.

Grainger smiled back imperturbably. "Mrs. Kendall used to let me trim the wicks on her lamps. I must say I enjoyed it. But I suppose there's never much fun in forced labor."

The Deepings came down, and she went into the kitchen to organize the other breakfasts. Peter had been clearing snow away from the front door. He came in, rubbing his hands, and she poured more coffee for him.

"Any sign of the weather clearing?" she asked him.

"It is blowing less hard." He held the cup between his hands to warm them. "I was right about the avalanche. A small slide, maybe three hundred meters west."

She nodded, and then thought about what he had said.

"West? But that wouldn't account for the power line going."

Peter shrugged. "Maybe another slide, as well, between here and the village."

George came into the kitchen, lighting a cigarette. He offered one to her, and she shook her head. He said, "Has anyone tried the telephone yet?"

"I didn't think of that."

"I'll do it."

When he returned, he said, "No joy. We're cut off, all right."

Mandy said, "We'll need to keep the children amused. I think maybe I'll have Marie clear the dining room as soon as breakfast is over, and they can do puzzles or play games in there."

"Fair enough," George said. He found a cup and poured himself coffee. "I'll do a recce as soon as the weather brightens up a bit."

The storm continued, though with diminishing force, during the morning. So far there was no particular sign of boredom among the guests; they seemed content to read, or talk, or merely to look out at the snow. Mandy adapted herself fairly easily to cooking on the solid-fuel stove. For the main course she prepared a casserole of beef, with sweet corn and jacket potatoes. She was a little short of green vegetables; this would have been the day for picking up supplies from Nidenhaut. There were three cabbages, a couple of large cauliflowers, and maybe three kilos of carrots in the cold store. On the other hand, there was a good supply of canned vegetables. Not that there was any cause to worry. Tomorrow, probably, they would be able to get through to Nidenhaut.

It stopped snowing during lunch, and the wind dropped a good deal. George announced his intention of going out to have a look at things.

They were drinking coffee in the salon. Ruth Deeping asked, "Are you taking the car?"

34

Her husband said, amiably contemptuous, "With six feet of snow up against the garage door? I don't know how he'd expect to find the road, either."

She said, "I suppose that was silly. I didn't think."

Grainger cut across her embarrassment. "Are you skiing down, George?"

"Yes."

"Down to the village?"

"If I can make it."

"How about getting back?"

"I'll walk it if necessary," George said. "The exercise wouldn't do me any harm."

Grainger said, "That removes from my mind the vagrant thought that I might volunteer to go with you. Walking up from Nidenhaut through this would do me quite a lot of harm."

Diana got up and walked restlessly to the window. "It really is clearing up," she said. "There's a break in the clouds."

Grainger went and stood beside her. "Where? I can't see any."

"There. Look." She leaned against him, Mandy noticed, while she pointed it out. How pointless it all was, and how sad. "Quite a big break."

"The girl's right," Grainger said. "Enough blue to make a bikini. Half a bikini, anyway. Let's get our skis and do a small local slalom, while George treks for help across the boundless wastes."

Mandy did not have her own coffee until everything had been cleared away and she had seen Marie well started on the dishes. She slipped into the bar while it was filtering. There was no one there; through the window she could see the Deeping children dragging a *luge* up the slope. She unlocked the cupboard, quickly poured herself a gin into the medicine glass she had brought with her, put the bottle back, and locked up again. Then, the need for haste gone, she took the glass over to the window, and looked out, holding it untasted.

The others were skiing farther off. She recognized the Deepings, the Graingers and Diana Blackstone, and Douglas Poole. No sign of Jane Winchmore; she must have gone to her room instead. She sipped from her glass, and felt a wave of affection for them all, for all humanity, whether soaring like a bird or slipping and sliding, falling in ridiculous humiliation. Even someone like Leonard Deeping was not bad, really. To know a little was to understand a little, to understand a little was to forgive all. She was amused at her own thoughts. Why, child, she told herself, you are becoming quite a philosopher. She tipped down the rest of the drink, slipped the glass in the pocket of her apron, and went to get her coffee.

The salon was deserted. It was nice to have the place empty for a moment, to be at peace and alone. She pulled a chair to the window, fixed herself a footstool, put her coffee on the table beside her, and settled down with a book. From time to time she looked up from its pages to the long sloping fields of snow outside, and the faraway peaks. She was surprised, on one occasion of doing this, to see a figure toiling upward: George returning. She looked at her watch. He had not been gone more than three quarters of an hour.

Mandy went to the door to meet him. He took his skis off and stacked them and scraped snow off his boots.

"What's it like?" she asked him.

"Half the bloody mountain's gone."

"At the corner?"

"Yes."

"No way of getting across?"

"Not without being a mountaineer, and you'd want to be well roped to go out on it."

"Then we are cut off."

"Not much doubt of that, my old love."

"For how long, do you think?"

George shrugged. "A couple or three days' work to clear it, at least. And they may not be able to start right away."

"Why not?"

"Well, I wouldn't be surprised to find they've got trouble of their own. This mountain's given itself a fair shaking, one way and another. I mean, there's two slips we know of—might be more, further down."

"So what do we do?"

He grinned suddenly. "Got a cigarette?" She found him one. "What do we do? We sit tight and wait. Not much else we can do, is there? How are we off for grub?"

"Not too bad." She thought it over. "I can feed them for a week, anyway. Out of cans, that is."

"And the Scotch will last even longer. Pity it's the Deepings who were to have gone tomorrow."

She had lit his cigarette, and now lit her own from it.

"Why?"

"Because Leonard, unless I miss my guess, will have it that the contract includes delivering him back at Nidenhaut. Failing which"—he went on, imitating Deeping's north-country accent—"I reckon we're being detained against our will, and in consequence of that I don't reckon we owe you anything for further board, in fact I'm not sure we don't have a claim for damages."

Mandy laughed. "I suppose he might say that. They will be able to open the road up within a week? You're sure of that? We don't have to start rationing food, or anything like that?"

"No rationing," he said. "They know down at Nidenhaut that we have supplies in for an emergency. If it were going to last long they would call in one of the helicopters to toss us a few boxes of provisions. These are the nineteen sixties, honey. We don't have to start drawing lots for who eats whom."

"Then there isn't anything to worry about?"

"Well, you'll have to worry about keeping them happy on tinned food." He put an arm around her shoulders; an ordinary gesture of affection, but she was conscious of strength and reassurance flowing from him. "Put you on your mettle, old love, but you can do the trick if anyone can. Tell you what, let's go and have a sustaining noggin before the horde comes ravening in for tea."

She protested. "At this time of day?"

He smiled at her, and she thought how silly it was to pretend. He must know, at least, about the bottle she kept in the bedside cabinet, and the lowered levels in the bar itself had probably not escaped him. She pressed her head back against his chin.

"I could do with a drink," she admitted, "at that."

One of the disadvantages of children was the need for preparing a separate evening meal. This evening, Mandy made them macaroni cheese; they had had it before and liked it, and macaroni and cheese were among the items in best supply in her store room. At least with the Deeping children she did not have to supervise the meal as well as prepare it. Ruth Deeping sat with them. Mandy brought her a cup of tea, and she smiled gratefully.

"Just what I needed. Thank you, Mandy."

Stephen, the faster eater of the two, had finished his macaroni cheese. He said, "Can I have some bread and jam?"

"Please, darling," his mother said.

"Please?"

Mandy said to Ruth Deeping, "Bread is one of the things we're going to have to be a bit careful with—just in case. Can they manage with one slice each? There's more macaroni and cheese, if they're still hungry."

"Of course," Ruth Deeping said, "they can do without bread."

Andy put his fork down. "I'd like some bread and jam,"

38

he said. He looked up at Mandy with a calm smile. "Can I, please?"

Ruth Deeping said, "Perhaps they could have the one slice you mentioned?"

Mandy said, "Of course. I'll get it."

The boys, when she came in again, had reverted to an earlier speculation about the length of time they were likely to remain cut off from the world.

Stephen said, "More than a week, perhaps. A fortnight."

"A month," Andy suggested.

"Six weeks," Stephen said, "and then we'll miss all the rest of term."

Their mother said, "Don't you worry, you'll be back at school by the beginning of next week."

"What do you think, Mrs. Hamilton?" Andy asked.

He had a trick of putting his head on one side when he asked questions, an inquiring, appraising gesture that, from so young a child to an adult, was almost but not quite pert.

Mandy said, "I think your mother's right, Andy. You won't be more than a day or two late in getting back."

"Swizz," he said. "I like it here." His gaze did not drop from her face as he smiled. "Thank you for the bread and jam. Black currant? I love black currant."

There was something in his manner, she thought, which was oddly flattering. As though, having a generalized contempt for the world of grownups, he exempted you from it. He was interesting in a way that not many small boys were and, of course, physically more attractive than his elder brother. She wondered, had they been hers, whether she would have favored him, as Ruth Deeping so plainly did. I had no favorites as far as mine were concerned, she thought— I left them all.

Stephen was tackling his bread and jam by eating his way around the crust first.

Ruth Deeping said, "Eat it properly, Stephen."

"I like leaving the middle part till last."

She said more sharply, "Do as I say." As though feeling a need to explain herself, she said to Mandy, "If I let him, he would eat his way round everything. It's important that they learn how to behave at table. Don't you agree?"

Mandy said, "Yes, I suppose it is."

Andy was eating his decorously, sitting up properly, his elbows tucked in. That made a difference, too, probably: one who had to be checked all the time, and another who did not need telling. She saw him wink at his brother, a friendly conspiratorial act, but one that did not exclude a certain awareness of superiority. There was a good deal of unfairness in life, Mandy thought. One had to get used to it; and one did.

For supper she served them baked ham, which was received enthusiastically. Afterward, as they had done the night before, they played bridge and dice, and once again the dice school lasted longer than the other. Mandy went up to bed at half past ten. It was all going very well, she thought—better than she had expected it would. No trouble so far, no friction from being confined together. She took the bottle out and measured her nightcap carefully; it was important not to become careless about it. Then she washed, and combed her hair, and knelt down to say her prayers.

3

A dedicated man, Selby Grainger thought, would be starting to worry now about the possibility of delay in getting back to work. He stretched back in the chair and gave a small grunt of satisfaction. Dedication, in his particular field, had a slightly comic sound—except, of course, in wartime. The day a week he gave to the Children's Hospital was more than balanced by the four days at the Clinic, not least financially. He put his mind lazily to the recollection of his list. Mrs. Enderby—breasts. Nathan, Levi, and Moncrieff—noses. Juliet Minchin—naevus. The last was the only one which was likely to give him any personal satisfaction. Breasts, however proud the patient might be of the improvement, did not usually go on public show, and he rarely felt entirely happy about noses. One would need to remodel the whole face for a really good result; as it was, the reshaped nose generally seemed wrong to him, however pleased the patient was. But a naevus was something else. Taking that ugly blotch off the girl's face was going to be one of the satisfying jobs.

He reached for the coffee, which Mandy had just brought out. Even for that, there was no hurry. Little Juliet had carried it around with her for twenty-seven years, and a few more days were not going to make the difference. The aunt who had died and left her the couple of thousand pounds which had brought her to the Clinic . . . for the rest of her life, the girl would bless her name. But she had left nearer twenty thousand to the nephew in Rhodesia, and since school little Juliet had looked after dear Auntie, and been a companion to her, and carried her head on one side to conceal that hideous right cheek. He would get rid of the blemish for her, but he was prepared to bet that, even as an old woman, she would look at the world with her left eye.

There was no point in dwelling on life's unpleasantnesses when one could do nothing about them. He drank his coffee and looked out across the snow. The weather was clear again now; a few small clouds clustered around the peaks on the other side of the valley, otherwise a vast, deep blue. All very nice. He was glad they had come here, despite his initial opposition. He had thought of Marrakesh or, if Switzerland, somewhere lively at least. But Elizabeth had had the Hamiltons recommended to her; she had liked the notion of an English enclave up in the Alps and, as always, she had been the one to watch the expense. If they were to get to Greece in late summer, they could not really afford to splurge on a holiday now. A point difficult to contest, especially since he was aware of his own private reason for wanting to go somewhere gayer and concerned that Elizabeth might become aware of it, too. And yet here he sat, he thought contentedly, in perfect weather, cut off from the world, with this sweet little black-haired creature sitting beside him. Admittedly, with Elizabeth on his other side, but he did not really mind that. The fact that Elizabeth was beautiful, while the Blackstone girl was no more than pretty, gave him a particular sensation of pride. And there was time, plenty of time.

His position with regard to Elizabeth was, he reflected, ideal. She knew that he had an eye for a pretty face or figure and, in the consciousness of her own superiority, was not worried by it. She knew that he flirted with women, and it amused her. She knew also that no woman could ever take her place in his life. All these things were true. What she did not know, and—he was determined—never would, was that occasionally the flirtation took a more intimate turn. He needed these little adventures, from which he returned to Elizabeth more loving and more appreciative than ever, but he never allowed the need to overcome discretion. So they did not take place with women of Elizabeth's own acquaintance, although, God knew, that was not for lack of opportunity, and he was careful in the kind of girl he picked. Diana's sister, for instance, although in fact more to his taste, he had ruled out almost at once. A young widow, as such, was a promising proposition, but this one had a seriousness about her which he was not prepared to risk.

No, it was Diana who interested him. She was not, he was prepared to bet, a virgin; on the other hand, not promiscuous. Her approach to life was fundamentally lighthearted and, from the fact that she appeared to spend no time writing letters and had no telephone calls, he was fairly sure that there was nothing of importance in her romantic life at the moment. Her trick of inviting attention from any male who was around was not significant, but the occasional surreptitious glance he had had from her was in a different category.

All that was necessary was to take things easy. Wait, and it will be granted you. Here, at Nidenhaut, a small harmless flirtation, under Elizabeth's indulgent eye. He turned to look at Elizabeth, with a smile and renewed admiration and affection. She was a wonderful woman.

He said, "Are we about ready for the slopes again?"

She shook her elegant head. "My knee's a little rocky from that last fall. You take Diana out. I'll sit and watch you."

He got up and stood before Diana. "Come on, girl. Time for action."

"I think I would just as soon rest, too," she said; but she hung on to his hands and he pulled her up.

She had not skied before this holiday, but had picked things up extremely quickly and was not at all bad. She would have good thighs, Selby thought, a clean lithe body. He touched her arm as they came out to get their skis, and felt the slight backward pressure against his fingers. Yes, he thought, with a pleasant tingle of anticipation, this one is going to be fun.

When they came in again, there was no sign of Elizabeth; she had probably gone upstairs to prepare herself for lunch. George had the bar open, and Deeping was sitting in there drinking a beer. Selby got Campari-sodas for himself and Diana, and took them out to the veranda. No one else was there. She was leaning against the wooden balustrade in a pose which, even wearing a bulky ski jersey, did a lot for her. He let his eye register its appreciation and she smiled, lips slightly parted.

"Thank you, Selby. I was looking for Elizabeth."

"She's upstairs, I should think, gilding refinéd gold, painting the lily."

"She is beautiful, isn't she?" But she did not sound worried about it.

Selby said, "Very. Enough soda in that, or shall I fetch the siphon?"

"It's lovely." She arched her body a little more. "I am enjoying this. It only seems a pity we weren't cut off at the very end of our holiday, like the Deepings."

"We still may be."

"No such luck. Back to dreary London and dreary work."

"What do you do? I mean, I know you're a secretary, but at what sort of place?"

"Accountant's office. Couldn't be duller. Not even big flashy tax-dodgers. Company audits, and very solid companies at that."

"Do you live with Jane?"

"Heavens, no. We wouldn't get on well for long. She lived in the country till Harry died. She's been floundering about in hotels since then. I think she ought to get a place of her own."

"Do you have that—a place of your own?"

"I," she said, striking a histrionic attitude, "live with a friend in West Chelsea. Fulham, that is. Walk up three flights, and there we are. Two rooms, kitchenette, share the bathroom. Her name is Sylvia Farley, and she works for a firm that sells diamonds. Alas, no samples. We have a gas cooker, a transistor radio, a rented TV, and we share a cat along with the bathroom. All the amenities. Friday nights, we wash our hair."

"All the amenities? That includes a telephone, I take it."

She looked at him, biting her lip. "So happens, yes. A pretty little pink one. Costs shared, but it's my name in the book. Blackstone, Diana, Finsborough one two three six. One plus two plus three equals six. Everyone says it's an easy number to remember."

He heard footsteps approaching from the salon, and recognized them as Elizabeth's. He permitted himself a faint smile before turning around to greet her.

"Yes," he said. "I rather think it is."

Elizabeth was not very keen on coming out in the afternoon, either, but Selby talked her into it. He had gone as far with Diana as, under the present circumstances, he wished to go, and could now concentrate on allaying any faint tremors of suspicion that might have crossed Elizabeth's mind.

He said boisterously, "Come on! You've got to work off some of that carbohydrate." Mandy, for lunch, had made them a rich stew with dumplings, followed by an apple-and-apricot pie. "Can't have you getting out of condition."

They headed, Diana accompanying them, for the top western corner of the bowl, from where it was possible to get a good run down—of well over a mile if one wanted, to the point where the road to Nidenhaut was blocked by the fall. In practice, they would not go far beyond the house, probably to the point where Jane, with Douglas Poole and the Deepings, was practicing on one of the easy slopes.

"One run," Elizabeth said, "then I shall leave you and Diana to carry on."

"Nonsense," Selby said. "It's the climbing that does you good. There's very little exercise in skiing down."

They reached their agreed departure point, and stood there, panting. They were about half a mile west of the house and at a slightly greater elevation; the sweeping curve of the bowl ran between, marred by the rubble of snow and ice and rock which had come down with the lesser fall. Fortunately it did not extend far enough to be in the way of their run.

The Deeping boys, Selby saw, had got the toboggan out again, and were using it to slide down the steepest part of the hillside, just beyond the fall. They were going quite fast, probably not entirely in control, but at least they were unlikely to do themselves any harm: the snow was deep about there. As though in confirmation, he saw the sledge buck, and bury itself, along with its passengers, in a snowbank. They climbed out pretty quickly, and their voices, excited and happy, carried thinly across the snow.

Elizabeth said, "They're having more fun." There was a note in her voice which came as near to wistfulness as her placidity allowed. "Sledging was what I always liked most about winter."

"Right," Selby said. "When we've made this run, we'll sledge. We'll get the big one out. George will lend a hand."

46

"The boys," Diana said, "have they found something?"

The little one, Andy, was grubbing in the snow. He had his back to them, and was bending over. He straightened up, and called to his brother, who was pulling the toboggan back up the slope. Then he bent down again, and slid forward gently on his face.

Some kind of a game they were playing, Selby thought, but there had been something disquieting about the way the boy had fallen. He stood there, irresolute, watching. Stephen came down to where Andy was, stooped, lifted and turned him. He squatted with his brother a dead weight in his arms, and looked up, as though seeking help. Selby wasted no more time, but dug his sticks in and started down toward them.

An ordinary syncope, he thought, seeing the white unconscious face, the limp body. Too much exercise too soon after lunch, or perhaps a delayed shock from the tumble off the sledge. He said to Stephen, "All right. I'll have him."

"He's fainted," Stephen said.

"Yes. He'll be all right in a jiffy."

He had stripped off his ski gloves and the boy's gloves, and his fingers went automatically to the pulse. He was shocked, incredulous. He bent his cheek to the child's mouth, slipped his hand up under the jersey and shirt to rest against the heart. He was holding him like that, the other arm supporting him, when there was a flurry of snow beside him and Diana was there, Elizabeth just behind her.

Diana said, "What is it? What's wrong?"

"He's fainted," Stephen repeated. "He just fell over."

Selby said to Elizabeth, "Undo my skis, would you? I'm going to carry him back to the house."

He kept his voice neutral, but he could tell from her face that she had guessed it was serious. She worked quickly and efficiently to unbuckle his skis. He stepped out of them, and carried the boy up through the snow to the house. Those who were down on the lower slopes had not apparently noticed anything, but Mandy came to the door to meet him.

"Is it an accident?" she said.

"I don't know."

She stood aside and he carried the boy through into the salon. He put him down on the carpet, in front of the fire, and stripped off the upper garments. He massaged the still warm chest, tried to blow breath into the collapsed lungs. But he knew it was hopeless long before he desisted and looked up. Elizabeth and Diana were there.

Elizabeth said, "Mandy has taken Stephen into the kitchen. Selby, is he dead?"

He nodded silently.

"But how? What happened?"

"His heart stopped. There may have been a history of weakness." He shook his head. "He didn't look like a heart case."

Diana said flatly, "I can't believe it." She turned her gaze from the small body and walked over to the windows that looked out across the veranda. "They're still skiing down there," she said. "Someone will have to tell them."

"I'll do it," Elizabeth said. She bent down and touched the dead boy's face, as though the touching would make the fact of death more believable. "Are you going to leave him here?"

"For the time being."

Waiting for the Deepings to come, he felt stunned himself. In the early days, in general theater, he had encountered his full share of sudden death, in all its forms. But that was years ago, and there had always been some warning, some explanation. Now he stared at the child's unmarked body in bewilderment and resentment. His own working days were spent in patching up imperfections in the human frame, winning small triumphs over nature's indifference, conducting a cool and measured campaign against ugliness. And here this child lay, delicate, flawless, dead. The supreme indifference, the final ugliness. Beside that, all he had done or hoped to do seemed derisory.

Until she spoke, he had forgotten Diana was still in the room. She said, "Do you think I should go—before she comes?"

He only half heard her. "As you think best."

"I can't stand scenes, and it isn't as though I can do any good." She gave a small nervous laugh. "And I feel I must have a cigarette."

"Yes," he said. "Go and do that."

Elizabeth came in with the Deepings. She was at her best in situations such as this: quiet, sympathetic, serene. She put her arm, unobtrusively but firmly, round Ruth Deeping's shoulders as she led her across the room.

No one spoke for the first few seconds. The silence was broken only by the crackle of the open fire, the ticking of the huge, elaborate cuckoo clock on the wall. Ruth Deeping had dropped beside her son, and raised his head to cradle it in her arms. When she looked up and spoke, her voice was reasonable, restrained.

"He's not dead," she said. "Only unconscious."

"I'm sorry."

"But he's warm!"

A piece of wood hissed in the fire, as though to mark the pointlessness of any reply. The blue eyes stared up, glazing now. Selby looked at Deeping. He had accepted it, all right. The acceptance showed in the hunch of his shoulders, the brooding sullenness of his mouth. Selby went to him, and said quietly, "I'm very sorry. There was nothing anyone could have done. He was dead when I picked him up."

Deeping wrenched his head around. "How?"

"Heart. Does he—had he had any trouble in that respect?"

The head shook slowly. "There's never been anything wrong with him. Never anything. Except chicken pox, measles—that sort." He stared at Selby, as though willing him to give some kind of explanation. "How did it happen? You must have some idea."

"There must have been a defect. Something which perhaps wouldn't show up except on a cardiogram. The only way of finding out would be"—he hesitated—"through a post-mortem."

Although he had been speaking quietly, Ruth Deeping must have caught his words. She said, her voice harsh, "No. No cutting. It's enough that he's dead. It doesn't matter what caused it."

Selby was relieved that she had come past the first terrifying point of recognition, but he would have been happier if there had been tears. The dry-eyed bitterness she was showing made him uneasy. He said to Deeping, "Perhaps you had better take him up to his room. Can you manage?"

She made no objection as Deeping lifted the body into his arms, and followed him quietly from the room. He heard them going upstairs, and remembered that the other boy was in the kitchen with Mandy. She should have gone to see him, he thought. It is the living who have needs. He went to the kitchen, and found the boy sitting with a glass of hot cordial. Mandy was busying herself with something. He caught her eye inquiringly, and she shook her head slightly. Selby wondered about that. It was the parents who should break the news to him, of course, not casual acquaintances such as themselves.

Stephen said, "Andy—is he dead, Mr. Grainger?"

There was some fear in his voice, and a lot of uncertainty. He would not, Selby decided, leave the telling until the Deepings returned from their vigil. He said, "Yes, Steve. I'm afraid he is."

"I thought he was." He hesitated. "It wasn't—because the sledge tipped over?"

50

Fear again, with an edge of guilt. Perhaps he had steered the sledge into the snowbank, or thought he might be blamed for it.

He said firmly, "Nothing to do with that." Though, of course, there could be a causal link, provided that there was a congenital defect. He went on, making his curiosity casual: "What happened after the sledge tipped over? How did Andy look?"

"All right. He was laughing about it. And then . . ."

"Then?"

"He called to me that he'd found something in the snow."

"What had he found?"

"I don't know. It looked like a blue ball."

Selby said, "You saw it?"

"Only a glimpse of it. Then Andy fell over."

"I see."

There was hardly likely to be a blue ball in the rubble brought down a desolate mountainside by an avalanche. A blue boulder, probably, sufficiently spherical to look like a ball. The only odd thing was that, if Stephen had seen it, so should he have when he picked Andy's body up. He had an exact recollection of the scene: the snow broken but homogeneous. No sign of blue in the white. No boulders.

"You didn't pick it up," he asked, "when you went to help Andy? Whatever it was."

"There was nothing there, then. But there was something before. Bright blue and—well, gleaming."

Some kind of illusion, Selby decided. He knew that sunlight on snow could play odd tricks with the eyes. George Hamilton came into the kitchen then, started to say something to Selby, but broke it off as he saw the boy. When he spoke again, it was in a more guarded tone.

"Can I have a word with you, Selby?"

"Of course." He said to the boy, "It didn't hurt him, you

know. It happened very suddenly. Drink the cordial Mrs. Hamilton has made you; it will warm you up. Your mummy will be down to see you very soon."

He hoped that was true. Hamilton led him through to the dining room, and said, "That's the bane of running a boardinghouse—lack of privacy. Pick a pew." They sat across the dining table from each other. "This is a bit of a shock."

Selby nodded. "Yes."

"Heart, I gather. Poor little chap. I suppose they had no idea of it being dicky?"

"None, as far as I can see."

"It's the way I've always wanted to go. But at that age! Bloody unfair. Still, nothing we can do about it." He looked restlessly at Selby. "Question is: what happens next?"

"In England, in circumstances like these, there would have to be an inquest. I'm not sure how things operate in Switzerland."

"Nor am I," Hamilton said, "damn it! I suppose I ought to be, but we haven't had a death before." There was a baffled expression on his face. "And we can't take official advice, not being in touch with anyone."

"You can't do anything with the body, anyway," Selby pointed out, "until the road to Nidenhaut is clear."

"Yes, I'd worked that out. It's a bit tricky."

"Tricky?"

"I've just seen Ruth Deeping. You know they've got the room next to ours, with the kids next door to them?" Selby nodded. "She asked me to have Steve's bed moved into their room."

"Well? The other poor kid's got to be put somewhere."

Hamilton hammered his large hands on the table. "Look. I can turn off the radiator, but the hot pipes run under the floor all the way along. I can't turn them off, without everyone freezing. This house was designed to be warm in winter. And

52

we don't know how long it's going to be before they get through from the village. It could be a week, by which time . . ."

"Yes," Selby said, "of course. Do you have a cold room somewhere?"

"In the basement. Northeast corner, and unheated. Nothing in there but tinned food, a few ropes, and general tackle. We can clear that lot out in a jiffy."

"That solves your problem, then."

"If we can convince Mrs. Deeping, it does."

"Yes," Selby said. He paused. "You think she might be difficult about it?"

"Don't you?"

"The alternative's not pleasant."

"Would you put it to her, Selby? You're a doctor, after all. You're used to this sort of thing."

Selby smiled wryly. "Not really. It's a good many years since I lost a patient."

"Anyway, you're a medical. You can put it better than I would. And she'll listen to you more easily than she would to me. Will you do it?"

"All right. We'll give her an hour or so to get used to things first."

"Good man." He snorted out breath in relief. "I'll have Peter get things ready down below. Get some ice in, set up a trestle table. And meanwhile I think I could do with a stiffish drink. How does the notion strike you?"

"Favorably," Selby said. "Very favorably indeed."

At first Ruth Deeping would not hear of her son's body being moved again. He would stay where he was, she insisted, until he could be taken down to the village. She was not going to have him put away in the basement.

Selby enlisted Deeping's support fairly easily, but this did not do much toward convincing her; she looked at her husband with angry resentful eyes, and said she did not expect him to feel as she did about Andy. He had put his own pleasures before the concerns of the boys all their lives, and it was natural for him to be indifferent to them dead. Them, Selby thought—as though she had lost both her children. Deeping did not attempt to reply to her, and looked sheepish. It was surprising how often submissiveness in women concealed a potential domination, particularly with unpleasantly cocky men like Deeping. Domination, and that same indifference she had charged him with showing to the children. Even before they were born, he did not think she could have felt anything for her husband.

He said, quietly but firmly, "It will have to be done, Ruth. You must accept that."

She shook her head, her eyes hating him. "No."

"I've seen the room. It's clean and cool. The best place, I promise you."

She said something which he did not catch. He asked her to repeat it. Her voice thick with horror, she said, "There might be rats."

He said, compassionately, "No. There are no rats here— George has assured me of that. And the room is quite bare. You can see that there's not even a mouse hole."

She stared at him. "No. I want him near me."

He put a surgeon's authority into his voice. "As a doctor, I insist." After a pause, he went on, "You were worried by the thought of rats. Have you seen what the human body looks like when it starts to corrupt?"

She closed her eyes, escaping from the image. Selby said to Deeping, "George has had a stretcher brought up. It's outside on the landing. Bring it in, and I'll give you a hand to get downstairs."

Deeping did as he was told. While he was gone, Selby put his hand on Ruth Deeping's arm. She was shivering slightly.

"Go downstairs," he said. "George will give you a brandy." She gave a slight shake of her head, and he said, "I prescribe that. I'm still talking as a doctor. Afterwards, George will take you down to the basement, and show you what's been arranged."

She remained motionless for a moment. Then she bent down and kissed the boy's face. After that, she left the room quickly; he heard her footsteps clattering down the stairs.

Peter, the handyman, took over Selby's part for the last flight of stairs; they were narrower, more sharply twisted, and Peter, going first, had to negotiate them with care. Selby followed them down, and into the room which had been made ready. It was at the far end of the passage. The door was open, showing a segment of light.

George was inside. There was an old table in the center of the floor, and a couple of large wooden boxes, their opposite ends knocked out, had been put together to form a rough approximation of an open coffin. Selby looked at it while the other two were putting the stretcher down. The bottom and the sides had been packed with ice. He looked at George, and nodded his agreement. Then Deeping lifted his son's body from the stretcher, and laid it in the boxes. The body had been put into pajamas, and Selby could not help feeling how cold and lost it looked.

Deeping put the sheet in also, and drew it up to cover the face. He stared down helplessly for a moment, and said, "Ruth will want to see him now. I'll go and tell her."

"I'll wait here," Selby said.

George waited with him. The air was chilly, after the warmth of the rest of the house, and silent except for a far-off sound which Selby recognized as the roar of the furnace. As much to break the silence as anything, he said, "The ice was a good idea. I didn't think of that."

"Nothing to it," George said. "My father was a butcher."

He looked at the makeshift coffin, his face expressionless. "Mustn't develop delusions of grandeur. A butcher's assistant. Though he was given a shop to manage in the end. He died the year after."

"How old were you then?"

"Fourteen. And there was a slump on at the time. I got permission to leave the Grammar School, and get a job as a clerk. Twelve and six a week. I could have got another half crown as a butcher's lad, but my mother wouldn't have that."

"You had a rough time of it."

George shrugged. "So-so. The war made the difference, of course. I was lucky enough to get into air crew, and qualify as a pilot. That was the difficult bit; the rest was a piece of cake." He grinned. "To use one of the many habits of speech I picked up in the process."

"First-class assimilation," Selby agreed. "Has it made you happy, do you think?"

With good-humored scorn, George said, "There speaks the man for whom a butcher's assistant was something in a blue and white apron at the back door, dodging the dog and making a pass at the scullery maid. My life may not look much of a success by your standards, chum, but it is by mine. Reasonable comfort instead of grinding poverty. And when I look out of my front window I see Grammont and Lake Geneva, not the other side of Crake Terrace with cur dogs peeing up against the gateposts. I bring my mother out every spring. She's as mad on these bloody mountains as I am."

Selby nodded. "I take the point."

"Do you? Maybe." He moved closer to the table, and looked down at the child's body. "The changes and chances are out as far as he's concerned, aren't they? Poor little sod. What a waste."

There were footsteps outside, and Ruth Deeping came in, her husband shepherding her. George moved away as she went to the table and stood there. Her face was white and still. George nodded slightly to Selby, and they went out together.

Afternoon merged into the heaviness of evening. There was a pall over the house, particularly depressing for one of Selby's mercurial and extrovert nature. The boy's death had been a shock, and he sympathized with what the Deepings, Ruth especially, must be going through, but this did not seem to him a sufficiently good reason for a general gloom. One could not, after all, deny the psychological fact that, where the loss was not personal, the death of another—even of a child— was a confirmation of one's own continued life. Hence the tradition of the wake, the funeral feast. Send to know for whom the bell tolls, and ask the ringer to jazz it up a bit.

Impossible counsel, of course, in the cramped confines of a snowbound chalet completely cut off from the world. All one could do was scowl and bear it. George opened the bar early, and Selby took Elizabeth and Diana for a drink. Jane Winchmore came in later with Douglas Poole. They seemed to be getting on well together, Selby noted, in a somewhat low-keyed fashion. It was difficult to imagine her accepting any more warm-blooded approach, or him initiating it. Finally Deeping joined them, and the tone was set for the dull, rather morose exchange of platitudes. Ruth Deeping, it appeared, was keeping a vigil by the side of the dead boy. The living one, in whom she seemed to have lost all interest, was being looked after by Mandy and the maid.

Selby went up for a bath early, and soaked there moodily for a long time, reading a copy of *Ladies' Home Journal*, which Elizabeth had bought at London Airport. He did not rouse himself in fact until she had rapped on the door several times and called him in her controlled but penetrating voice. He dressed slowly, trying to spin the minutes out.

Ruth Deeping did not come to supper, either. George had put a chair in the basement room for her, and she had said she wanted to stay there. She had accepted tea that Mandy had made for her, but insisted that she could not eat anything. Selby himself had a raging appetite, and Mandy had made an extremely nice steak pie, but the gloom, the muted voices were progressively more difficult to bear. Both for the general good and her own—not to mention his own in particular—Ruth must, Selby decided, be got out of the way. He went down to the basement with a firm step and a determined mind.

She was sitting with her head resting against the side of one of the boxes, and did not look up as he came into the room. He took a firm hold on her arm, and said, "I'm taking you upstairs now, Ruth. You must lie down for a little while."

She still did not look at him. "No."

"I insist." He levered her to her feet. "You can come down again later, if you want to."

She had not resisted. She said, her voice helpless, "There must be someone with him."

"There will be. Leonard will come down."

Her eyes were large in a face haggard enough for a woman fifteen years older than she was. She said, "If he comes first." She rocked her head from side to side. "I don't want him to be alone."

Selby nodded, and went upstairs to fetch Deeping. She said nothing to him, merely watched as he took her place by the coffin. Then she let Selby guide her from the room and upstairs. She refused to undress, but consented to slip her shoes off and lie on the bed. He had the maid bring her a strong brandy and hot water and, from the supply he always carried with him, produced half a grain of Nembutal. She took the yellow capsule with some sign of alarm.

"I don't want to be put to sleep," she said.

"Your nerves are bad," Selby told her, "inevitably. This is a

58

mild sedative. Something to steady you. Swallow it quickly. Here's a glass of water."

When she had taken it, he watched while she drank the brandy and water. Then he persuaded her to get her head down on the pillow. He left her, and went downstairs for his coffee. When he came up again, twenty minutes later, she was fast asleep. He managed to get her, still clothed, beneath the blankets. She stirred once, but showed no sign of waking.

Deeping was sitting, looking uncomfortable, in the chair in the basement room. Selby said, "It's all right. She's sleeping. I should come upstairs if I were you."

Deeping looked ill at ease. He said, "She didn't want him to be alone."

"Look," Selby said, "she's had a terrible shock. She'll feel better when she wakes in the morning. There's nothing you can do for the boy now—you know that. With the door closed, nothing can touch him." As the man continued to look hesitant, he said, "Or were you thinking of spending the night down here?"

"If she wakes up, and comes down . . ."

"Does she take sleeping pills normally?"

"Sleeping pills? No."

"She's got half a grain of Nembutal in her, and a very large brandy on top of that. She won't wake just yet."

Deeping allowed himself to be persuaded. Upstairs, the atmosphere was lighter, but still on the grim side. Selby drank a lot of whisky in a fairly short time, keeping up with George, who was on large brandies. They were all drinking more than usual, he noticed, even Jane Winchmore. He looked at her with reflective admiration. It was a pity about that temperament. His eye caught her sister's; she gave him a look briefly complicit. Yes, he thought, more rewarding altogether.

There was a general move toward bed at an early hour. Selby looked in on Ruth Deeping, and found her heavily

asleep. He went to his own room, to find Elizabeth already undressed and in her bed. She was wearing a nightdress he particularly liked; diaphanous, trimmed with silk almost the color
of her flesh. Kissing her good night, he thought of making a
more positive approach, but she had a strange and rigid sense
of sexual proprieties and he felt he might offend her. Later, in
his own bed, he heard her toss and turn, and thought he might
have been mistaken. But it was too late to do anything about
it now. And he was tired.

Someone was screaming in a nightmare, so loud that it
woke him. As he fumbled for matches to light the lamp beside
his bed, he realized that the screaming was actual—a woman,
somewhere in the house. Elizabeth said something to him, and
he mumbled a reply as he took the lamp out to the landing.
The screaming was still going on, from downstairs, he realized. He saw that there was a light down there, a lamp. Ruth
Deeping was holding it, and the screams of agony and grief
were coming from her. Selby raced downstairs to her; he put
his own lamp down on a table and took hers from her also.
Putting his arm around her, he said, "It's all right." He shook
her, sharply and savagely. "Listen. Everything's all right."

The end of the screaming was almost as disconcerting as
the sound had been. In the quietness, he was aware of other
people appearing upstairs, of Elizabeth following him down.
Ruth Deeping opened her mouth, and he thought the screams
would start again. But she spoke sensibly, though in a voice
hideous with wretchedness.

"He's gone," she said. "Someone has taken him."

She had woken up and gone down, then found the wrong
room in the basement. An easy thing to do, especially with her
mind shocked, and clouded by the sleeping draft he had given
her. He guided her with his arms, as he had done earlier that
day.

60

"No," he said. "He's here still. Come, and I'll show you."

She offered no resistance. The door to the room with the coffin was just ajar. He pushed it open, to show her. The lamp hanging from the ceiling hook was burning. But the coffin was empty, as empty as the room.

In part, a birth; in part, a reawakening.

First there was an awareness of life, of sentience, some-
where close, and with the awareness came hunger. The hunger
grew, and made its soundless cry—a command, an appeal, a
wheedling, and an enticement—to the mind whose presence
had brought it into being. Awareness quickened. There was
response: curiosity, pleasure, and a coming nearer, nearer.
And then contact. Flesh. Living cells. Nerve endings . . .
The moment of consummation—swift, naked, intense—as the
essence of the Possessor entered the Possessed, and found it
good.

After that, for a time, quiescence. For the Possessor, the
immediate hunger sated, there was calm, appraisement, the
slow growth of memory. And the learning of this body, of its
parts and purposes, all the things that would be necessary for
control. For the Possessed, there was a kind of death. The
heart stopped beating, lungs pumped no longer, flesh cooled,
blood ceased to flow. But did not congeal. And the cells, the

millions of cells that were the units of this superb construction, still lived. The house seemed tenantless, but was not. It had two tenants now, master and slave, shocked by their collision into inactivity, for the present functionless. But alive and waiting.

Waiting, also, to be left alone. After one learned the nature of the body, one learned its use, and this must be done unhindered, unobserved. The senses, first. Hearing . . . small distant sounds swimming up from the silence—the creak of old wood, the muted furnace noise, the soft thud of snow falling on snow. Touch . . . the smoothness and jaggedness of ice, the rougher texture where part of the hand lay against wood, the softness of the sheet against the face. Smell . . . a slight mustiness and another, fainter odor. Tea? One of the boxes from which the coffin had been made had held tea. Possessor and Possessed learned these things together, in a silent communion of question and answer.

Sight . . . Another stage required, the finding of the small muscles that would open the eyes, and then the directing. A strangeness here. Question and answer again. A heaviness, unknown before. Then, touch? Something that rested there, smooth—metal? The other muscles: arm, wrist, fingers. The hand moved slowly, lifted, plucked the coins first from one eye, then the other. Now the eyelids could open. Tears flowed from their ducts, the eyes blinked again and again. Sight came slowly, a blur of light, resolving itself, as fingers dragged the sheet back, into the shape of the lamp hanging from the ceiling.

A pause. Immobility, a brief exhaustion. The Possessed was shocked still, from time to time essaying a hopeless resistance. There could be no resistance, the Possessor's calm thought said. But the Possessor was patient. A long time of partnership lay ahead. The little flutterings of fear and defiance would fade into the glow of union.

Movements, the next time, were more purposeful. The synaptic paths were known and charted, muscle and sinew took their orders more easily, acted more deftly. The body pushed up, bracing against its elbows. It rose awkwardly, stepped from the coffin to the table, from table to chair, and so stood, upright, on the stone flags of the floor.

Those who had known the child would have thought him unchanged; and physically there was no change. Except in metabolism. For the Possessor's memories were of a colder, heavier world than this. Heart and lungs worked more slowly, body temperature stabilized at a little over seventy degrees. This was a blessing the Possessor brought: the creature would live longer now, much longer, and in better health. The Possessor thought of this, with serene benevolence. Already it had become fond of its collaborator, its dwelling place, its slave.

The Possessor willed muscles to act, and they acted. Control was complete. But the movements would always be sluggish, judged by human standards, because of the Possessor and the Possessor's heritage. The new entity that had been Andy Deeping walked with an unchildlike deliberation across the room, put out a hand, turned the handle, and opened the door. It walked through to the passage and stood, for a moment, considering.

Survival meant propagation, assimilation, but from now on it could not be swift, annihilating, sure. Possession, for the future, would have to be achieved through that which was already Possessed and could not be done quickly. It was unfortunate, the Possessor thought, that the first should have been a child, with only a child's strength. Force was out of the question; there would have to be guile. The mother . . . But the mother was not alone, and the others, inevitably, were the enemy. Until, in time, they too submitted.

At present it was necessary to get away from them, to es-

cape. In the house there was danger, but outside there would be safety and the opportunity to make plans. The cold was no handicap, but the body would need fuel.

The Possessor's knowledge was the knowledge the child had had, and the child, playing in the basement during the blizzard, had seen the food store. Question and answer: such a thing was nourishing, good, this other not. A means of carrying—there was an old basket behind the door. The small arms reached up and pulled it down, filled it with the things that had been chosen.

Then that which had been Andy Deeping walked, a little stiffly, to the basement door, drew back with difficulty the iron bolts, lifted the latch, and walked out into the dark, freezing night.

4

Of the sisters, it was Jane Winchmore who was awakened first. She sat up in bed, pulled the cord on the bedside light before she remembered that it was useless, and felt fear grow in her. There was moonlight outside, but Diana had insisted on having the curtains drawn across the windows. The room was dark, and she was conscious of the darkness of the house all around her.

Diana said, from the other bed, "My God! What is it?"

The familiar voice, the realization of not being alone, was a relief. She slipped her feet out of bed, and went to draw the curtains. Enough light came in to enable her to find her slippers and dressing gown. She said, "I don't know. Better go and see, though."

"No! Stay here. It scares me."

She went to Diana's bed, and they held hands. When the screaming stopped, she said, "I'll go and see what's wrong. You stay."

"I'm not going to be left. I'll come with you."

There were others on the landing—Douglas Poole and Elizabeth Grainger—and George Hamilton came noisily down the stairs from the floor above. Douglas had brought a light out, so they could see each other and, to some extent, their surroundings.

She asked him, "What's happened?"

"I don't know. It was Ruth Deeping. Hysterical, I imagine. Grainger's down there with her, and he seems to have succeeded in quietening her."

The child, she supposed. She felt at a loss. Her own bereavement gave her no insight into this different, so much more passionate one; and, of course, she herself had never had a child. Women did, she knew, sometimes go mad with grief, though surely they would be more unstable to start with than Ruth Deeping had seemed. Looking down the well of the stairs, she could see Grainger, half supporting Ruth and talking to Hamilton. His voice was pitched low, and did not carry up to the landing. Hamilton said something, and Grainger took her off to the room that was used as a bar. Then Hamilton called up to all of them, "You'd better come down, I think."

They gathered in the salon. Embers still glowed in the fireplace, and Mandy set to work with sticks, coaxing them into life. It was not cold—there were radiators in this room as there were in the others—but the prospect of a fire was cheering. Marie was lighting the two big oil lamps.

Hamilton said, "Are we all here?"

Deeping began, "Ruth . . ."

"Selby's giving her a brandy next door. I should leave her with him, for the time being. She's had a pretty severe shock." His gaze took in the small figure, standing beside his father. "Mandy, I think it's caught now. Will you take Steve out and give him a hot drink?"

When they had gone, and the door closed behind them,

Deeping said, "For God's sake, what is it? Not what she was afraid of? Not . . ."

"He's not there any more." He spoke as though trying to convince himself as much as the others. "The coffin's empty. And the room."

"It can't be!"

Deeping stared for a moment at Hamilton, turned, and went out. They heard him running downstairs to the basement. Hamilton closed the door, and stood with his back to it.

"Doesn't make sense," he said, "does it? A body doesn't just disappear like that. It has to be somewhere."

Douglas said, "He couldn't have been dead, in that case. Catalepsy. Haven't there been cases where people have been put in their coffins, and then recovered?"

"Yes," Hamilton said, "so I've heard. Mind you, Selby said he was dead, and he ought to know. And he looked dead to me—as dead as anything I've ever seen. But we could have been wrong. The point is: where is he? If the kid woke up, found himself lying down there on a table, he'd go up to his mother, wouldn't he? Or make some row, at any rate. But there's just no sign of him. Far as I can make out, Ruth woke, and felt she must go and have another look at him. And found nothing there."

Elizabeth said, "He might be badly shocked, surely. He might not quite know what he was doing. Gone off somewhere to hide."

"Yes," Hamilton said, "that's the only way it starts to make sense to me, too. That's why I've asked you all to come down. We'll have to hunt round the house till we find him. All the cupboards, under the beds. I'll do our floor, and Peter will do the attics. The rest of you do the first floor. Then we'll all have another good look around the lower regions."

Diana stayed close to Jane, and she stayed near Douglas. Elizabeth, who searched the first floor with them, made a separate check. Aware of her own weakness and uneasiness, Jane felt a touch of resentment at the other woman's capability and calm. It was hard to imagine anything ruffling her. She chided herself for her lack of charity, and furiously pulled dresses to one side in her wardrobe-cupboard.

Diana objected. "He can't be in there."

"We're supposed to look everywhere." She detected a sharpness in her voice, too, and said more quietly, "We're directly under the Deepings' room. He might have mistaken the floor, then got scared and gone into the cupboard."

There was no sign of the boy. They went down and were joined by the others.

Hamilton said briskly, "Well, he's not upstairs, and he's not here on the ground floor. Mandy's checked that. The basement is the only place left. There's that big room next to the washhouse with all those crates and things. I suppose he may have got into or behind one of them. Leonard will want to help, of course, and Douglas can lend a hand, too, but we shan't need the ladies. You can stay here, or go back to your beds, as you choose."

Elizabeth said, "I'd prefer to come and help you look."

Hamilton shrugged. "As you like."

"We'll all come," Jane said. "There's no point in thinking of going back to bed while the child's missing."

They covered the other rooms in the basement first, looking behind rows of tins, sacks of potatoes, and big sugar and flour canisters in the food store. The room that Hamilton had mentioned was a jumble of crates and boxes, stacked almost up to the ceiling in some places. They worked as systematically as possible through them, moving them from one side of the room to the other. It took about half an hour, and although there was no radiator, they were sweating by the time they finished. Hamilton looked at the rearranged junk, and shook his head slowly.

"I really thought he might be here. It's next door to the one he was in."

They went out silently, and were heading for the stairs. On their left was the small bare passage leading to the basement door; the lamp Hamilton was carrying gave enough light to make it plain that no one was there. But the thought came to her, and she said automatically, "The door . . ."

They all stopped. Hamilton said, "What about the door?"

"Could he have gone outside? It's probably silly."

"In weather like this?" Hamilton asked. "And I don't see that he'd have the strength to draw those bolts. All the same . . ."

He went past her along the passage to the door, and lowered the light toward the floor.

"They've been drawn, all right." With his back to them, and stooping, his voice sounded odd. There was a resonance in the passage. "I don't like the look of this."

Hamilton lifted the latch with his free hand, and pulled the door open. It swung heavily toward him, and they shivered in a blast of freezing air. Outside there was the long slope of snow, lit by a half-moon. Hamilton stood looking out, and they crowded after him.

"Footprints?" Douglas suggested.

"If you can tell new prints from old. Everyone's been out there since the last fall. The boys, too. They were playing there yesterday morning."

"He would be barefoot," Elizabeth said.

"Doubt if that would show either, in this kind of snow. You don't see any sign of anything, do you? Anyone?"

Diana repeated, "Barefoot . . ."

"Yes," Hamilton said, "and wearing pajamas. The sheet is still in there. I think some of us had better go and put some warm clothes on."

Grainger listened to Hamilton in silence. When he had finished, he said, "What's the temperature out there?"

"I've not checked the thermometer. I'd say at least fifteen centigrade below—twenty more likely. And a nasty wind from the east."

Grainger shook his head. "Even in shock, he wouldn't go out into that. It's absurd."

"The bolts were drawn. I wouldn't have thought he could draw them, for that matter."

"Perhaps he didn't."

Hamilton stared at him, with what might be the beginning of anger. His nerves had been frayed, Jane thought, as all their nerves had, and she suspected that underneath the bonhomie there could be sensitivity and a quick temper.

"What the bloody hell do you suggest happened, in that case?"

"Someone might have taken the body outside. The child was dead, in my judgment."

"And who would do a stupid, filthy trick like that?"

"I don't know. But it's rather more probable than that the boy was alive, and that he got up and walked out into snow."

"Not to me, it isn't. Anyone would have to be a maniac to do it."

"A sleepwalker would do as well. Or someone with an obsession about not being under the same roof as a corpse— your chap Peter, maybe. How does a Swiss peasant's mind work? I don't know."

He sounded tired, himself overwrought. Calming Ruth Deeping had probably taken it out of him. He had managed to get her to take more Nembutal, Jane gathered, and Mandy was with her now, having got Stephen back to bed and asleep.

Hamilton, on edge but in a different way, said, "Is that what you're suggesting? Are you seriously putting that one up as a proposition—that Peter came down from the attic, and carted the kid's body out into the snow somewhere?"

In a sharper, colder voice, Grainger said, "All I'm doing is suggesting alternatives to your own incredible story. The fact that they are almost as unlikely is beside the point. As things stand, we don't know what happened. We can only guess."

Beside her, Douglas said, "Can't we leave the theorizing for the time being? If there's even a faint chance that the boy's alive out there, surely the important thing is to try to find him."

Grainger said, "Yes. You're quite right, of course." He rubbed a hand across his forehead. "I'm not thinking very straight. I'm sorry, George."

Hamilton, mollified, said, "I reckon we're all a bit off beam. Need a little something to help us zero in properly. Come on through, and I'll pour us all a noggin."

Jane refused a drink for herself, and insisted on only a very small brandy being poured for Diana. Hamilton produced strong tots for the men, and for Elizabeth. The latter, looking completely controlled, said, "Yes, I do need it." She drank it down quickly, making a small face.

Hamilton's suggestion was that the hunt should be conducted by the five men, four of them searching the area near the house, and Peter, who was an expert skier and used to snow slopes at night, covering the outlying regions. Grainger nodded to this.

"Fair enough. Though he won't have got far, if he is out there. Not possible."

Elizabeth again intervened, insisting on being included. Jane and Diana pressed their claims, also. Jane said, "One extra person might make the difference between finding and not finding—or finding in time. And better out there than waiting."

"Right," Hamilton said. He tipped his drink back. "Then we might as well get cracking. Upstairs, and wrap up warmly. Meet down here as soon as you're kitted up."

Coffee had been made by the time Jane came down again. She drank it gratefully, and listened to Hamilton's instructions.

72

They were to go in pairs or threes, to prevent, as he put it, the possibility of someone falling, breaking a leg perhaps, and there having to be a further search party on top of the present one. They were given general areas to search. Diana had already attached herself to the Graingers and was to concentrate with them on the area east of the house. She and Douglas were told to beat around to the west. Hamilton himself, with Deeping, was taking a wider sweep both above and below the chalet.

Outside, it was colder than she had thought it would be, and brighter. The half-moon light, reflected from the snow, meant that she could see a fair distance in front of her. To the south, the Alps were faint but real against the horizon. Clear of the house, she looked down toward the road to Nidenhaut, and saw that the shoulder of the mountain which cut them off from the village was quite sharp. The sky was already beginning to pale a little, there in the east.

Although visibility was better than she had expected, the strangeness of the light played tricks, interfering with her memory of the contours. Within twenty yards, she missed her footing and slid into a hollow. Douglas came down to help her to her feet. She said ruefully, "That's what George meant, I imagine."

"You're all right, though? Nothing strained or broken?"

"Nothing like that."

He held her arm with his gloved hand for a moment, and then let her go. To her relief. Not, she thought wryly, that she stood in much danger of a romantic approach at this time and under these circumstances. But it had troubled her a little that they were apparently being thrown together. Diana, whose determination to form a trio with the Graingers had a lot to do with it, had commented on it the previous night. The comment had been only partly arch. She had said seriously, "You do get on quite well with him, don't you? I mean, to

73

talk to." Which could be translated, Jane felt, into, "How nice for you to find someone as stodgy as yourself in the party."

It was true that she found him pleasant company, and restful. Because of that, she felt it the more important to avoid the possibility of anything else creeping in. She had lived with her body long enough to know that most men found it physically attractive. There was a probability that Douglas, who seemed to be unattached, would do so too. Unless, bearing in mind that most men in their middle thirties could be expected to show signs of attachment, or having been attached, he was uninterested in women. She was surprised to feel a small twinge of disappointment as the possibility crossed her mind.

Well, that was normal. One preferred a man to be male, with all that implied, even when not personally interested. And the very notion of being interested in him, in any man, was a depressing, draining one.

Harry's death, after so short an illness, had inevitably had a numbing effect—for a couple of months she had gone around in a daze. But during that time she had understood what was happening to her, and that it had its limits. The sense of shock would pass; life would fall back into normal, undistorted patterns. What she had not guessed was that the numbness would be succeeded by her present apathy, by the nagging insistence somewhere at the back of her mind that everything was pointless, nothing worth striving or working for, life itself only bearable on a basis of living from day to day.

Her relations with other people formed an extension of this. Providing they made no demands, they could be tolerated. In some moods, in fact, the company of another was preferable to her own. And where the tie was the simple tie of blood relationship . . . she had not resented Diana's boisterous reintrusion into her life, had accepted her attentions passively and, after persuasion, allowed herself to be talked into making the trip. The decision was one which she neither regretted nor was glad of. She had skied a little out here, idled a lot, had drinks which she would not have had in England, talked to people and been talked to. None of it made any difference to the way she felt.

She had felt moved, for a while, by the death of the child. The unfairness of it had angered her: that the boy, in apparent good health, with everything to live for, should have been deprived of life, which to her was a burden, a necessary unwanted routine. This had passed, and the faint possibility that the boy might be alive still had not revived it. To care about the boy would have been to commit herself, and there was nothing, she knew, worth the committal. Had he lived, it would have been to perform stupidities, to make choices which, whether selfish or noble, ended in wretchedness and boredom. There was no alternative to this.

They turned to head back in the direction of the chalet, and the east wind was bitterly cold on her exposed face. Pajamas, she thought, and bare feet. He could not still be alive out here. This, like everything else, was a waste of time and effort. Perversely, she was glad of the fact that it was also uncomfortable.

Douglas, a few feet above her on the slope, said, "It will soon be light."

The mountain spur in front of them was delicately touched with rose, the stars fading overhead. On the glimmering slopes, she could see other figures—two together well below the chalet, three higher up and farther off. Physical fatigue and lack of sleep had made her a little lightheaded. She said, "Douglas."

He turned his head in her direction. "Yes?"

"What is worth doing? Anything?"

It was a ridiculous question, regretted as soon as voiced. Either he would simply be bewildered by it, or else embarrassed. She had a wave of despair with herself.

But he said, after a pause of consideration, "It varies, I suppose, with different people, doesn't it? For me? Well, sticking

75

to things, I suppose. And not giving in to other things. That more, really."

Well, she had got it—precisely the answer she could expect to get from a rising provincial unmarried solicitor. A worthy man, a solid man. Like Harry, in some ways. Oh God, she thought, it's so cold. And I'm so tired.

When she did not reply, Douglas went on. "I don't think one person's reactions can be much help to another. The reactions themselves are different, at different times. Patches, phases. When one is in a bad one, it's impossible to imagine being out of it—you can't conceive there can be a way out. One does get out, though, eventually. It's more or less a certainty."

With unhappy irony, she thought: he's being kind. Commiserating with the unmerry widow. He thinks I'm grieving for Harry, and he's being nice about it. Disinterestedly nice. She thought for a moment of trying to explain that it was really not like that at all, but decided not to. Explanations were pointless, as pointless as questions asked on a snow-packed mountain slope in the freezing pre-dawn.

She said, "That's George and Leonard Deeping down there, isn't it? They seem to be heading back towards the chalet. Shall we do the same?"

They had all drawn blanks. While they ate the breakfast Mandy had prepared during their absence—porridge laced with treacle, and thick rashers of gammon and fried potatoes afterwards—they talked about it.

Hamilton said, "I reckon we've covered everything within a reasonable distance. And Peter didn't find any sign of anything on the outlying slopes. We can have another hunt in a while, but I'm not very hopeful."

Grainger emptied his cup of coffee, and poured more in from the pot. He said, "We were over two hours out there.

76

With the time we were hunting through the house, and so on, that makes it more than three." He glanced at Deeping. "I'm sorry, but even if he weren't dead yesterday, he can't possibly be alive now. It's a medical certainty. And in fact he was dead yesterday."

Deeping said nothing. He was eating the food in front of him, his face expressionless. Stoicism, Jane wondered, or callousness? Or neither of these, perhaps, but a dull realization of the way in which the death of the child might become a central inescapable feature of his future life with a woman deprived of her purpose and meaning, and so—having no more to lose—prepared to hate. She halted these speculations. A growing cynicism about the motives of others was one of the more depressing side effects of recognizing one's own lack of motive.

Douglas said, "That doesn't explain why we none of us found anything." He, too, glanced at Deeping, and went on in a quieter voice. "We'll presume Andy's death. It does seem reasonable. But even so, where is he? Not in the house, and not outside—in the immediate vicinity, at any rate. Then where? And how?"

"He could be somewhere outside," Hamilton said. "You can miss things pretty easily in the kind of light you get before sunup. You couldn't tell whether a drift had been disturbed, for instance."

Elizabeth said, "Do you mean that someone might have put his body in a drift? But why?"

Grainger said, "I've told you, there could be half a dozen reasons. All of them batty, of course, but the situation is batty, isn't it?"

"You were wrong about old Peter," Hamilton said. "He's more upset about it than anybody. The Swiss like death to be ceremonious, I gather."

"He was just one possibility. All the same, a show of concern doesn't rule him out. We're all actors, and we all under-estimate the acting ability of the next chap."

"What you're really saying," Douglas said, "is not that we're all actors, but that one of us is a particularly unpleasant maniac."

"What I'm saying," Grainger said, spearing a portion of potato, "is that I can't see a sane solution that makes sense. It doesn't mean there isn't one."

They went on talking afterward over fresh cups of coffee. Jane listened to them, with no more than slight interest. She was very conscious of her tiredness, and of the soft warm bed upstairs from which she had been dragged after only half a night's sleep. Even the element of puzzle in the situation did not mean much to her. It was shocking that the boy should be dead, shocking, in a different way, that his body was missing. She registered both facts, but neither of them engaged her.

The coffeepot, she noticed, was empty, as was her own cup. The solution to that, under normal circumstances, would be to pull the braided bell rope that hung beside the huge orna-mental tiled stove. Circumstances, though, were nothing like normal. She decided that the least she could do to help out was to take the pot through to the kitchen herself; it would be some break from tedium and the action might help to wake her up. Hamilton, when he saw what she was doing, said, "I'll see to that, Jane," but accepted her smile and shake of the head, and went on talking. She picked up pot and milk jug —she preferred black coffee to the addition of the watered-down tinned milk which was all that was available now, but some of the others could tolerate it—and went out into the passage.

She saw Ruth Deeping outside the door that opened into the bar. That was not surprising. She had been left sleeping on the sofa there; and presumably she had woken again, found herself alone, and come out to look for the others. What was surprising, though, was that she was heading neither toward the salon nor the stairs, but in the direction of the front door. As she reached the inner door, and wrenched it open, Jane called to her, "Ruth! What is it?"

There was no reply, not even a backward glance. She went through the entrance lobby, and began fumbling at the heavy iron ring of the outside door. She was still dressed as she had been earlier, in a light wrap over a nightdress, and bedroom slippers.

Jane saw that there was a ledge over a radiator near her; she slammed down the things she was carrying and raced along the hall. Ruth had managed to get the door open by the time she reached her. They wrestled on the threshold, the frigid air blowing around them, and she called for help from the others. Before they came, she had been dragged out into the snow, and her neck was hurting where Ruth had clawed at her.

The men between them subdued Ruth and managed to get her back into the bar. She struggled against the restraint they put on her and swore at them as a child might—the words not very bad in themselves but obscene in the way they were torn brokenly from her. Grainger tried to calm her.

"It's all right," he said. "You've been asleep, and you've had a bad dream. You'll be better in a moment. Easy. You're hurting yourself."

"You bastards!" she said. "You bloody bastards . . . he's out there. Andy's out there in the cold."

"We've been looking for him," Grainger said. "And we'll look for him again."

Hamilton had detached himself and now brought a glass of brandy to her. "Here. Get this down, and you'll feel better."

She was still for a moment, and then made a fierce effort to free herself. She did not succeed, but the glass went spinning across the floor.

"Let me go, you bloody swine," she said. "Andy . . . he's out there. I tell you, *I've seen him!*"

She said it with a chilling conviction. Even knowing it was nonsense, a delusion brought about by shock and grief and the drug Grainger had given her, Jane found her eyes going automatically to the window. It was much brighter out there, though the sun had not yet risen.

In a quiet, humoring voice, Grainger said, "Where, Ruth? Where did you see him? We're trying to help you. Truly we are."

She strained to move in the direction of the window. Grainger nodded to the others, and they gave her her head. They went with her, and stood around her. She pointed out across the snow.

"There. He was there. I woke, and looked out, and I saw him." She turned to look into their faces, her own drawn, desperate. "I'm telling you the truth. I'm not mad! He was there."

"Near the place where the little avalanche came down?" Hamilton asked.

"On the other side of it. I couldn't be mistaken."

Douglas asked her, "What did he look like?"

"Like Andy! How else could he look?"

"I meant, what was he wearing?"

"Only his pajamas." A sob racked and tore at her. "In that bitter cold. And he was carrying a basket."

It was this last which was the touch of nightmare. Jane felt herself shiver uncontrollably as she in turn looked out. The white slopes were empty. The wind, which seemed to be getting up, whipped a faint powdery spray from the rubble which marked the place where the avalanche had descended—apart from that there was nothing, no movement, no hint or sign of life. A boy in pajamas, carrying a basket. An illusion— what else?—but the thought was terrifying.

There was a silence, which Hamilton broke. He patted

Ruth on the shoulder, a warm, comfortingly ordinary gesture.

"Right," he said. "In that case, we'll go out again, and have another look. And you must promise to stay here, and watch us. You'll be able to see everything that goes on."

"I want to come with you!"

"You're not dressed," Hamilton said. "And, more than that, you're not well enough." He looked at Grainger, who gave a small nod. "Leonard and Douglas and I will go out—right away. Three of us will be enough. It's pretty light now. And the others will stay and wait with you. You'll get Ruth a cup of tea, Jane, will you?"

"Yes, of course."

Ruth was quiet for a time, but became more and more restless, watching the three figures as they moved up and down the slopes. When at last they came back, she burst into another paroxysm of sobbing and accusation: they had not looked properly . . . he was there, and they would have found him if they had looked.

Grainger watched her for a moment, then said, "We'll go and look for ourselves. Will that do?" She nodded, still sobbing, unable to speak. He glanced at Elizabeth. "Take her upstairs, and get some warm clothes on her."

When they had gone, Hamilton said, "Should she go out, do you think? The kid's not there. I can tell you that."

"It may help if she's shown that he's not there." Grainger shrugged. "On the other hand, of course, it may not. At a certain point, a fixed delusion is no longer susceptible to disproof. But I think we ought to give her the benefit of the doubt. At least, it will ease her a little. She's under a pretty heavy strain."

In the end, apart from Mandy and the servants, they all went. The chalet still lay in the shadow of the mountain, but to the west the snow was lit by the morning sun. It looked warm and cheerful out there, although the wind, Jane found, was keener. It brought tears to her eyes, and a smart to her lips.

They hunted for over half an hour, but it was plain from the start that their task was hopeless. The snow stretched bare and empty before them, smooth except where it was broken by ski- and footmarks, and by the rubble of the avalanche. Some of the footmarks were small enough to have been the boy's, but, of course, this was the part where the two of them had been playing, before Andy had his attack. There had been no fresh fall of snow since then.

Ruth seemed to recognize the hopelessness of it all, and when, eventually, Grainger went to her, took her arm, and said gently, "Time we went in, I think," she made no protest. They returned in silence to the chalet. Mandy was waiting for them in the hall, and she and Elizabeth took Ruth upstairs.

When they had gone, Grainger said, "I hope she'll get a good sleep this time. But someone had better stay with her. She still could do something rash."

"Mandy's doing that," Hamilton said, "while I look after things down here." He added, to Deeping, "She's putting her in our room for the present—thought it would be best. Hope that's all right?"

Deeping said quickly, "Yes, of course."

Hamilton looked around the circle of his guests. "I should think you could all do with a rest."

"What about you and Mandy?" Douglas asked.

Hamilton laughed. "All in the day's work. You learn to manage without sleep in this business."

Some of the party chose to go to bed; others stayed up. The Graingers split on this, he deciding that, with the new day well advanced, it was absurd to think of sleep; she, yawning like a great sleek cat, declaring that she found no temptation in the sunlight when she had had less than her due of rest. "Yes," Grainger told her, "off you go and renew that beauty."

She smiled, patted him lightly on the cheek, and took her graceful way upstairs.

Diana, rather obviously not looking at Grainger, said that she, too, felt it pointless to go back to bed. There was no need, Jane thought, to worry about this. Diana was a girl who enjoyed flirtations and, she was fairly sure, knew how to keep a firm hand on them; while Grainger, whatever his gallantries, was not likely to stray far from his decorative and capable wife. Her own first decision was for staying up, but she altered this when it became apparent that Douglas was staying up also. In part she disliked the thought of being credited with a similar maneuver to her sister's; rather more, though, she felt a lingering embarrassment over her question to him when they were out on the snow together, and his clumsy, would-be sympathetic reply.

She undressed quickly, and climbed into bed. There was the keen voluptuous pleasure of feeling the warmth and weight of blankets over her, and, this coinciding with a wave of drowsiness and fatigue, she thought that she might be able to get to sleep. But the coffee had undone her, as she had suspected it might. Time and again she rolled to the very edge of oblivion, only to snap back into wakefulness. When she had looked at her watch and realized it was nearly an hour since she had come up to bed, she recognized the inevitable, sat up, and reached for her book.

There were occasional sounds from outside—people moving about the house. Footsteps, once, going past her room in the direction of the bathroom. The book she was reading was of the kind she enjoyed, but which these days seemed a rarity: written about fairly pleasant people in fairly pleasant prose. It crossed her mind as a little strange that she could be interested in the doings of these fictional characters, and not in those of real people. But perhaps the fictional ones were nicer: the proposition, she admitted, included herself.

She did not, at first, pay any attention when the activity outside increased and became noisier—voices raised, someone hurrying. But a feeling of urgency gradually communicated itself. She got out of bed, put on wrap and slippers, and opened her door. Douglas was coming up the stairs, and she called to him, "What is it? Have they found the boy?"

The impression he usually gave was a boyish one—slim and dark with a clear skin under a quiff of rather curly hair—and being tense, as he was now, did nothing to change that. He still looked like a boy, but a worried one. He stopped when Jane spoke, and looked up at her.

"No," he said. "They haven't found the boy. But we've lost Ruth now."

5

Ruth would not agree to being undressed again, but Mandy persuaded her to lie down, on top of her bed, and have a blanket pulled over her. Then she drew up a chair beside the bed, and talked to her. She never had much difficulty in talking to people; George had reckoned that a major asset when they had decided to become guest-house proprietors. The secret, although she did not understand it herself, was that she had very little vanity, and so could talk about herself without either embarrassment or aggressiveness. And she did not look to the other person for approval or disapproval. She rattled on about herself, and George, and the odd but comfortable life they had lived together. Ruth listened to her—it was difficult to gauge with how much attention—and at last said, "Of course, you have no children."

The tone was bitter. Mandy hesitated before replying. The twelve years before George was the part of her life she did not talk about. And one kind of loss was different from another—

speaking of it would give no comfort to this one bereaved. She shook her head.

"No, we haven't had children."

Something in her voice had given her away. Ruth said sharply, "Was George your first husband?"

She said reluctantly, "No. We've both been married before."

"And children?"

"Not George."

Indeed, not George; the notion of Phyllis with children would have been either laughable or sinister. Poor Phyllis had been created for wartime R.A.F. officers' mess dances, for prangs and beat-ups, and a brave recognition that there was no future in anything. What was it George had said? "Three fiancés shot away from over her—but the war had to end sometime."

"But you," Ruth said, "did you have a child in your first marriage?"

"I had three children," Mandy said, and recognized the tense she used, as she always did.

"What happened to them?"

"Their father got custody."

"Couldn't you have fought that?"

"No." She thought about it. "Not honestly."

"Does honesty have anything to do with it?"

"I think so. I hope so. It was the best thing for them."

"You don't seem to have minded much."

There was as much incredulity in it as contempt. Mandy said, "They were happy, fond of their father. And very American. George and I . . . we've had fun, but I wouldn't say it's been terribly stable, the right kind of background for growing children."

"It sounds very objective."

"As bad as that? There was something else as well, of

86

course. I was the guilty party. I'd run off with a foreigner. Could you see any American court giving me custody in those circumstances?"

There was a silence before Ruth said, "It's not the sort of thing I'm very good at understanding, I'm afraid."

"No," Mandy said. "I'm not very good at explaining, either."

She thought that Ruth would pursue it, but she did not. It seemed, in a way, that the passage—the total failure of comprehension, communication—had eased her. Her face, as she lay back against the pillow, was strained and miserable, but less so, Mandy thought, than it had been. And after a time her breathing became more even, deeper, and Mandy saw that she had dropped off to sleep.

She watched the sleeping woman, trying to think of some meditation which would pass the time. But the good memories, for the moment, had been driven out by the bad; and she would not surrender herself to those. She had looked at her watch when she first noticed Ruth was asleep and, glancing again, she saw that only five minutes had gone by. The realization was depressing. She needed—she really needed—a little something to cheer her up.

With a shock of surprise and then of pleasure, she realized something else: that she had not had a drink so far that day. There had been the hurried rising in the middle of the night, with Ruth screaming at the foot of the stairs, and from then on she had been too busy, too preoccupied, to think of it. And, of course, she was glad of that. It showed that, even though it had become a habit, it was a habit that could be broken. Through the window she saw the distant peaks, bright with morning sunshine. Perhaps the mountains had something to do with it. They had always frightened her a little and, between seasons when she had time on her hands, they oppressed her more than ever. It was between seasons that the drinking crept up on her; when there were guests in the house she drank no more, if anything, less.

Maybe if they went somewhere else . . . The Camargue, perhaps. Or Greece—one of the smaller islands. The sound and sight of the sea, she thought, would be comforting. Up here there was either silence or the inhuman howl of the wind. And cowbells in the summer, far-off, melancholy.

She took the bottle from its place, taking care not to chink it. It was less than half full; she had not realized the level had got so low. She poured her tot into the glass, and then poured a little more. After all, she still had something in hand. She took tiny sips, one after the other. It warmed her, and the mountains in the distance looked less frightening. Then she tired of sipping, and drained the rest, feeling the brighter, heavier glow inside. She held the empty glass in her hand, and stared at it. It was very quiet; she could hear nothing but the breathing of the sleeping woman, and the ticking of her own watch. She looked at it. Only a quarter of an hour. The thing to do, she decided, was to pour another drink and not to touch it for—how long? Another quarter hour? Half an hour, perhaps? What was important was to see it in front of her, available, waiting on her act of will.

She started drinking the second glass after ten minutes, and her failure so depressed her that she drank it all quickly and poured another. This time she set no time limit and was surprised and pleased to find the temptation less. She had needed to relax, and perhaps the two drinks had been enough to achieve that. She felt relaxed now, and physically tired—not sleepy, but it was wearisome sitting up in a chair. She took the glass and walked quietly around to George's bed. She put the glass on his bedside table, and lay down. She could see both Ruth and the glass at the same time, and the softness of the bed was a comfort. George's bed. She thought of him with affection. I am not an unhappy woman, she thought—with George, who could be? Perhaps it's just that some things have to be paid for, and some of us don't have the money. So we go bankrupt. She reached for the glass, brought it down, tilted it to her lips without spilling it, and had a little drink.

When she awoke it was to the guilty realization that, having dozed off like that, Ruth might have herself woken, and seen the glass on the table between them. This was the first part of the shock of seeing the other bed empty: Ruth had woken, perhaps gone to the bathroom, and Ruth had seen that she was drinking. She felt a sweat of shame break out on her. It took a moment or two of waiting, listening for returning footsteps, wondering how to carry it off, before she remembered why she was here—that she was supposed to have been watching.

She got up then, quickly, not bothering about the glass, and hurried out of the room. The bathroom door was closed. She rapped on it, received no answer, and turned the knob. The door opened, and the room was empty. She checked the other rooms on the floor, but without much hope. The bathroom on the first floor . . . she might have thought this one was occupied, and gone there. It was a slim chance, but she went, anyway. That door was also closed, and once again there was no answer when she knocked. But this time it did not budge when she tried to open it.

George, when she told him, wasted no time. He raced upstairs, threw himself against the bathroom door, and burst it open. Following close behind him, Mandy saw that there was no one in the room, and also that the window on the far side was open. A little powdery snow was blowing in; falling from the roof presumably since the sky was clear and blue.

It was the easiest way to get out of the house unobserved. There was a lean-to roof three or four feet below the window ledge, sloping down. The drop from that to the ground was not more than eight feet, and into thick snow. It was possible to trace her progress: snow scuffed along the roof and a hole marking the place where she had jumped down.

Mandy said wretchedly, "I'm sorry. I ought not to have fallen asleep like that."

He put an arm around her shoulders, and gave her a hug.

"You were tired, lovey. Not to worry. I don't think we shall have much difficulty in picking her up." He turned from the window. "That wasn't what I was afraid of."

"She's gone to look for the boy again?"

"What else? But if we found the poor little devil now, I'm not sure she'd believe it. Anyway, let's go and see Selby."

From the house, they could see no sign of Ruth. Elizabeth was still sleeping, and Stephen, but the others were present downstairs. Diana, who was hanging on to Grainger, said, "If we go in pairs, it will be best, don't you think? And all go different ways."

Grainger said impatiently, "No need for a major search party. It's fairly obvious where she's headed for."

Douglas Poole said, "Obvious?"

"I think so. Up beyond the avalanche. It's where she claimed she saw the child before."

"This time she might think she'd seen him in the opposite direction."

"Doubt it. A pretty fixed delusion, I should guess. She's not likely to vary it."

Jane said, "An odd one. Carrying a basket."

Mandy felt a chill of unease. She said, "Is that what she said—that the boy was carrying a basket?"

Grainger said, "Yes. It's the odd touch you get with a certain kind of fantasy-hallucination. Absurd and plausible at the same time."

Mandy said, "But there is a basket missing."

They looked at her. George said, "Are you sure?"

"I noticed it when I was down checking the food. The old wicker basket that used to hang behind the door."

There was a silence. George said, but not unkindly, "Maybe you didn't look in the right place. Maybe someone moved it."

They were all uncomfortable, contemplating they were not sure what. Grainger said forcefully, "It's ridiculous! Quite ridiculous."

Jane said, "I wonder . . ."

"What?"

"You suggested someone may have moved it. Andy may have taken it—before all this happened. To play with, or something. And Ruth could have seen him with it. So she could have imagined him with it this morning."

The atmosphere of relief was palpable. Grainger said, explosively commendatory, "Takes a woman to find the logical answer. Plainly, that's it. You can't be sure it wasn't there yesterday, can you, Mandy?"

"No."

It was true: she could not be sure. On the other hand, she felt herself that it had been there. And there was the matter, which she had not mentioned, of food being missing. Cheese, biscuits, two small tins of corned beef. She had thought that someone had taken them as a precaution against their being cut off for so long a time that food became scarce. It was the sort of thing that she could imagine Deeping getting up to. That might still be the explanation. In any case, there was no point in saying anything.

George said, "Let's get back to the important thing—finding Ruth and bringing her in. You're probably right about where she's gone, Selby. There isn't much cover in other directions, for that matter. Better have all the chaps come along, I suppose?"

She found chaos in the kitchen, and Marie quietly weeping. Things, it appeared, had become too much for her: their being cut off, the child's death, the lady screaming in the night

. . . and now the dough would not rise for the bread which Madame had asked her to prepare. It sat in tins on the rack above the cooker, the covering muslin sagging sadly. Tables and floor were in a clutter. She soothed the girl, made her hot coffee from a fortunately boiling kettle, and set her to work clearing up the mess. The explanation of the dough was simple; she had forgotten the yeast. Fortunately flour was one of the items in good supply; and she could probably work more fat in and make pastry from it. Not the kind of pastry of which she would be very proud, but edible at least.

Order had more or less been restored when she heard her name called from the hall. Diana's voice, and excited. But happily excited, she thought, as she went to see what was the matter. Diana met her outside the door leading to the bar, and pulled her in.

"Look!"

She pointed out of the window. Figures were coming across the snow from the direction of the avalanche. The four men who had gone out. And Ruth. And . . . She stared, unable to believe what was so plainly visible. George, in his strong arms, was carying a small pajamaed figure. Andy. And the boy was alive. There could be no doubt of that. She saw him turn his head to look at his mother.

Jane was there, too. She said, "I don't understand. How could he . . . ?"

The wave of happiness and relief was so great that Mandy felt tears welling in her eyes. Relief, and remorse. She said, blaming herself, "And we wanted to stop her going out there to find him . . . She knew. But he might have died while we kept her in the house." She blinked her eyes vigorously. "They must both be freezing cold. I'll go and get hot drinks ready."

As she turned, Jane said, in a puzzled voice, "The basket . . ."

Mandy looked again. The boy, carried in George's arms, was holding the basket that had been missing from the basement. She said happily, "You see—she was right about that, too."

"It doesn't make sense," Jane said.

"It doesn't matter! I must go and get something ready for them."

She told Marie, who was as incredulous as she had been and then, accepting the fact, wept again. When they heard the front door open, they both went out and joined the other two women to greet them. They were taken into the salon, everyone jostling and laughing and talking at once. Mandy went to take the child from George, but Ruth reached for him at the same time. She said, "Let me have him." Her voice sounded thick and heavy, presumably in the anticlimax of emotion. "I can look after him now."

Mandy had touched the boy's face. She said, "He's so cold! Bring him up close to the fire. Pull the settee forward, George. We must warm him."

"I am all right," Andy said. "I'm not cold."

It was as extraordinary hearing him talk as seeing him. She remembered the white, seemingly dead little figure of the previous day, and could not link it with the living boy. Although he was so cold, he was not shivering.

Mandy looked around at them all. "But where was he? How did you find him?"

George said exuberantly, "Ruth found him. They were sitting together in the snow when we fell over them. Just the other side of the avalanche."

Jane said, "But we looked there! We searched all round, this morning."

Grainger was staring at the boy, deeply puzzled. So much for doctors, Mandy thought lightheartedly. He had said the boy must be dead. They could be wrong. Probably he was a

93

little miffed over that. But they could be wrong. Life still had its surprises. Tears stung her eyes again.

"Little beggar had buried himself in the snow, apparently," George said. "That's how he lasted out. A good thick blanket of snow over him. And he had a spot of grub with him, so he didn't lack for nourishment."

"But why?" Jane asked. "Why did he go out into the snow? What happened?"

In an expressionless voice, Ruth said, "It was the shock, I think. He woke up down there in the basement, and found himself alone. He didn't know what he was doing. I suppose the last thing he remembered was being out there, by the avalanche. He just went out there again. He was shocked, you see."

Grainger said, "But not too shocked to get hold of a basket, and fill it with provisions, before he went."

George said, "No limit to the things you can get up to when you've had a blackout. I knew a chap who brought a Lancaster back with two engines out and three-quarters of the controls shot away. And he didn't remember a thing after the flak hit him over Berlin."

"Not quite the same, " Grainger said quietly. "He was continuing a routine action."

"Not exactly routine."

"But not irrational. Ruth, I think I'd better have a look at him now."

She seemed reluctant to part with the boy; as was, Mandy felt, no more than natural. She herself remembered that she had been going to get something hot and nourishing for him. There were a couple of shell eggs she had been hoarding. Beaten up with hot milk, and a little brandy . . . She slipped away while Grainger was reaching for the boy.

When she returned with the drink, Grainger was just completing his examination. He was frowning, as though trying to

94

work out a problem in an unfamiliar idiom. Mandy came past him, and held the glass for Andy.

"Try and drink it right down," she said. "I've made sure it's not too hot. You'll feel better after this."

The boy drank obediently.

Grainger said, "Pulse slow, heartbeat down. And he's damnably cold." He turned to Ruth. "I think we ought to get him to bed, right away, and keep him there. I would very much like to have someone else look at him."

Ruth said, "He's all right now." She spoke with flatness and conviction. "I shall look after him."

Mandy said, "I know you will. But he'll be best in his bed, won't he? There, he's drunk it all. Feel a little better, Andy? George will carry him upstairs for you."

"No," Andy said. His voice sounded strange, too, but it could be expected to do so, after all he had been through. "I can walk up, thank you."

"If you're sure . . ."

He took his mother's hand, and they left the room together.

Mandy said to Ruth, "I'll bring a drink up to you."

"Don't bother." She looked at Deeping, who was trailing after them. "I'll take him up and we'll lie down together. We both need the rest more than anything else."

Deeping hesitated, then nodded. "You're sure there's nothing I can get you?"

"Nothing."

The two of them went upstairs, slowly, as though tired. Which they would be, Mandy thought. And Ruth, whatever she said, could do with something warm inside her. A cup of tea, and perhaps a touch of rum with it.

She went back to the kitchen, and made the tea. The kettle was still simmering on top of the stove. While she was waiting for the tea to brew, she helped herself to a quick drink from the bottle with the wine vinegar label which she kept behind the jar of vanilla sugar. She slipped it back just before Marie came in from outside. Warmed and relaxed, she told Marie to get some rum from Monsieur, poured the tea, added a generous tot, and gave the bottle back to her to return.

She decided to take the tea up herself. She was climbing the second flight of stairs when she heard the child's voice raised in alarm. Not Andy's voice, though—Stephen's. She hurried, spilling a little of the tea into the saucer. The door to the Deepings' room was partly open, enough for her to realize that some kind of a struggle was going on in there. She pushed the door open with her elbow. Andy and his mother were on either side of Stephen, holding him, with Ruth bending down as though pushing him back into the bed from which he was trying to rise. They turned and looked at her as she came in, moving with an odd kind of unison. Their hold on Stephen slackened, and he broke free, flung himself off the bed, and ran full pelt for Mandy. His head bulleted against her stomach, and he clutched at her, sobbing.

"Why, easy," she said, "you're spilling all the tea."

Over his head she handed the cup to Ruth, who took it, her eyes riveted on Stephen. Ruth said, "He woke suddenly, and was frightened." Her voice was harsh, strained. "Seeing Andy . . . he must have thought . . ."

"Poor old chap," Mandy said. She rubbed his head, comforting him. "But Andy's all right, you know. There's nothing to worry about. Nothing for anyone to worry about."

Stephen said something indistinguishable into her apron. She bent down to him, and took his head gently between her hands. He looked up at her, quickly. As though reassured by what he saw, he said, "I want to come downstairs with you. Please, Mrs. Hamilton."

She looked at Ruth. "I guess he can get up now, can't he? He's slept long enough."

"Quite long enough." Ruth put her hands out toward the

boy. "I'll send him down to you when he's got washed and dressed. Thank you for the tea."

Stephen said, "No!" He faced his mother, his body pressed against Mandy's. "I don't want to stay with you."

Ruth looked more angry than anything else. And that was understandable, too, Mandy thought. After this terrible time with the younger boy—thinking he was dead, and then missing, and finding him at last out in the snow—her nerves must have been worn ragged. But for little Stephen, also, it had been grim enough. His brother dead, his mother crazy with grief, and to discover Andy standing by his bed, touching him . . . the Andy who had always been the favored one.

Mandy said to Ruth, "He'll be all right when he's properly come awake. But I'll see to him while you put Andy to bed. His clothes are in the next room, anyway, aren't they?"

Ruth stared at her, and the boy, and turned away. "All right." Her voice was cold. "I'll leave him to you, in that case."

They went through to what had been the boys' bedroom, and Mandy closed the door. Remembering the physical modesty of the pre-pubertal boy, she said, "Your clothes are over there, Steve. Would you like me to leave you to get washed and dressed? I'll go down and see about rustling up some breakfast for you."

"No!" The edge of fear was in his voice. "Please stay with me."

"Just as you like. But you will have to get ready pretty quickly, because there are lots of things I've got to do downstairs."

He said earnestly, "I'll be very quick."

While he was dressing, Mandy looked out of the window. The far peaks were clear, sharp, and white against blue, but cloud was beginning to form at a lower altitude, thickening up in the valley below them. It would be a dull gray comfortable day down there.

97

She said, "It's wonderful about Andy, isn't it?"

"Yes." His voice was indistinct.

"It does happen sometimes. With animals and birds, as well as people. I remember when I was very small—younger than you are—I went for a walk with my father one cold winter's day. I found a wren by the side of the path, on its back with its little legs stretched out. I put it in my pocket—I was going to bury it when I got home. And just before I got home, I felt something flutter in my pocket, and there it was, quite alive. I put my hand in, and lifted it out, and it pecked my fingers and flew away."

She could remember how happy she had been: the feeling of having given warmth and life, as though a part of herself had gone into this small creature, flown away on those suddenly beating wings. She thought about it with rekindled pleasure. She did not mind thinking about those days. They were so long ago. And no one had been hurt by them, no one betrayed.

She turned around. Stephen was dressed, and trying to comb his hair, looking at himself in the mirror over the washbasin, his face screwed up in concentration and frustration. Her heart moved toward him.

"Let me help you, Steve." He suffered her ministrations patiently. "There. You look just fine. Shall we go in and see your mummy and Andy before we go down?"

He shook his head. "I'd rather not."

"Well, then, we'll go and find some breakfast."

As they came to the first-floor landing, she heard a noise and looked up. Ruth was gazing down from above. She looked tired, her eyes showing fatigue and a kind of emptiness.

"We'll look after this one," Mandy said. "You go to bed and get some rest."

After the alarms and excursions with which it had started,

the day was settling down to normality—insofar as normality could be stretched to cover their continuing to be cut off from contact with the outside world. On that point, George organized a sortie to see what progress had been made, if any, in the opening up of the road from Nidenhaut. He went on skis, and took Grainger with him and, on her last-minute insistence, Diana. Grainger then asked Elizabeth, who had finally emerged from their bedroom, if she would not come as well, but she shook her head, covering a yawn.

"Still much too tired. If you do manage to get to the village, bring some of those Florentines back from the patisserie. I feel a craving for them."

"Not a hope." He looked at his wife with frank and unstinted admiration. "You're getting far too fat."

She smiled back at him, over the head of the much shorter Diana.

"Darling, you know I'm your mother figure."

Over lunch, they reported what they had found. The way was still completely blocked and the curve of the rock face prevented their seeing what things were like farther down. George had had a shot at venturing out on the slope of rubble to see if it could be traversed, but it had begun to slide, and he had given up the attempt. Mandy felt both relieved and annoyed with him, hearing that. He was much too willing to take chances with his safety.

Douglas Poole said, "Did you hear anything of activity on the other side?"

"No." George shook his head emphatically. "Not on the other side. There was a sound of what could have been clearing work, but a good way off. They've probably got at least one other section to clear before they get on to this one."

Deeping said, "So we're stuck here indefinitely."

The familiar, slightly grousing note, absent since Andy's collapse the previous day, had returned to his voice. George looked at him with irritation, and said, "Yes. Lucky we're well stocked with food. And all good jolly companions. Aren't Ruth and Andy coming down to lunch, by the way?"

Mandy said, "No. Andy's still asleep, and Ruth is staying up with him for the time being. She says she isn't hungry just yet. I'm keeping some for them."

Deeping said, still sounding querulous, "I'm not feeling particularly hungry myself. A broken night always upsets my stomach. I don't think I'll have any sweet, Mandy. Just coffee."

Mandy sighed. "That's another thing. We'll have to go easy if there's no sign of them getting through yet. Coffee in the morning, and after supper, but we shall have to cut it out after lunch, I'm afraid. Fortunately we're not short of tea."

Deeping stood up from the table. "I'd rather have had coffee," he said, "but I suppose it can't be helped."

"No," George said, "it can't, can it? By the way, I've made your bill up to yesterday afternoon. Since then, board and lodging's been on the house."

Deeping looked at him, flushing. "That's not necessary. I can pay my way."

"Think nothing of it," George said.

Getting him alone later, Mandy said, "You were a bit unkind to him, George. He's had a pretty bad time the last twenty-four hours, with Andy and Ruth."

"Don't talk about that bastard. 'I'd rather have had coffee.' The only person he's ever likely to worry about is Len Deeping."

She shushed him. Stephen was standing in the entrance to the kitchen. "What is it, Steve?"

"Do you mind if I go downstairs, Mrs. Hamilton, and play with the race game?"

The race game was an old Escalado, kept along with a number of other adjuncts to time-passing in bad weather, in a room in the basement somewhat optimistically referred to as the games room.

"Why, yes," she said. "Can you set it up?" He nodded. "Don't stay down too long and get cold. There's only one small radiator down there."

Which was the principal reason why the games room was little used during the winter season. She said to George, as she had said before, "We must do something about getting more heating in there before next winter."

"The boiler is pushed to the limit as it is. More important to keep the upper part of the house warm."

"We should have had a bigger boiler."

"The hell of it is we're undercapitalized. And we're not making too much profit at the moment. Not with me standing on my dignity to Deeping, and the people who should have taken their place lining the pockets of old Mueller, at the Buffet de la Gare in Nidenhaut. Maybe we ought to send a cable to Aunt Mandy."

She smiled at the familiar joke, the only reference to her American background that they normally permitted themselves. Aunt Mandy, married at nineteen to a wealthy coal owner and now nearly fifty years widowed, had written one letter to the niece who had been named after her, on hearing that she had left her husband for George. The letter had been long, but businesslike rather than reproachful. She had listed her assets, valued them, and arrived at a sum of three hundred and twenty-two thousand seven hundred and fifty dollars, as the nearest approximation. This was the estate which, in her previous will, had been left to her beloved niece, Mandy. It had been replaced, she explained in an un-American copperplate, acquired at Miss Hudnut's Academy for Young Ladies of the City of Boston, by a new will. She wished to advise Mandy that her name did not appear in this one.

"Do you mind being poor?" Mandy asked him.

He grinned. "That should be my question."

And, of course, he was right: it should be his question.

She smiled again. "Doesn't worry me. Doesn't worry me *at* all."

"What does worry you, Mandy?"

He spoke gently. She knew what he meant, and wished there were some kind of answer she could give. He was such a good person. She had known that when she met him and now, seeing him more clearly because no longer blinded by that which had overwhelmed her, and glorified her, and destroyed her, knew it with greater certainty.

"Nothing," she said. "Nothing worries me. Honey, off you go and look after our guests, while I look after the kitchen."

Ruth came down a little later, bringing Andy with her. Mandy asked her if they would have lunch now, but she refused.

"Surely Andy will have something to eat," Mandy said. "He's had nothing but the milk and eggs this morning."

"No. That is, he ate some chocolate upstairs. Where is everyone?"

"Most of them are outside, skiing. I think your husband is in the salon, though."

"And Stephen?"

"He went downstairs to play with the Escalado."

"We'll go down and look for him, I think."

Mandy watched them go, feeling faintly uneasy. They both still had that funny way of walking—a slowness, deliberation —which made her think they were not properly recovered from the recent events. They ought to have eaten something, too. She wondered if she should not go after them, and try to persuade Andy at least to have something; after what he had been through, he must need hot nourishing food. But she decided against it. Ruth was a woman not very much younger than herself, and with very positive ideas of her own. She would not take kindly to having someone tell her what was best for her son.

She was looking at the new batch of bread she had put out when she heard the cry. It was indistinct, but she recognized Marie's voice. Where was she, though? Outside? She remembered: she had sent her down to the food store to check up on various things before planning the following day's meals. The voice called again. "Madame!" Mandy pushed the last tray back and hurried to the stairs.

The voice was louder, crying for help, and there were other sounds. They came from the games room. Through the open door she saw a tangle of struggling figures—Ruth, Marie, the two boys. She could not think what had happened and, bewildered, called, "What is it? What's happening?"

The faces of the two women turned her way as she came through the doorway. Marie's was shocked and frightened, Ruth's . . . What she saw in that instant horrified her. It was not hatred, but a coldness, a terrible blankness. And a hunger. It scared her, but she took a step forward nevertheless.

"Ruth . . ." she said.

There was a moment of balance, of immobility, and then it broke. Figures erupted toward her: not only Ruth, but little Andy. They had gone mad, she realized, both of them, and shrank away. She wanted to cry for help, but could not. They came at her, reached her and, buffeting her out of the way, were past. Their footsteps retreated along the passage outside, in the direction of the basement door. Marie was weeping, the other boy white-faced. Mandy pulled herself together, and went to them.

6

Skiing, Douglas had more or less decided,
was not for him. It was a conclusion he had tentatively reached
on his earlier essay, during his Army service, but the years between had eroded the recollections. He was learning all over
again that his sense of balance was not very good, and that
loss of contact with solid ground was something to which he
found it difficult to become accustomed. And, of course, that
snow—as a medium to land in heavily—was both colder and
wetter than one would think from looking at it.

Now that he had given up trying not to think about Caroline, he could be honest with himself over his reason for coming here. Tony, her husband, had been a keen skier—the an-
nual two weeks in January had been one of the bad things,
casting its shadow over Christmas—itself, necessarily, a bad
time—to be endured grimly and without grousing. She had always said that she hated going away, but he had guessed that
this could not be entirely true. She had every kind of physical

excellence, and would inevitably get pleasure from skiing. Very possibly she was skiing now, in the United States. They had winter sports resorts within reach of New York, surely? And here he was, floundering about the baby slopes on a mountain slope in Switzerland . . . it was laughable.

He had never been able to understand what part he played in her life. He had swung between seeing it as something very large, and something very small. He had believed her, and still believed, when she said that he had been the only man in her life apart from Tony. She was not the kind of woman who went out of her way to attract male attentions. And the awareness of this had given him, at the beginning, a feeling of triumph and of confidence. There was the boy, but he was four —she had married very young—and due to go away to Tony's old prep school at eight. He had not, at the outset, pressed for any kind of assurance of the future, because he had assumed he knew what it was to be. With Rodney away for two-thirds of the year, there would be nothing to hide the emptiness of her marriage. Tony, whom he had met once or twice, was a pleasant, civilized fellow. He would give her a divorce when she asked him for it.

It was a couple of years later that his confidence began to show signs of fraying at the edges. It was not due to any signs of withdrawal on her part—she remained as loving as ever and as available as the exigencies of her life allowed—but rather to a growing sense of involvement on his own. He was no longer content to wait for the telephone call to his office which would tell him when he could see her. Her prohibition on telephone calls to her—the girl might answer, her mother was always dropping in on them, Tony himself was sometimes back at odd hours—which he had accepted readily enough, suddenly became irksome. He felt more and more that he was tied to her life—tied, for that matter, to the girl, and her mother, and even Tony—while she was free of his.

The first crisis came not when he asked her to go away with him, but a week or two later. He asked her in the cool blue and white bedroom of the house in Blackheath, Tony being away in Paris, and the girl on her afternoon off, and her mother visiting her other daughter on the other side of London, and she smiled, and said how nice it would be if they could. When he asked her why not, she said why, of course, Rodney. Even for this afternoon she had had to get a friend to pick him up from school and take him back with her little boy to tea. He had put his hands on her breasts, and said, "All right. But when he goes away . . . Promise?" They would see, she had said, and he admired her honesty as he had done before. She would never make empty promises. It would be lovely, but so many things could happen. They would see. Her tongue flickered, and her nipples stiffened against his fingers.

But he had gone away dissatisfied, out of sorts, and the dissatisfaction and uneasiness had grown during the following week, in which he did not see her, nor speak to her. A brief meeting after that had not helped. When he saw her properly again—in his own flat because she had come down ostensibly to visit the Winchester aunt who had been the means of their first meeting—he was in a state of nervousness and determination. This sort of life was no good to them. There had to be a permanence, a belonging, if not at once then in a future which one could envisage, and to which one could look forward. If they could not have that, it was better for them to break off now, cleanly.

He was not sure how he had expected her to react, but he recognized the reaction as the only one possible to her. She had neither consented, nor been angry. She told him, and the truth of it was inescapable, that she was giving him all that at this time lay within her power. Things might change in the future, but one could not offer guarantees. Life was too uncertain altogether.

In that case, he had said, end it now. She had smiled, sadly he thought, and said, "Whatever you think best." There had been silence, not really awkward but oppressive, a load weighing on mind and body. On the mantel the four-hundred-day clock twirled its silly little brass spheres around, clockwise, anticlockwise, marking seconds that suddenly were longer than they had been before. "Three o'clock," she had said. Her smile was mischievous this time. "My train isn't till six." She had never looked more desirable.

He said, "There's a fast one to Waterloo at three thirty."

"Well," she said. The smile had not left her lips. "Will you take me to the station, or must I find my own way?"

He had telephoned her three weeks later, breaking the prohibition which she had laid down. His mouth had been dry, and he had stumbled over his words when he talked to her. She had not been angry. She had seemed pleased, in fact, although only willing to talk in brief unemotional phrases, and not for long. She had cut him off, saying she would ring him when she had the time.

And that had been the following morning. She could see him, in London, at the week's end. They fixed a place and time. He took her back to his hotel room, and they made love. He tried to explain himself, to apologize, but she put her hand over his mouth. There was nothing to explain, she insisted, nothing to discuss.

There had been a similar crisis the year that Rodney went away to school. It followed the same pattern, except that he only waited two days that time before telephoning her. And the year after, he had not even let her go away, but had run after her down the street, stupidly, like a schoolboy. Thinking of it now, he was amazed at the level of banality to which his relationship with her had reduced him. And, as a final absurdity, a skiing trip! Picking himself up, for something like the twentieth time, he began to unstrap his skis with cold, clumsy fingers.

Jane called to him, "Are you going in?"

He looked up at her. "Yes."

"I think I've had enough, too."

They made their way up to the house together, and stacked their skis in the rack. It was, he told himself, comforting to reflect that there were still pleasant and attractive women in the world. Comforting, not challenging. With a drop into unhappiness, he speculated on one aspect of his future. Prostitutes? Scuffling liaisons with junior typists? Or a wife, perhaps? Someone suitable—good-looking, capable, not too young. Someone like Jane, perhaps. Comely young widows were always thought suitable, weren't they?

The door opened before he reached it. Mandy stood there, breathless, disheveled. She said, "Did you see her? Ruth?"

"No. Why?"

"I think she's gone crazy. And the boy."

Her obvious confusion made him feel confused himself, and at a loss. It was Jane who took charge of the situation. She said quietly, "Tell us what happened, Mandy."

He listened, and gathered that Ruth had run amuck in some way, which was not altogether surprising. There was something about the boy, Andy, which made less sense. She had left the house and taken him with her? Well, yes, she probably would.

Jane, turning to him, said crisply, "I'll look after Mandy. Do you think you can call the others in? Selby, at least."

He nodded. "Yes, of course."

They came readily enough to his call. Diana skied up hard on the heels of Grainger, with Elizabeth trailing some twenty yards behind. She was glowing from the sharp air and the exercise and looked, he thought with detachment, very pretty.

"Tea?" She took her cap off and shook the dark curls free. "It seems awfully early."

He said to Grainger, "More trouble, I'm afraid. With Ruth. I'm not quite sure what."

Jane was with Mandy in the salon. Deeping was there, too. He had a crumpled look, the bounce, the knowingness, knocked out of him like the wind it was. Although not liking the man, he felt some pity for him. He was coming in for heavy punishment.

Grainger said, with authority, "All right, Mandy. Tell us what it's all about."

George came in while she was telling her story. When she had finished, he said, "I've seen Marie. She's with Steve. They're both all right. A bit shaken, but all right."

Diana said, "I saw them. They were climbing up the slope, at the back of the chalet. I thought they were just . . . well, walking in the snow."

We'd better go after them," George said.

Grainger put his hand up. "In a minute. Mandy, how did you say she looked? Her expression?"

"It's hard to describe it. Empty, blank—and yet wanting . . . I don't know what."

"Look," George said, "you can do the trick-cyclist stuff later on. The important thing is to find them and bring them back, before they do themselves an injury. She's got the child with her, after all."

Grainger said, "I want to know what we're looking for."

George said impatiently, "A woman who's been driven a bit round the bend, and understandably."

"And the boy?"

"She took him with her. That's understandable, too. But dangerous for him."

Grainger addressed himself to Mandy. "That's not quite right, though, is it? She didn't take him with her. He went with her. And his expression?"

Mandy closed her eyes, shutting something off. In a low voice, she said, "The same as hers. Empty, and wanting something."

"You imagined that," George told her. "After all, you only saw them for a moment or two. She rushed out, and the kid rushed after her. He would do."

Grainger asked, "Do you think you could have imagined it?"

She shook her head silently.

George burst out, "Look, it doesn't make sense! Does it, now?"

Mandy said, "I've been wondering . . ."

"What?"

"If it could be some kind of illness—that Andy had got it first, perhaps, and Ruth picked it up from him." She looked at Grainger. "Is that possible?"

"Theoretically. On the other hand, the symptoms don't add up to any kind of illness that I've met or read about. And where do the boy's collapse and coma fit in?" He paused. "I'd like to see Marie. And Steve."

"I'll get them," Mandy said.

George said, "I haven't got your professional interest, Selby." There were red spots on his cheeks. "I'm taking Peter out there, to look for her and the poor unfortunate bloody child. Are you coming, Len?"

Deeping said, "Yes. I'll come."

Grainger said calmly, "Three of you will be enough, I should think. If you find them."

"And why the hell shouldn't we?"

"I was thinking of the previous occasion. It took some time finding the boy. In fact, we didn't find him. He turned up again, with Ruth."

"What's that supposed to mean?"

"I don't know." Grainger screwed his face up. "I wish I did."

Had George asked him to go with them, Douglas would have agreed. But George whirled out of the room, not looking

110

at anyone. Deeping followed him but, under the circumstances, Douglas did not feel like doing so. Three, as Grainger had said, was presumably a sufficient number to find the woman and child in broad daylight. And he was interested in seeing what Grainger was trying to discover. There was also the fact of personal disinclination: he had had enough of snow for the time being.

Stephen was composed when he was brought in, Marie less so. Her reasonably good English had deserted her, and she answered Grainger's questions in a spatter of French. From it, Douglas was able to glean her main charge—that Madame was possessed, and the little one also. She had always been told that there were devils in the mountains. This was well known among the Fribourgeois. A school friend of hers had an uncle who had gone as a priest to a village in the Pays d'Enhaut, and several times he had to exorcise devils . . .

"Did Madame attack you?" Grainger asked.

"Because I defended the boy from her." She had recovered enough to speak English again. "They attacked the boy. Both of them did so."

Grainger said gently to Stephen, "What happened, old chap? Before Marie came along."

"It was the same as in the bedroom." His voice was low but clear. "When I woke up and found them by my bed. They were both pressing against me."

"Trying to hurt you, do you think?"

"I don't know." His brow wrinkled. "They didn't try to . . . hit me, or anything. Just to press against me. But I was scared. And they felt funny."

"How, funny?"

"Tingly." He shook his head. "I don't know how to say it."

"Did they say anything to you?"

"No. I suppose that's one of the things that made me frightened. Just stared, saying nothing." He looked at

111

Grainger. "Then Marie came, and they still tried to hold on to me. But when Mrs. Hamilton came, they let go and ran off. Do you know where they've gone?"

"Somewhere outside. People are looking for them. Listen, try not to worry about this, Steve. Your mother . . . is not very well just now. People sometimes do strange things when they're ill."

"And Andy? Is he ill, too?"

"Yes, in a way."

He motioned to Marie, and she took the boy out of the room.

When they had gone, Mandy said, "So it is an illness?"

Grainger drew in a deep breath. "Well, yes. If we define illness as the absence of what we call health—mental or physical. But it doesn't get us a great deal further."

Douglas was in entire agreement with that. It was all confusing. Were there diseases which turned people mad? He was too ashamed of his medical ignorance to ask Grainger; and Grainger, in any case, seemed as much at a loss as anyone. Hydrophobia . . . a mad wolf? But the symptoms were different, surely, and there were no wolves in these mountains, no dogs higher up than Nidenhaut.

Jane, voicing his thoughts to some extent, said to Grainger, "It still doesn't seem like anything you recognize—any particular disease?"

Grainger said wryly, "No. Not like anything I recognize. Perhaps if I write it up for the *B.M.J.* they'll call it after me. Grainger's Lunacy. Or perhaps Marie is right, and all will be made well when a black-robed monk heaves into view, leading a convoy of bloody great St. Bernards and scattering holy water."

"Which falls," Elizabeth murmured, "as tiny tinkling icicles. It's a pretty thought."

Diana said, "*Seriously,* Selby. You must have some idea of what's wrong with them. I mean . . . well, you *must.*"

112

"You mean, ruling out diseases unknown to medical science, along with mountain devils? Not much, I'm afraid. Communicable hysteria? But I wouldn't have thought Ruth was a hysteric type, and that degree of communication is improbable. But I imagine it's our best bet."

"When they bring them back," Mandy asked, "what's the best thing to do?"

"Lock them up, I suppose, until we can get them down off this mountain top to a place where they can be given proper medical attention."

"Together?"

"Yes, that's a point. There's no indication of her having an inclination to injure this child, but one can't afford to risk that."

Mandy said, in a worried voice, "I don't really know where we could put them—a safe place. The attics, perhaps, and move Peter and Marie downstairs somewhere." She looked at Grainger in appeal. "But there are no bars or anything on the windows."

"Easily fixed," Grainger said. "Let's get them back here first."

George returned, with Deeping and Peter, empty-handed and out of sorts. He went into the bar, opened up, and poured drinks for the other two men and himself.

"We're opening early today," he said. "I have a feeling that it would do me no harm to get a slosh on. No harm whatsoever."

Douglas, with Grainger, had followed them in. Grainger said, "You can do me a whisky while you're about it. No sign of them, I take it."

George did not answer immediately. He poured the drink for Grainger, and held the bottle up, his eyes on Douglas.

"Anything for you?"

"Yes," Douglas said. "I think I could do with a whisky."

"Let's all get a slosh on," George said. "No, we saw neither hair nor hide of them. Which was what you predicted, wasn't it?"

Grainger said, "I didn't predict anything. Let's say, I'm not terribly surprised."

"All right. Why aren't you surprised? Let's have some sort of rational questions and answers."

"Did you find their tracks?" Grainger asked.

With disgust, George said, "The sodding mountain's covered with tracks."

"Up past the spur, I meant."

"Up there, too, from those other searches. Come on, answer up. Why aren't you surprised?"

"I told you: the boy was missing for all that length of time. And then appeared, all bright and chipper. Well, fairly bright and chipper."

"Having found himself a hole in the snow and gone to sleep there. You're not suggesting that the pair of them have dug in and gone to sleep? Look, you're the doctor wallah. You ought to know what makes sense, and what doesn't."

"So I ought," Grainger said. "So I ought. Unfortunately I've never been as strong on the triumph of orthodoxy as some of my colleagues. You've heard of Count Mesmer?"

The others looked blank. Douglas said, "Mesmerism?"

"A celebrated nut case," Grainger said. "Started off as an astrologer, and went on to stroking people with magnets. They ran him out of Paris in the end. But twenty-five years after that, mesmerism was going so strong that they had to have a government commission investigate it. The Société Royale de Médecine appointed a committee, made up of able and cautious men, and they went into things. They sat for six years, and saw hundreds of people, and they produced a report.

"Their chief charge had been to investigate the therapeutic possibilities of mesmerism. They found them proved. But they
114

didn't stop at that. They said that telepathy and clairvoyance by means of mesmerism had been demonstrated as well."

Incredulously, Douglas said, "A French medical commission said that?"

"It was taken care of," Grainger said. "The report was never printed. I expect it's still moldering away in the manuscript archives in Paris. They appointed another committee, and put a chap in charge who'd gone on record as saying that mesmerism was nothing but fraud and chicanery. They examined two subjects, under pretty hostile conditions, and rushed a report out. The Society printed that one. It said that there was nothing in mesmerism, and that the first committee were all nuts. And that wound up the scientific investigation of that particular subject."

"There's hypnotism," Douglas said. "It's much the same, isn't it? That's pretty widely accepted, surely."

"Hypnotism," Grainger said, "is mesmerism, cleaned up and cut down to size. The point about mesmerism was that it involved what was called rapport—operator's and subject's minds all tangled up with each other, subject in deep trance, but operator in mild trance, too. The modern medical profession likes a comfortable distance between doctor and patient; or what kind of authority would the weaker brethren be able to command? So Braid worked out a method for getting some of the mesmeric phenomena by remote control. He found that if you put a bright object before the eyes of a subject and got him to gaze at it persistently, he went into something like mesmeric sleep. You could then control him by suggestion, induce analgesia, that kind of thing. But none of this telepathic or clairvoyant nonsense. Best of all, he gave it a new name, derived from a nice reassuring Greek root, like all the best scientific terms."

George said morosely, "I don't see what all this has got to do with Ruth and the kid."

"I've been talking about my personal views," Grainger said. "I think modern medicine is pretty good on the the structure of the body, not quite so good on the structure of the mind, and distinctly inadequate on the relationship between the two. Sorry if I've been boring you, but I've been trying to explain why my being the doctor wallah doesn't help in this case. My own branch of medicine is strictly physical. I've not looked much at the psychological fields, because I mistrust their premises."

Douglas said, "Fair enough. But it was you who said the boy was dead in the first place, and you who said it was a medical certainty that he couldn't have survived being out there for that length of time."

"Not so extraordinary. We are all conditioned to the usual. Catalepsy of that order is a very rare state. Surviving several hours' exposure to a severe winter night is rare, too, when the subject is a little boy in pajamas and bare feet. The exceptional is not something you go looking for. You wait till it's thrust down your throat, and then you forget it, or explain it away, as soon as you can. I knew a Freudian psychiatrist once who saw a ghost. He had it accounted for, of course—a trick of light and sound, making up an hallucination—but he was honest enough to admit that, for some hours until day broke, he had believed that what he thought he saw had reality. When was he right—when he had had time to marshal his defenses and rationalize things, or immediately after the experience itself?"

"Ghosts," George said. He poured more drinks for himself and the others. Douglas put a hand over his own glass, to prevent this. "Look, Selby, all we're asking you is what the hell's going on?"

Grainger took his glass, contemplated it, sipped and smacked his lips. "Afternoon drinking," he observed, "has a *frisson* all its own. What's going on? Well, something odd."

116

"Christl! We know that."

"And if anyone knows any more than that, they have me at a disadvantage."

His blandness was exasperating; it was having an irritating effect on him, Douglas realized, and George was a more irascible type. He said, "You've been doing all the talking, but it hasn't had much application to the situation, has it? Do you feel we ought to do nothing—not even go out and look for them?"

"No, we have to do that, of course, and before dark. In fact, as soon as we have sunk these particular drinks, I think we ought to make a start." He nodded toward the window. "The sun's within spitting distance of Grammont. The night cometh, when no man can work."

Douglas went out with the others. They covered the long slopes of snow again, marked, as George had said, by the criss-crossing tracks of their earlier searches. The scene had a strange beauty. The sun's more level rays lit up a landscape heavy with shadows, displaying a kind of weary grandeur. The distant peaks, above which the sun's disk was hovering, had gold in their whiteness, and a deeper gold overlaid the thick fleece of the cloud bank which covered the whole of the valley floor and the lake. The sense of isolation that one had up here was heightened; one was conscious of the brilliance here and on the far horizon, and of the aureate carpet covering a darker world between. Darker, but more human.

The sun slipped down behind the peaks, light drained from the sky, and George's waving arm called them back to the chalet. The cloud in the valley was a thick ugly-looking gray, and higher, Douglas thought, as though it were rising to engulf them. He himself was tired and dispirited. There had been no sign of Ruth or the boy. They had called, as the other groups had, and heard their voices echo thinly back over the snow. Figures moved, distant and tiny, in a great emptiness.

After the first five or ten minutes, he had no expectation of finding either of them.

They reassembled in an atmosphere of gloom. Mandy was going about the house, lighting the oil lamps. They had seemed attractive at first, but now Douglas was more conscious of their inadequacy, of all the shadows in the corners which their light did not properly reach. George opened the bar again, and was joined by Deeping, the Graingers, and Diana. Not feeling like drinking, Douglas went into the salon, where, at least, the fire was cheerful. Jane accompanied him there, and sat opposite him. She did not pick up a book, but sat looking into the fire. Her hands were folded on her knees. There were two lights on her face—firelight and lamplight. She had a good face, he thought. It was a pity that goodness was so irrelevant in a woman.

He said, "I suppose she may come back, when the night properly falls."

"Yes."

"If she can find her way."

Jane stirred. "It's horrible to think of them being out there. Horrible."

"Can you think why . . ." He broke off. "I mean, one could have understood it if the boy had still been missing, if she had been crazed with grief. But not this way."

"There are time lags sometimes." Her voice was dry and concentrated, as though she were reviewing something long known but never properly understood. "One wakes up and realizes that something terrible has happened, that one failed to see it at the time, but it has happened, and things are never going to be the same afterwards."

"But she had the boy with her. She'd found him again, alive and well."

"Yes." She nodded. "That's true, of course."

He waited for her to go on, but she stayed silent. She had not been talking about Ruth, he guessed, but about herself.

She had had her own loss. She was a woman capable, he thought, of an enduring and single-minded devotion. It would have been a shattering thing to lose its object so comparatively early in married life.

The silence between them, with this consideration, became awkward. He tried to think of something to say that would be suitable, but the words and phrases spun emptily in his mind, at once banal and outrageous. He told himself he would stay mute and then, compulsively, found himself talking.

"We should all have training, I think, in the appreciation of impermanence. And some kind of punishment whenever we try to make the transient things into enduring ones."

"Should we?" she said. "What are the transient things, for that matter?"

"Everything passes. And a good thing. If happiness lasted, grief would last as well. As it is, there's always a monochrome to look forward to. The ordinary is only just around the corner."

And there, of course, he was talking about himself, as he had suspected her of doing. He saw her look at him; his voice, probably, had given him away.

She said quietly, "And if a person chooses the monochrome, deliberately, turning away from brightness—and then loses that, too. What then?"

"The monochromes are self-perpetuating. They renew themselves very quickly. That's their big advantage."

There was another short silence before she said, "I think I'll go and take a bath. Will you excuse me?"

Her face was preoccupied, a little tense, and he wondered if something he said had offended her. But she turned to him from the door and smiled warmly enough.

"See you at supper, Douglas."

"Have a drink first," he said. "Quarter past, in the bar."

Jane nodded. "Love to."

119

The atmosphere remained heavy, not helped by the fact that the bones of iron rations were beginning to be evident beneath the gloss of Mandy's cooking. There was a nourishing soup, but the main course, while a tribute to what could be done with corned beef, was corned beef for all that. They had tinned grapefruit to follow, which kirsch made palatable. An excellent dinner, really, in view of everything, but nobody seemed to enjoy it much. Afterward there was an attempt by George and Grainger to carry on with the drinking they had started earlier, but their hearts were clearly not in it. They were all tired.

Just before ten, Mandy said, "If nothing more is wanted, I'll get off to bed." She looked at Deeping. "We're leaving the downstairs light on all night, just in case . . . And I thought I would leave Stephen in the cot in our room rather than disturb him. Is that all right?"

Deeping said, "Yes." He yawned. "I think I'll be going up, too."

There was a general exodus, which Douglas joined. Grainger gave some indication of being prepared to stay on, but Elizabeth insisted on his coming with her. George was left below, having poured himself another whisky not long before. He had got through a fair amount during the evening, but showed little sign of it.

In bed, Douglas thought at first of the woman and child, somewhere outside in the bitter night. Cloud partly obscured the moon now, and the wind was rising again; looking from his window he had seen the brightness come and go in the cloud surges. But the image, terrible though it was, did not come to life. It existed in a vacuum, and the characters themselves were unreal. The woman was mad, and madness alienated sympathy. The boy . . . the image of him lying dead was stronger than the later sight of him alive.

So, abandoning the present, he returned to Caroline, and

120

the amalgam of past and future which he had begun, laboriously but with delight, to build. Remembered scenes mixed with scenes envisaged, and after a time it was difficult to tell one kind from the other. Not that he wanted to do that. This was unreal also, but an unreality where he felt at home. When he got back to Winchester, there would be a letter . . . no, Mrs. Williams would have left a note on his telephone pad . . . he would call—not the Blackheath number, of course—a hotel? Not a Winchester hotel—the improbability of that made the whole image shiver on the verge, for a moment, of dissolution. A London hotel, the sort that she would be likely to move into, coming back from America on her own. The Royal Court, perhaps; she liked Chelsea. He worked times out sketchily. The plane getting in to London Airport just before midday, Customs cleared and through to the air terminal around one, lunch, and there was a train about three thirty, wasn't there? In the flat by six. If he telephoned right away, got through to her, he might make the six thirty back to London, be with her for dinner . . . Somewhere special. The White Tower, perhaps. The Étoile. Or, in a sentimental mood, Au Père de Nico . . . and walk back together afterward through the dark, quiet streets, pavements glistening with rain in the lamplight, her scent, and the click of her heels . . .

He awoke, hearing a sound that he could not place at first, but metallic, familiar. Of course—the door handle being turned. The door opening. Footsteps. Not just of one person; two at least. Drowsy with sleep, he said, "Who is it?"

Deeping's reassuring Yorkshire voice: "It's all right, Douglas. Not to worry."

But spoken quietly. And the footsteps coming nearer, toward the bed. He sat up, and said sharply, "What do you want?"

There was a faint light from beyond the window—moonlight behind cloud. Two figures silhouetted themselves against it. Deeping, and . . . Ruth!

"She's come back, then," he said. "And the boy? Is Andy all right?"

There was no reply, but a third, small outline crossed the faint rectangle of light. It was only then that he felt fear. That the Deepings should be in his room at night, unheralded, was strange, but the strangeness of it was offset by their familiarity. What danger could there be in the Deepings? The child was different. The child's presence tilted the incident from strangeness into nightmare. And with that, their failure to reply to him took on a frightening significance as well.

He could hear Deeping's breathing as he approached the bed. In a moment the man would be beside him. In Douglas's mind, fear and self-preservation warred with the conditioning of a lifetime—nursery, prep school, public school, university. Don't show fear. Don't cry out. Avoid embarrassment, above all else. The English ethos.

He yelled just before the hand reached for his face, yelled for help at the top of his voice, twisted away, lashed out. And yelled again, and again, hearing his voice reverberate in the room and through the house. And the hands broke away, feet scuffled, retreating. Out of the room, and down the stairs.

7

They got together in the salon again. Glancing at the cuckoo clock—he had left his watch by the side of his bed—Selby saw that it was five to four. The still small hours, he thought, with a twinge of nausea. It reminded him of the far-off days of being an intern, of being wakened from his truckle bed by a new arrival in Casualty, of irritability and a bad taste in the mouth. He had them both now. Mandy was lighting the second lamp, Marie remaking the fire. Selby looked around the room, checking them. Peter, gaunt and watchful by the door. Jane and Diana, the latter looking sleepy and, he thought, with a small but positive surge of pleasure, quite delectable. Elizabeth, yawning. George, carrying the tousle-headed Stephen. And, of course, Douglas Poole, whose surprisingly stentorian shouts for help had brought them all staggering from their beds.

He said, "Right. Now let's have a slightly less confusing picture. What happened, Douglas?"

George said, "Douglas has told me a bit of it. I think I'll bed Steve down first." He moved to go toward the hall, then checked. "I'll put him on the settee in the bar for the time being. Fetch a blanket, Mandy, will you?"

George carried the boy through the connecting door, and closed it after him. Mandy went off, too, presumably to get the blanket, and Marie followed her out. She seemed to have reached an extreme of apprehension which was only allayed by Mandy's presence.

Douglas said, rather shamefacedly, "I'm afraid I kicked up a pretty horrible din."

"Reasonably horrible," Selby said. "But it wasn't just a nightmare, I take it? More to it than that. And it concerns Deeping."

"All three of them. Ruth and the boy, as well. They were in my room. I spoke to them, and they didn't answer. Just came towards the bed. That's when I yelled."

"Didn't answer at all?"

His brow creased, remembering. "No, I'm wrong. I heard someone in the room, and asked who it was. Deeping said not to worry. It was afterwards I asked what he wanted, and said something about Ruth and Andy. That was when there was no reply."

"And when you sang out?"

"He had just made a grab for me. He broke away. They all cleared off, downstairs."

George had come back into the room, closing the door again. He said, "He's asleep. He didn't properly wake up at all, which is just as well. They went downstairs. It looks as though they went right down to the basement. I found the basement door open."

Elizabeth said, "I don't get it. They were going to attack Douglas in his bed—the Deepings, that is—and Andy was with them—and they ran off when he called out—out of the

124

house . . . but why go all the way down to the basement? Why not the front door?"

"There are two doors there, both pretty heavily bolted. The basement door's a single." George looked at his hands; he kept his nails well manicured. "Someone was in a hurry to get away."

Diana said, "But it's silly. Why should they attack you, Douglas? And if they were attacking you, they wouldn't have Andy with them. And how did Ruth and Andy get back into the house, without anyone knowing? Though I suppose Leonard knew, didn't he? I mean, did he go down and let them in?"

"I think I've got the answer to the last bit," George said. "And it gives another reason for them heading on down to the basement. There's a little window down there Mandy leaves open for the cat—not really open, but ajar. It's wide open now. An adult couldn't get in through it, but the boy could, if he were given a leg-up from outside. And then he could open the door. So on the way out there wouldn't even be a single bolt to draw."

"That's silly, too," Diana said. "We were looking for them yesterday afternoon, calling for them . . . I mean, there was no need to break in. If she had rung the bell . . ."

"We should have know they were in the house," Selby said. "And that, apparently, was not the idea."

Jane said quietly, "What was, then? *Would* they have attacked Douglas, if he hadn't cried out?"

Douglas said, "Perhaps they wouldn't have. I suppose I panicked a bit."

"Leonard," George said. "That's the thing I don't get. Ruth hasn't been normal since—since the boy collapsed. But Leonard was sane enough. A bit too sane, if anything."

This aimless slamming away at disconnected points was not, Selby felt, advancing their understanding of the situation;

125

the reverse, if anything. There had to be a logical explanation, but it would need working out, step by step.

He said, "Let's tackle this bit by bit. We can make assumptions as we go along, and test them by the evidence. Two, to start with—that Ruth got in by pushing Andy through the little window and having him open up to her, and that Leonard is now in the same condition that she is in—whatever that may be."

George objected. "We don't know much about Leonard's state of mind. None of us has seen him—Douglas was half asleep when all this happened."

"True," Selby said. "And yet Leonard, along with Ruth and the boy, ran like hell when the alarm was raised. Just as Ruth ran this afternoon."

"Your communicable hysteria?" Jane murmured.

"Or Marie's devils, or the disease unknown to science. Let's take things back a little. Marie finds Ruth and Andy apparently attacking Steve yesterday afternoon. They grapple with her, but Mandy comes on the scene. So they flee. They manage to hide somewhere outside—perhaps by digging holes in the snow, as the boy did before—and in the night they come back to the house. They get in, quietly. They go quietly upstairs to Leonard's bedroom. And then . . ."

Jane said, "Then it becomes ridiculous. I mean, all the rest can be explained as some kind of brainstorm in Ruth—the boy would follow her automatically."

"Would he?" Selby asked. "I don't think so. But let that go. Leonard is by himself because Steve has been left with George and Mandy. Perhaps he wakes up, realizing they are in the room with him. Even if he does, why should he raise an alarm, against his wife and son? Or perhaps he is sleeping more soundly than Douglas. Anyway, something happens in that room. The devils claim another victim. Or the sickness infects him. Or the hysteria communicates. However you de-

126

scribe it, there are three of them now, instead of two."

Elizabeth asked, "Three what?"

Selby said restlessly, "Whatever it is, it can be passed on. And there is an urge to pass it on. The attack on Steve, the— the recruiting of Leonard, the threat to Douglas. Why Douglas? Probably because apart from Peter and Marie in the attics—and Peter is a light sleeper and the attic stairs creak like hell—Douglas was the only person in a room by himself. And therefore vulnerable."

In a shaky voice, Jane said, "If he hadn't called for help— what do you think would have happened?"

"I can't even make a guess about the details. But pretty obviously, whether it's infection, or possession, or multiple hysteria, the process itself is contagious. There has to be, at the least, a laying on of hands. They might have been able to do it while he was asleep. Or, if awake, a hand over his mouth, or round his throat, to keep him quiet while it was happening. We must presume that, but for the fact that he gave an alarm which woke the house, whatever happened to Leonard would have happened to Douglas in turn."

"And then," Elizabeth said, "there would have been four."

Selby admired, as he had done many times before, the calm perceptiveness in her, underlying her apparent indifference and lack of interest. He said warmly, "Exactly! Three of them adult. I wonder where they would have turned after that? To the girls? But they would still have been outnumbered, in the event of an alarm being raised. Perhaps they would have waited for the morning, for people getting up. Peter, and Marie, and then Mandy. And then George, and they would have the top of the house to themselves. That wouldn't have given the rest of us much chance."

The door opened, and Marie came in with a tray, Mandy following her. Mandy said, "I've made some cocoa. And there are biscuits. Only cheese biscuits, I'm afraid. We're down to our last packet of sweet biscuits, and I thought I'd keep those for the children . . . for Steve."

George said, "Good show. Cocoa's very nice, for them as likes it. But I think I need something a little stronger after listening to Selby trying his hand at blood curdling." There was contempt in his voice, as well as flippancy. "I'll just nip next door and get a bottle."

Marie set the tray down and hesitated. Mandy said, "Stay with us, if you'd rather." She looked apologetically at the others. "You don't mind, do you?"

They all accepted cups of cocoa. George, returning from the bar with a bottle in his hand, noticed this.

"Am I the only one drinking?" he asked. "Selby? Shot of Scotch in your cocoa? Douglas?" When they showed their refusal, he said, "Anyway, I want to take you two away for a few minutes. Something I want to discuss. We can go next door into the dining room. Peter, look after the ladies."

His voice had the ring of military authority. He would have had a good war, Selby thought. A nonentity before, and a nonentity of a different kind after, but when the keynotes of the times were urgency and violence, George must have been pretty good. Although the tone was brusque, the words a command rather than an invitation, he saw no point in arguing or refusing. George held the door to the dining room open, and Selby went through, Douglas following. George produced a box of matches, and lit the lamp that stood on the table. Looking at the box, before returning it to his pocket, he said, "Something else we're running low on. Well, we can always make do with spills. Shut the door, Douglas."

They sat down. George had fetched a glass from the sideboard. He poured neat Scotch into it, drank it, and refilled the glass.

"If either of you wants to chase that cocoa, go and get yourself a glass." He paused. "I'm surprised at you, Selby."

128

Selby sat back in his chair. "Are you? In what way?"

"Spreading alarm and despondency among the ladies. You were scaring little Diana out of those frilly nylon panties she probably wears."

It was spoken lightly enough, but the iron edge—contempt, resentment?—was even more evident than before.

Selby said, "What do you suggest I should have done? Told them there were now two dangerous lunatics wandering around outside instead of one, and they should just toddle back to bed, and forget about it? There had to be some kind of explanation once they knew both the Deepings had cleared off."

George said, "You need only have said that Ruth had got into the house with the kid, that she had woken Leonard— he'd been following her round the house, perhaps trying to persuade her to go back to bed . . ."

"And all three of them converging on Douglas's bed?"

"Well, why not? Douglas spoke to him, and he said not to worry. Then Douglas let out a yell, and that scared Ruth. She skidded off downstairs with the kid, and Leonard chased after her. Down to the basement and out through the door she'd left open."

Douglas said, "It wasn't quite . . ."

George cut in. "Maybe not. But you would have kept your trap shut, wouldn't you? What's the point in frightening people unnecessarily?"

Selby said, "In the first place, you are underrating the ladies' intelligence. It's a habit with a lot of professionally male males—always unwise, and in some cases dangerous."

George flushed slightly, but he remained controlled.

"In the second place?"

"For their own safety—for the safety of all of us—they've got to realize that the Deepings are now a menace. Do you deny that?"

There was a silence. George said, "At four o'clock in the morning, I'm not prepared to deny anything, or agree with it. This is the second night running they've been dragged out of bed by some uproar." He glanced at Douglas. "No one's fault, but they're bound to feel a bit ragged. The obvious thing to do is soothe them and get them back upstairs. Not frighten the hell out of them with talk about menaces, and what might have happened if Douglas hadn't yelled for help."

"Back upstairs?" Selby said. "Nicely tucked in, and asleep. And if the Deepings come back, in an hour's time, say? Even if you bolt the door and close the window downstairs . . . what's to stop them breaking a window to get in?"

"Nothing," George said flatly. "You're not too bad at underrating intelligence yourself. I don't know whether the Deepings are dangerous to the rest of us or not. We didn't know them until they came here, or anything about them. Maybe they carry on this way back in Dulwich. But obviously we don't run risks. Another reason for getting you two out here is to decide the best way of handling things." His glance flicked sharply at Selby. "I'm not sure what being professionally male means, but I still don't see any need to involve the ladies. What is pretty plain is that we need to have somebody on guard at night. I don't mind taking what's left of this one. After that . . . there are four of us, with Peter. Roughly two hours a head."

Douglas said, "Do you mean you think we'll still be—well, on the hook—tomorrow night?"

"Maybe not," George said. "Maybe tomorrow morning there will be a ring at the doorbell, and the Deepings will be there, nice and normal and asking for hot coffee. Or maybe a party will have got through from Nidenhaut."

Selby said, "I like your first alternative better, though I can see some snags in it."

"Do you?" George asked. "What don't you like about the second?"

"They have changed," Selby said slowly, "in some respects. Body temperature, pulse rate. And the ability to withstand cold seems to be much greater. But they still have most physical limitations. They break into a house by ordinary human methods, flee as a human being would flee."

George produced a pack of cigarettes, and offered it to Douglas, who took one. He held his lighter for both of them. While Douglas was drawing on his, he said, "Just what are you trying to say, Selby—that they aren't human? What the hell do you mean by that?"

His voice was steady. So was his hand. All the same, Selby felt he had an explanation of the resentment George had been showing to him. It was not on account of scaring the women; that had only been the excuse. It was the voicing of his own deep terror that upset him. He was a man with very little fear of anything in the natural world, but with a dread of the supernatural. Realizing this, he felt more charitable. He said mildly, "I don't mean anything. Let's say it's a sickness, and contagious. The fact is, they're different in some respects, but only in some."

Douglas said, "Aren't you taking some things for granted, Selby? You didn't examine Ruth for temperature and pulse rate—only the boy. She seemed cold, I agree, but she had been outside looking for him. And you don't know anything at all about Leonard, except that he's gone off with them— with his wife and child."

"And temperature and pulse rate in the boy could have been connected with his collapse and coma," Selby said. "Fair enough. I've been abusing the rules of evidence, or something. It doesn't alter my point about not being particularly keen on seeing a rescue party from Nidenhaut at the moment."

"Why?" Douglas asked.

Selby got up and went to the sideboard. He got two glasses and brought them back to the table. He looked inquiringly at Douglas, and poured drinks for both of them. Then he said,

"Because as long as we are cut off from the rest of the world, so are they. If that road gets opened, then they can carry the sickness to Nidenhaut. And from Nidenhaut . . ."

Douglas said, "You think there could be an epidemic? Isn't that . . . ?"

George broke in. "You're pretty good at making the flesh creep, Selby." His voice was heavily sarcastic. "I thought you medical men were all strong and silent. And trained in controlling the imagination, rather than letting it run riot."

Selby said amiably, "You're thinking of the medical men with patients who wake up in the night with a bellyache and at once diagnose cancer. My line is helping to make day dreams come true, not stalling off the nightmares of the death wish. No point in my being strong and silent."

George said, "Ah, hell!" He took the bottle and poured more into his glass. "This is not getting us anywhere. I suggest you two, and the ladies, clear off to bed. We can talk about it in the morning."

Selby thought of George, alone down here with the whisky bottle, and the flickering lamplight, and the creaking and groaning of wood in an old house. He said, "You have more to do during the day. I'll stay up."

"No!" It was a little too emphatic. "This is my show, Selby."

Their eyes locked. A silence was broken when Douglas said mildly, "I don't mind staying up." He paused. "We could toss a coin for it. Or play dice."

George laughed suddenly. "I never say no to a round of dice. I'll go and get the dice and the pot."

While he was away, Douglas sipped his drink and then went to the sideboard to dilute it. He said, "You really think there is a danger, Selby? To others, as well as to those of us here?"

Selby said, "I don't know. I'm against underrating things, though. Dangers, as well as intelligence."

132

"Do you think it is a sickness of some kind?"

Selby shook his head. "I don't know."

George returned, rattling the dice in their leather pot. He looked more cheerful; in fact was grinning.

"The ladies think we're round the bend now. Except Diana. She wanted to come in. Three lives?"

"One," Selby said. "Otherwise we'll be up all night, all of us. Aces up and kings towards."

They each flicked the dice in front of them. Selby and Douglas both turned up knaves, George a king. He took the pot, gathered all the dice, shook them, slammed the pot down and, cupping it between his hands, examined his throw. Then he slid the pot across the table to Selby.

"Three jacks."

He was smiling, his eyes watchful. Selby nodded, and took the pot. There were two knaves underneath it, with queen, ten, nine. Unhesitatingly, he brought out the ten and nine, and threw them open.

A knave and a queen came up. Selby said, "Four and a queen."

Douglas took the pot, looked under it, hesitated, and displayed the dice. Leaving the three knaves on the table, he threw the queens under the pot.

George looked at him. "Well?"

Douglas looked under the pot. "Four jacks and a king."

George took the top off. "Bad luck." There were a queen and nine there. George scooped up the dice and put them in the pot again. Shaking it, he said, "You and me, Selby."

He looked, and pushed the pot across the table.

"Low straight."

His eyes were fixed on Selby. Selby tapped the leather base of the inverted pot with his fingers. It had been a very quick glance, but that meant nothing; even with dice faded as these were, George had the eyes and the alertness to pick out a straight without hesitation. But there were other considerations. The previous call, of three jacks, had been pre-emptive, and false, but he had been able to pass that on to Douglas. With only two of them left in, things were a good deal more critical. And if a low straight were there, only one course would be possible to him: rolling the nine under the pot in the hope of an ace, and calling a high straight. Odds of five to one against. And, of course, there might not be a straight there at all.

He took the top off. Ace, king, queen, ten, nine. A broken straight.

"Too bad," he said.

George nodded. "It was a chance. I'll leave you the bottle. Go and get another from the bar, if you kill that one. I've left the key in."

The bottle was three-quarters full. "If I kill that," Selby said, "I won't be able to walk as far as the bar."

When the others had gone to bed, Selby poured himself more whisky, and idly rolled the dice along the table. Three aces. A good first throw. He thought about the game they had just played, and about George. George did occasionally make pre-emptive false calls, especially in the end game, but he had never known him to call a straight before. There was only one explanation that fitted: it had been done deliberately, knowing that Selby, unless he were playing with a lunatic recklessness, must whip it. It had been called to lose. And there was only one reason for that. Fear. He had desperately not wanted to be left down here, alone, but pride had made him claim the post. And the dice had provided a means of getting out of it without losing face.

Which was fair enough. Weaknesses in others were things one recognized, noted, but did not linger over. No harm was done as long as the recognition itself went unrecognized. He was pleased with the fact that he had not showed anything to

George, that he had sent him off to bed with honor satisfied.

A distant creak of wood reminded him why he was there. He had checked the basement, and made sure that the door was bolted, all the windows firmly closed. In this quietness, the sound of a window being broken would be easily heard. At the same time, it occurred to him, he was not in the best vantage point. He really needed to keep an eye on the stairs. He could, he supposed, actually sit on the stairs, but the bar, with the hall door open, would be good enough from that point of view, and far more comfortable. He picked up his glass and, after a moment's thought, the bottle, and headed for the bar.

Through the double-glazed window, he looked across the hillside. The moon was clouded. There was barely enough light to make out the line of the slope, no possibility of distinguishing figures unless they came very close. But would they do that? Faces outside the window, pleading to be let in? Or possibly grimacing and horrible. Something out of a horror movie. Selby sipped his drink, and smiled. It was ridiculous. The Deepings, a middle-class suburban couple with their middle-class surburban child . . . one could not relate horror to them.

And yet, they were out there in the snow somewhere. There was an external thermometer fixed to the side of the window here; he carried the lamp across, and peered at it through the glass. He could not be sure, but it looked like minus seven or eight. A suburban couple, and their child . . . And for the child, the second night in the open. There was horror enough in that, whether one thought of a normal small boy, suffering from the biting cold, or of a changeling, weirdly impervious to it. An absurd, senseless horror.

There was also, he thought with grim humor, a kind of retribution in this, as far as he was concerned, anyway. The years of lighthearted unorthodoxy, of poking mild fun at the

135

shibboleths of medicine, or gently dynamiting overearnest colleagues, narrowed down to this focus, and left him as helpless and ignorant as the most devoutly orthodox G.P. More helpless, possibly, because he had no defense against the bizarreness of it all, no means of retreat into complacency. Something had changed the Deepings—changed them both physically and mentally—and what that something was existed no more in his philosophy than it had in that of poor old Horatio. A disease? Hysteria? One might as well settle for Marie's Alpine devils. A more embracing, and therefore more satisfactory theory.

A sound disturbed him, and he looked up quickly. From the stairs. But from the upper part of the house, not the basement. He had a moment's apprehension—that they had somehow got past him, that everyone up there had been changed, leaving him terribly alone—but pulled himself together. Most likely it was George, kept awake by conscience and coming down to make sure everything was all right. Another sound. Yes, someone coming down. But not George. Too light of step. Bedroom slippers, a glimpse of white ankle, a blue silk housecoat.

She came downstairs and, unhesitatingly, crossed the hall to the bar. Her face, Selby noted, was made up, her hair brushed to neatness. He said quietly, "What is it, Diana? Couldn't you sleep?"

"No." She leaned against the bar, and looked across the room at him. Her voice, too, was quiet; nothing so conspiratorial as a whisper, but deliberately pitched low. "Jane is asleep, but I was restless. I wondered . . . do you think a drink might make me more sleepy?"

Selby pondered this judiciously for a moment.

"Do you know, I wouldn't be surprised if it did. Not at all surprised. Let me get one for you."

He had to pass close to her to get behind the bar. The scent she was wearing was one he had encountered before, but not on her. She normally used a light scent, girlish; this was much heavier. Femme? Something like that—he could never remember their names. And fairly liberally applied. He was a few feet from her now, but it was still strong.

"What'll it be?" he asked her. "I'm drinking whisky, but George has left me *carte blanche.*"

"Whisky will be fine."

"If you wouldn't mind bringing my glass over, I'll join you."

That kept the bar between them. This was not, Selby thought as he poured a whisky for her and weakened it with water, at all characteristic of the girl. He was sure he had not been mistaken about her; she was—or he would be very much disappointed—seducible, but she was no man-eater. And yet there could be no mistaking what this visit was all about. It was not merely the scent and the careful grooming. There was provocation in her manner, restrained, but very obvious. Her fingers touched his as he passed the glass to her. The house-coat covered the top of her nightdress. The vee was deep, showing a little of the white curves of her breasts, the beginning of the valley between them.

Selby took a deep breath, and raised his glass.

"Cheers."

"Cheers," she said. "There's something funny about being awake when everyone else is asleep. Don't you think?" She looked about her. "And with this lamplight . . . It makes everything strange . . ."

Her voice trailed off. ". . . and romantic," Selby decided, was to be inferred. No, not characteristic. She might even say no, if he did pick up the cue, though he did not think she would. It was the crisis atmosphere, probably, which had done it. Weren't some forms of danger supposed to have that effect on women? But there was no point in wasting time in abstract

137

speculation. The situation demanded action or, rather—if everyone were to be kept happy and future doors, at the same time, kept open—some fast talking.

He said, "Is your sister a fairly heavy sleeper?"

She rose to that one, and bit hard. "Jane? Very heavy."

"Yes, I would have thought that. People are sometimes a bit misleading, though. Take Elizabeth. Very restless at night —always waking up. And given to wandering. I'm surprised we haven't had her down here already."

An arrant lie, but one of which, he was fairly sure, Elizabeth would approve. He looked across the bar, and held the girl's eyes for a long moment. She smiled at him, and gave a tiny shrug. Accepted, he thought with relief. The danger was over.

She said something about the Deepings, but perfunctorily, and soon switched to a less disturbing topic. The good thing about taking a holiday at this time of the year was that one got back home to find spring beginning—trees budding, evenings drawing out . . . The office in which she worked was near Marble Arch, and she liked walking across the Park and getting a bus in Knightsbridge. When she wasn't burdened with midday shopping, that was. Though that was easier now that they had a delicatessen quite close to the flat, which stayed open in the evenings and on Sunday mornings.

She chattered on, and Selby listened to her with pleasure. She was a pretty, lively little thing, and there would be a proper time and place for doing something positive about that. For this hour, it was quite enough to have her company, to listen half-attentively to what she said, to be aware of future possibilities and, at the same time, stay smugly armored in present virtue. Where had she got to? The summer. It was attractive to contemplate the summer.

"We eat sandwiches in the park," she said, "or in the queue if it's a Beethoven night."

138

"The Proms?" Selby said. "I wouldn't have taken you for a Prommer."

She said, with some indignation, "This will be my fifth year."

He was delighted. "And do you queue all night for the last performance? And wave banners at Sir Malcolm Sargent?"

"I don't wave banners. I was picked to give him a bouquet last year, though."

"I'll bet you were. Can I come with you once or twice next summer? Not on a Beethoven night. I'm getting too old to queue for things."

"But queuing is part of the fun! You get to know people." She looked at him seriously. "What kind of music do you like?"

"All kinds, as long as it's a big orchestra with lots of luscious strings. Tchaikovsky, even."

"I like Tchaikovsky!"

She spoke with a fascinating indignation, leaning toward him across the bar counter to emphasize her point. For the moment, quite irresistible. Selby leaned forward himself, and kissed her. She was taken aback, then smiled, tongue delicately held between teeth. He kissed her again, at greater length and more effectively. But the effectiveness was considerably limited by the barrier between them. He released her, with the intention of doing something about that. Drawing back, he looked, past her head, at the window. The face stared at him through the glass.

Neither suppliant nor menacing; but much worse. A face expressionless, calm, observant. Like a marine biologist gazing through the plate glass of an aquarium. Except that this was the face of an eight-year-old boy, and the temperature out there nearly ten centigrade degrees below freezing point.

He said to Diana, "You've finished your drink. I should think you will sleep all right now."

She looked slightly disappointed, but his voice carried a decisiveness which she accepted without demur. He watched her go upstairs before he went to the window. He did not expect to find anything: the face had dropped at the moment of realizing that it had been seen. And there was nothing—nothing but darkness and the pale glimmer of snow. He thought about the position of the window. The ground fell sharply away there; the bottom ledge of the window would be, on the outside, six feet from the ground. So the child had been lifted up, perched, presumably, on his father's shoulders. A very ordinary, human act. Selby shivered.

He poured himself another drink, and then went the rounds, carefully checking doors and windows.

In the morning, he told George and Douglas about the appearance at the window, although not, of course, that Diana had been downstairs at the time.

Douglas said, "Not trying to get in?"

"No. Merely looking."

"Seeing what you were up to," George said. Selby glanced at him sharply, but there was nothing behind the remark. "A recce party."

"Something like that."

"No sign of them this morning?" Douglas asked.

"No. Not that one would see much, in this."

They were in the bar. Selby gestured toward the window. Outside, gray mist swirled in small currents of air. The mist had come down or, more likely, up from the valley cloud, toward dawn, and was thick all around the house. Visibility was about ten yards at most.

Douglas said, "One really does feel cut off."

There was an uneasiness in his voice which reflected, Selby felt, the mood of all of them. They had been looking to have their anxieties put to rest by day, by the sight of the empty sunlit snow slopes, the reassuring immutability of the distant peaks. Instead they had the mist all around them, cutting them off from the world more completely than the night's darkness did. At night there was a chance of seeing the moon, stars, the lights of St. Gingolph on the faraway shore of the lake. Now there was nothing to see but the mist itself, eddying, coldly seething, but never changing. It was depressing, and unnerving.

George said, "I thought they might have come back."

A silence followed. Each minute that went by, Selby reflected, hammered one more nail in the coffin of the comfortable satisfying solution they all so desperately wanted to find. He said sharply, "What sort of weapons do you have in the house?"

George looked up. "Weapons?"

"Any guns?"

"A twelve-bore. I do a bit of rabbiting in the summer."

"Cartridges?"

"A couple of boxes. Look, Selby, what are you driving at? There are only three of them, one a kid. They're not likely to attack us."

"Not when we're together, I agree. We outnumber them too greatly. But if anyone were to go out on his own, I think he would need protection."

Douglas said incredulously, "Protection? From the Deepings?"

But there was apprehension in his voice, as well as incredulity. There was a danger, Selby thought, which was independent of any particular menace the metamorphosed Deepings might present: the danger of panic here in the house. To that extent, George had been right the previous evening, and he had been wrong. But they had to realize a menace existed. He thought wearily, I'm not seeing straight, probably. Two nights running with no more than a few hours' sleep. He

141

shook his head, and drank the coffee Mandy had brought them.

George said, "No one's going out. It would be lunacy to go out in this, anyway. All we can do at present is sit tight, and see what happens. In the end, they'll have to come to us. Hunger will bring them. At the rate they rushed out, they didn't have time to pick up any rations."

"You may be right in the long run, but I wouldn't bank on quick results."

"Why not?"

"As far as subjective hunger's concerned, I don't see why it should bother them any more than cold appears to do. They just aren't responding to ordinary physical stimuli in the normal way. Even so, they would still need food as a fuel, of course, but probably not as much. That lower metabolism rate means less energy expended. And they may be able to blank things out much more when there isn't a need for activity. Remember the boy's coma, and his little hibernation stunt when he dug himself into the snow? And they can probably utilize reserves. It's not so much the case with the boy, but the two adults have enough body fat to keep them going for quite a long time, on the basis of which they seem to be operating."

George said, "That's bloody cheerful, I must say. How long do you think?"

"I've no idea."

Douglas said, "We're discussing them as though they aren't—well, human."

There was no point, Selby felt, in commenting on that. George appeared to take the same view. He said, to Selby, "But they would still take food, if they got a chance, wouldn't they? They must have it at some stage."

"The boy took food out with him, the first time he left the house. Yes, they will need food eventually."

"I wondered if we could figure out some way of trapping them," George said. "Put food out as bait. Something like that."

"You could try." Selby yawned. "We don't know very much about the way their minds are working, but it wouldn't do to regard them as being any less intelligent than they were . . . before they changed." He paused, remembering the face he had seen. "No, it wouldn't do at all." He drained his coffee. "God, I'm tired. I'm going up to get some sleep. Give me a shout if anything happens."

He fell asleep almost as soon as he climbed into bed, and slept heavily, dreamlessly. Elizabeth had to shake him to rouse him. He opened his eyes, and looked at her muzzily.

"Twelve o'clock," she told him. "That's when you said you wanted calling." She smiled unsympathetically. "You look a bit bedraggled, though. How much whisky did you get through during the night?"

"Thirsty," he muttered.

His glass was empty. She took it to the tap, filled it and returned it to him.

"Would you rather have lunch in bed?"

He shook his head carefully. "No, I'll get up." As she turned to leave, he asked, "Anything happened while I've been asleep?"

"Nothing. And we're still fogbound."

His gaze went to the window, a bleak gray square. Not very encouraging. But it was a relief to know that the morning had passed uneventfully.

Selby bathed, dressed, and went downstairs. He found Douglas and George in the bar, the former with a beer, the latter with what looked like brandy and ginger ale. George said, "All fit? What will it be?"

"Beer for me, too, I think. I gather all is well."

"So far. I wish this mist would clear."

"How long does it usually hang around?"

George shrugged. "You can't tell. It stuck with us for a week once."

"That's cheering."

"Yes." George poured himself another slug of brandy and, after a moment's consideration, added a little ginger ale. "This is our third day of being cut off. Since they haven't been able to get through by road, this is about the time I would have expected them to send a chopper in—making sure we're all right, maybe dropping provisions, that sort of thing. But they couldn't risk it in this muck."

"No," Selby said, "I suppose not."

It was tantalizing to think about it. One could have got some sort of message out, alerted people somehow. And a helicopter could search for the Deepings far more effectively than people on foot. Still, the mist must lift eventually. And they were forewarned now, and holding their own.

Mandy came into the bar. Her face was hot from cooking, and there was a smudge of flour on one cheek. She said, "George?"

"Yes, love."

"Peter." He raised his eyebrows. "Did you give him a job to do?"

"A job? No. What kind of job?"

"I thought he was downstairs. But . . ."

Selby saw George's face tighten, and felt his own tighten also. George said quietly, "How long is it since you last saw him?"

8

After breakfast, Elizabeth had got hold of Jane while she was smoking a cigarette over the remains of her coffee.

She said, "Ah, there you are. I've found a Monopoly set, and I thought we might organize a game." She added, by way of explanation, "For Steve's benefit, chiefly. Something to do on a miserable morning."

Jane nodded. "Yes, of course, I'll play."

It was typical of Elizabeth, she thought, and tried to make the thought wholeheartedly admiring. While they were in their parents' care she had paid less attention to the Deeping children than anyone else in the party; not seeming to notice them apart from an occasional remote, tolerant smile. Now that Stephen was left alone, however, she had taken him over briskly and efficiently. The boy, for his part, was clearly appreciative of her attentions, and felt flattered by them. She had confidence in her power over the male, Jane thought, of whatever age group, and the confidence was far from being misplaced.

Diana played with them, in the salon. She seemed tired, and was yawning a lot. Jane did her best to repress her annoyance at this. Uninhibited yawning in public was one of the things she most disliked, especially in a sister, but there had been two broken nights and at her age she needed a full measure of sleep. In the end, though, she said, "You could go back to bed, if you're tired."

"Tired?" Diana said. "I'm not tired."

"You seem to be."

"Just yawning." She yawned again, noisily, then grinned. "You must be the tired one—grouchy like that. Or envying me my property. Steve, I'll have another house on Piccadilly before Jane gets round there."

Stephen gave her the house and put the money in the bank. He said, "They aren't going to come back, are they?"

There was no need to ask who "they" were. In the silence that followed, Elizabeth rattled the dice loudly. She said at last, "We don't know, Steve. They're ill, and they've gone away. They may come back."

"Perhaps they've found a way of getting down to the village."

"Perhaps. Steve?"

"Yes."

"Mandy told you, didn't she, that if you did see them—you know, near the house—you shouldn't go to them? Even if they tell you to?"

"Yes. It's because they're ill." He thought about this. "Dad as well?"

"I'm afraid so."

He said, "I know about it. It's their brains being sick. A chap at school—his father was like that. They took him to a hospital and gave him electric shocks, and he got all right again."

146

Elizabeth said, "That's probably what will happen with your mother and father. Except that they aren't really electric shocks—not the kind that hurt you."

"And Andy?"

"I'm not sure about Andy. I should think he'll just get better. But we shall have to find them all, and look after them, until they can be taken to a hospital. If you see one of them, you'll tell us, won't you? And keep away from them yourself."

"Yes. If they have got down to the village, they'll look after them there, won't they? And take them to a hospital?"

"Yes. Of course, they will."

Elizabeth threw, a seven.

"Mayfair!" he said excitedly. "That's mine. Fifty pounds rent, please."

Jane, as the play continued, took stock of herself unhappily. She had thought she was living in an emotional vacuum, but did nature, perhaps, abhor this kind of vacuum as much as any other? Twice in a short space of time she had found herself reacting—to Elizabeth's competence in dealing with Stephen, and to Diana's yawning. Two very different things, but the reaction, in each case, had been one of resentment. Could it be that resentment was becoming the keynote in her life, the automatic reaction to other people being successful, other people being natural and unabashed? The thought appalled, and scared her. But what was the alternative? Getting outside herself, taking an interest in others—being positive and active, instead of negative and withdrawn? The prospect was wearisome, the effort of will required daunting. And for no conceivable reward.

The dice came to her, and she shook them.

"I was on your property," Stephen said gleefully, "and you forgot to ask for rent! Six. That's Fenchurch Street station. You can have that."

They finished playing at about a quarter to twelve, and she decided to use the time remaining before lunch to write to

Wendy Gabriel. Wendy was the only one of her old Oxford-shire neighbors with whom she had remained in touch, and even this link, she was well aware, had been kept in being by Wendy, not by her. She had scribbled a brief note, in reply to two long letters, mentioning the impending Swiss trip, and another fat letter had followed her out here. It was full of news about the people who had once rounded out her life, but whose doings now failed completely to interest her. Her first thought had been that a picture postcard would provide sufficient reply, but in the aftermath of her moments of self-criticism she decided to write a letter instead.

Consciousness of virtue got her to the point of sitting down with pen and paper and writing the salutation, but could not take her much further. The bizarreness of what was taking place up here, she found, inhibited the telling of it. To say that one had been cut off by an avalanche would be easy enough, but to go on from that and recount the rest of it—a boy apparently dead, but resurrected, the mother gone mad and attacking her other son, the father apparently catching insanity from her, and the three of them wandering out somewhere in the mist-enshrouded snow—she felt irritated by the absurdity, the irrationality of it all. Letters to be successful required the ordinary, the undemanding; as life itself did. She put her pen down with a sigh of exasperation.

Douglas, at this point, came in from the bar, and she turned to him with relief. The letter would keep, until it was all over and could be set down briefly and tidily, bracketed by the commonplace and, if possible, reduced to it. She greeted him lightheartedly before she noticed the tense, worried expression on his face. He said abruptly, "Have you seen Peter?"

"Peter? No. Why?"

"He seems to have gone missing."

It took a moment or two for the implications to sink home. She said, "You don't mean . . . ? Along with the Deepings?"

"Mandy thought he was seeing to the boiler. But according to Marie, he said something about going out to get more logs."

She got up from her chair. "I'll help look."

Diana and Elizabeth and Stephen were apparently upstairs. They found the others in the basement, near the boiler. George was saying to Marie, "I told you both to stay indoors. You remember that, don't you?"

The girl was in tears. "I will not go outside. I promise you, monsieur! But I cannot tell Peter what he must do."

"Damn it, you could have told Madame that he was going out! Couldn't you?"

"But it was for the logs only. Not more than ten meters from the door. I will not go myself, but it is different for him, a man . . ."

"How long?" Marie looked at him, dazed and uncomprehending. "How long since he went outside?"

"I . . . I am not sure. Perhaps half an hour. I went upstairs."

George whirled from her to Selby and Douglas. "We'll have to go and look for him. But I'm taking that shotgun. Wait here."

Mandy said, while they waited, "He does wander off sometimes. He's a bit odd in his ways."

She was flushed, and her speech, while not exactly slurred, lacked precision. It crossed Jane's mind that she might have been drinking. She chided herself for the thought: have charity. Cooking and looking after the house and guests with only two servants were enough to make anyone seem confused, even without the present attendant circumstances.

Elizabeth came down with George, and the women, grouped together by the door, watched the three men go out into the mist. George warned them, before they went, to keep the door closed, bolted, until their return. Mandy pushed the bolt

149

home, and they went to the store room, which had a window looking out. The figures of the men were disappearing into the mist, and in a moment had gone. They watched the meaningless curve and heave of gray.

Mandy said suddenly, "Steve?"

"Diana's with him," Elizabeth said.

"One gets on edge," Mandy said. She looked flustered. "I must run upstairs and see how lunch is coming."

Elizabeth, when she had gone, said, "How long has he been missing?"

"About half an hour, according to Marie," Jane said.

"It may be all right, then."

"Yes."

But waiting, and staring at the mist, were fraying her nerve ends. It was her ears, she realized, that were attentive rather than her straining eyes: she was listening for a sound. For a gunshot, in fact. The discovery was shattering: that she had accepted that there was a real menace outside there, an enemy. The thought made her feel sick. Not only through fear, although she was, at this moment, afraid. There was a revulsion, also. To see danger in others was to be involved with them.

Elizabeth said, "Do you know if anyone has had a weather forecast from the wireless?"

"Not that I know of. George is keeping the wireless off as much as possible. The battery's getting low."

"Yes, I suppose it would be." She stared through the window. "It doesn't look much like change out there."

They fell silent. It seemed a long time before the figures of the three men rematerialized outside, but, looking at her watch, Jane saw that they had not been gone much more than ten minutes. Three, not four. So they had not found Peter. She went around with Elizabeth, and they opened the door to let them in.

Douglas and Selby were both shivering with cold. Selby

said, "I shall be ready for my lunch. And something to warm me up first."

George slammed the bolt back into place, and turned the heavy iron key in the lock. He straightened up and looked at them.

"A spot of exercise will do the trick," he said.

"What did you have in mind?" Selby asked.

"Nailing planks over the windows down here."

Douglas said, "Do you think that's necessary?"

Selby said slowly, "Yes, I think you've got something there. Right away, do you think?"

"Do no harm."

The fear again, and the revulsion. Jane said, "Is this turning into a siege, or something?"

Elizabeth said, "You saw no sign of him? Or them?"

Selby shook his head. "Not that you can see more than half a dozen paces in front of you. But he's not anywhere near the wood stacks; and I don't think he's near the house. We went all round."

"So they've got him," Elizabeth said.

Her remark fell into a silence. Then George said briskly, "Luckily we've got all that half-inch wood that we were going to use for a new shed. Some of the short lengths will do as they are. We'll slam them across on the diagonal—shouldn't need too many."

Selby said, "Except that any gap left must be too small for a small boy to wriggle through. We're wasting our time otherwise."

George looked at him grimly. "Yes. We are, aren't we? I'll show you where the hammer and nails are, and you and Douglas can get started, while I saw some of the long ones."

She went upstairs, but the noise of sawing and hammering followed her. The writing pad was lying, where she had left it, on the table near the window. She sat down, and looked at it. "Old Peter, the handyman, has disappeared now. It looks as though he's gone mad, too, so that there are four of them wandering around in the mist. So now the men are barricading the basement, in case they try to break in . . ." No, there was nothing to say, nothing to communicate. Except . . . I am beginning to be afraid. And lonely. She thought of Mandy, struggling with the preparations for lunch, and decided she would go and ask her if there was any way in which she could help.

Mandy was alone in the kitchen. As Jane came in, she was using the small steps to arrange something on one of the shelves. She turned quickly, putting a hand to her breast, and for a moment was in danger of losing her balance.

"Oh . . ." She smiled nervously. "You scared me, I guess."

There were jars on the shelf, some with preserves, a couple apparently full of sugar. Jane said, "I'm sorry, Mandy. I wondered if I could help in any way."

"Why, thank you, Jane. I think we're managing all right, though."

She moved the steps from where they were to a position under the window, for no apparent reason. Jane said, "Will they want to bar this window, as well?"

"Do you think so?"

"If they're worried about someone breaking in. It's the ground floor on this side."

"There's always someone about here."

"During the day. But at night . . ."

"Dear God!" Mandy said. "Barring windows against them —the Deepings—the boy—and old Peter . . ."

Jane said dispiritedly, "Yes. Though I suppose there's nothing to stop them coming to the door, if they want to come back."

"It's Andy," she said. "He might want just to creep in . . . I can't believe that he could do anything bad, a little boy like

152

that. And to think of him being out there—cold and hungry—it's terrible."

George, coming through the door from the hall, said, "What's terrible?"

"Andy out there."

Hammering still came from below. George said, "Yes. Selby and Douglas are finishing off. I've asked them to come up to the salon after that." He looked at Jane. "Can you round the others up? It's nearly lunchtime, anyway."

When they were together, George said, "I don't want to labor things unnecessarily, but there are one or two items we might get straight. In the first place, I don't think there's anything we really need to worry about, provided we use our common sense. If Peter has—gone over, there are three of them out there. And eight of us here."

Selby said, "Three, and the boy."

"And Steve to cancel things out. I wasn't counting the boys. The point is that we outnumber them by a lot. It's only as individuals that we could be in danger."

Elizabeth had her arm around Stephen's waist. She said, "Do you need Steve and me for this little chat? If there's anything important, you could tell me afterwards."

"I think Steve ought to stay," George said. "We can't go in for niceties. We've probably been a bit lucky over Peter."

Elizabeth said, "Lucky!"

"That he was noticed as being missing. Look, this change, whatever it is—we don't know how long it takes, but not long. I mean, Leonard had already been changed by the time he came down to Douglas's room. And Ruth had almost certainly been changed when we found her out there with the boy—and she couldn't have been out there much more than half an hour. If Peter had just come back . . . we shouldn't have spotted anything, probably. Marie would have kept quiet about his going outside. Or he would have quietened her."

He looked round their faces, bleakly and intently.

"Peter would have been in the house. One of them, and none of us suspecting it."

Mandy said, "You think maybe he would have come back? Then might he not still?"

"It's unlikely. Even if they weren't aware of us tramping around looking for him, they will see the bars across the windows and realize we know what's happened."

Douglas said, "We could have left the windows till later, surely. He might have come back, and we could have grabbed him."

"I don't think so," George said. "I don't think they are taking any chances. And we mustn't take any. None of us must. That means you, too, Steve. You follow that?"

Stephen nodded. "If I see any of them, I'll come and tell you."

"And if they are somewhere they can reach you, yell. Yell hard. That's what we grownups are going to do, so you see if you can yell louder than we can. It's not really your mother and father and Andy out there at all."

"I know. They're sick."

"Sick," George agreed, "and they can hurt you. We must all of us keep together as much as possible. Especially don't go down to the basement alone. And no one must go outside under any circumstances except by agreement."

Diana said restlessly, "How long do we have to keep this up?"

"We don't know. Not long, I hope."

She stared toward the window. "If only this mist would clear . . ."

Selby said, "It will." He spoke with confidence. "Tomorrow, if not today. And they will probably send a helicopter up from the valley, and we'll be all right. But meanwhile, as George says, we're in a pretty strong position as long as we behave sensibly. We've got food and shelter, and the advantage of numbers. We only have to sit things out."

Diana said, "But this sickness, whatever it is . . ." There was an edge to her voice, a nervousness not too far from hysteria. "They may have left germs in the house!"

"It's not that kind of sickness," Selby said.

"But you don't know! You said you didn't know what it was."

"I know what it isn't." He went to her, put his hands on her shoulders, and shook her gently, affectionately rather than chidingly. "We are all right, all of us, as long as we stay together. Or keep our distance from them. And we've fixed things so that no one can get into the basement without making a lot of noise, and this afternoon we'll do the same for the back of the house on this floor. And after that we sit tight and wait." He glanced at George. "And we do as George tells us."

There was a relief, Jane thought, in having things spelled out, and in the realization that the men had stopped bickering and would co-operate. Selby released Diana, and Jane moved closer to her. She had a rare feeling of protectiveness toward her.

George said, "Stay in the house, and keep together as much as possible. That's all." He looked at Mandy. "Lunch nearly ready?"

"In ten minutes."

The afternoon dragged its way into an evening marked only by the draining of what little light there was from the gray mist that surrounded them. The lamps were lit, making the darkness press closer against the windows. Nothing had happened out of the ordinary; there had been neither sight nor sound of those outside. Mandy was in the kitchen with Marie. George had opened the bar, and Selby and Elizabeth and Diana were with him. Stephen, too. It had been agreed that he should stay up and have supper with the grownups. Jane, not wishing to drink, settled by the fire in the salon, and Douglas joined her there. The fire was warm and cozy, and curtains had been drawn to keep out the night, and whatever lurked in its shadow. She had a book—Walpole's *Rogue Herries* in a scratched leather binding—but did not feel much like reading it. She was not quite sure how she felt. The disturbance and fear of earlier had subsided but had left her restless, somehow drained. In part, she wished she could be alone; in part, she was glad of Douglas's company.

She had an impression that he was restless, too, although he did not show it physically—he sat in the armchair opposite her, staring into the fire and saying nothing. It was she, in fact, who spoke first. She put the book down, and said, "What has been decided about standing guard tonight?"

He said, not looking up, "I expect George and Selby and I will share it. Though perhaps George and I will take it between us. Selby did his bit last night."

"We could all take a turn. Except Mandy and the maid. They have enough to do during the day."

"I don't think George would agree to that."

"That's ridiculous. This is not the time for gallantry."

"I don't know that it would be. Gallantry, that is."

The center of the fire collapsed, leaving a hole, and Jane stooped down and put another log on it. She said, "George is a pretty solid type. Protective and simple with women."

"Do men fall into types, as far as women are concerned?"

"I think so."

There was a silence, and then he started talking. She realized, with a qualm, that she was beginning to receive confidences and about, of all things, an unhappy love affair. She wondered what had brought him out in this; she did not think he was the kind of man who would normally talk about his

156

private concerns to someone who was no more than an acquaintance. The circumstances, probably. The tension they were all under might, she supposed, compel him to find some discharge for another, different tension. And she had no choice but to listen.

It was all very ordinary, although to him, of course, it must seem unique. She said, at the appropriate moment, "These things can be hellish. But, in a way, there must be a feeling of relief as well. After all, there wasn't much future to it."

"The relief doesn't have much chance to operate at present. It probably will, eventually. As to future—well, no, not by normal standards. But one gets used to a way of life, or half-life."

He was drawing the contrast with what he saw as her own normal happy marriage—with what, she reminded herself, she had seen as such. Keeping away from that, she said, "It all happened suddenly—her husband being transferred to New York?"

"No, I don't think so. Suddenly to me, of course. But when I look back . . . there are things that make sense. I think she probably had several months' warning."

"I suppose she thought it was better for you that it should happen in the way it did. And was right."

He said wryly, "On the premise that when I knew I would make another strenuous effort to get her to come away with me, yes. And that she had made up her mind about it. She only had a couple of hours to contend with after she told me."

"Try not to be bitter." She paused. "It's rather silly saying that, isn't it? But for your own sake . . ."

"Yes, I know. I don't think that is my main reaction. The loss—a certain numbness." He looked up. "I'm being pretty selfish, aren't I?"

"Selfish?"

"Talking about loss. After all, I know she's alive. The finality is not such a terrible one. And you can talk yourself round it. I do. Whereas with you . . ."

The new log she had put on the fire caught, and burned brightly. Resin glistened in the leaping yellow of flame. Jane said, "I was fond of my husband. I thought I would miss him."

She saw him look at her, and look away. It was his turn to be embarrassed. She wondered what could have made her say that, and felt a flush of acute shame, as though she had paraded her naked body for him to see. There was an impulse to get up and go away, but she controlled it. She was waiting for Douglas to say something, make some comment, knowing that anything he said would only make things worse.

But he said nothing and, looking again, she saw that his eyes had come back to her. And that she could bear them. She knew also that she could not leave it like that.

"I married young," she said. "And not knowing much about it. I was very shy in my teens. Harry—my husband— I admired him tremendously. He was fifteen years older than I was, already settled. A horticulturist—tomatoes, lettuce, flowers, some peppers and aubergines. He worked hard, and was good at it. I had a comfortable life."

She paused for a moment before going on. "I met someone when we had been married a year and a half. We got to know each other, found we had much the same tastes and interests. And there was physical attraction. Eventually, he told me he loved me, and I thought I loved him."

"Only thought?"

"Very seriously thought. He wanted me to go away with him. He was sure Harry would be willing to give me a divorce, and I think he was right about that. His own wife would have been only to glad to divorce him. They had one child, a daughter, away at school. Harry and I were childless. It all seemed quite simple."

"What went wrong?"

"Nothing. Everything went right. I stopped seeing him, and got on with the business of being a faithful wife. Hard going at first, but smugness is a great help. It would probably have been a good deal harder if I had gone to bed with him. But I have very respectable parents, and I never wanted to rebel against them. Bourgeois standards, I'm afraid."

He said, "You make it sound easy."

"You mean, there couldn't have been anything very strong there to begin with? Perhaps not. It seemed strong to me. I lost weight—couldn't sleep—in the end had a minor physical collapse and went home to mother. Harry was very good, very patient. For a time, I thought he might have known something—you know, like the husband in *Brief Encounter*—but I'm pretty sure he didn't. He couldn't imagine there being anything wrong with our marriage; and that was comforting, too. I stayed with my parents a couple of months, and then they packed me off back to him. And I made more good resolutions, and kept them this time. Life settled down. I slept at night, put the weight back I had lost." She smiled. "To the point of having to diet a little, in fact."

"And no regrets?"

"I think regrets need fairly constant attention to survive. I made sure I didn't look at mine."

"It sounds like a new morality tale. I'm not being nasty."

"I know. No happy ending, though."

"When your husband died . . ."

"It was a shock, of course. Bronchitis, which turned to pneumonia, and the drugs didn't work in his case. For a time, one doesn't realize what has happened. Eventually I came out of that stage. I found I accepted his death quite easily. What I couldn't accept was the pointlessness of my own life. Nothing seemed worth doing. Nothing does."

"How long had it been since—"

"Martin? A couple of lifetimes. Eight years."

"You'd lost touch?"

"Oh, yes. His marriage broke up, he remarried, and went to live in Canada. But that wasn't important. I'd killed that long ago. The point was that nothing was important. All the effort and misery was a waste. And there was nothing to put in its place, and no prospect of there ever being anything. Does this sound like nonsense?"

"No."

She looked at her hands. "I'm amazed at myself—telling you all this."

"I started it."

"Yes. Do you feel any better?"

He thought about that. "No."

She laughed. "Nor do I!"

But at least she felt grateful to him, for listening, for not saying the wrong things. And to feel this small degree of indebtedness, to another human being, was presumably better than nothing. She had a wave of tiredness, and a desire for solitude.

"I think I'll go up," she said, "and take my bath. I'll see you at supper, Douglas."

9

Mandy worried about Stephen, and about George.

It was a terrible thing for the boy to have the familiar reassuring figures of his parents replaced by bogeymen he must guard himself against—much much worse than it would have been to lose them entirely. She wanted to fuss him, in an attempt, admittedly inadequate, to make up for it, but, of course, during the day she just did not have the time. The scatterbrained side of Marie's nature had come increasingly into evidence during the past few days, and after Peter's disappearance she was almost useless. She had to be told the same thing over and over again, and then was as likely as not to drift away from whatever she was doing halfway through. It meant watching her all the time.

She had thought that she might take care of the boy after supper, while Marie was clearing up, but by that time Elizabeth had established herself as being in charge of him. This was reasonable; she had had the time to devote to him during the day. And she was good with him, and he seemed to like her. It was just that she belonged to that class of English-woman that Mandy found depressing. The Graingers, like the Deepings, had two children, a boy and a girl, but theirs were away at boarding school and had been, she guessed, from the age of seven. She had shown no anxiety—as Ruth would cer-tainly have done in her place—over the fact that the ava-lanche had put her out of touch with them. When they came home for the holidays she would greet them with a bright wel-coming smile, and a careful eye for clothes that needed mend-ing or renewing. She would be calm and kind with them, a friendly stranger.

There was no doubt that as an approach it had something to commend it. Her calmness communicated to the boy, and made him calm also. Convenient for the rest of them, bottled up here with who-knew-what outside, but wrong, she was sure —truly wrong. He was only ten, after all. There should have been storms—tears and helplessness—and someone to soothe him, and make things just a little bit better.

Marie left the kitchen to get the rest of the things from the dining room, and there was time—not much, but enough, and without snatching or gulping—to get herself a drink from the bottle behind the jar of vanilla sugar. It was nearly empty, she saw. Enough for tonight, but she would have to get some more in the morning. She contemplated herself for a moment with melancholy and sad disgust. What, in any case, could she have given the boy? What could she give anyone? Even George . . .

She could see that the strain was beginning to tell on George; the small tic, unnoticed probably by the others, that pulled from time to time at his left eye was a sign of that. And he was drinking more—not ostentatiously, as he usually did, but with a quiet compulsiveness. And as he drank, he became morose. When Jane, after supper, sought to press the suggestion that the women should stand guard at night as well as the men, he rejected the idea with a sharpness that was almost vicious. He said coldly, "No. And we won't discuss it any more. I'll decide who goes on watch, and when."

She was relieved that no one challenged him. In this mood, had one of the men done so, there might have been violence. She had seen George hit a man, without warning, simply for smiling at something he had said. And yet he was not by nature a violent man—no one knew that better than she did. Not even, normally, in drink. But drink and this mood together were the danger.

In the end, it was fixed that the three men should stand guard on the basis of two hours on duty followed by four hours off. Douglas was given the first period from ten o'clock until midnight, and George was to follow him. Selby would have the middle watch, from two to four, but was not required to do any more that night.

They arranged the details of this, and Selby said, "Just after ten o'clock now. You're on, Douglas. And I think I will go up to bed and get what sleep I can before George comes looking for me. Don't forget to leave the whisky out, George."

There was a general move to follow him. Mandy herself felt tired; the day had been exhausting in more ways than one. She lingered, though, until only George and Douglas were left. She said to George, "Are you coming up?"

He stared at her. "Later." She did not move, and he said irritably, "I've said I'll come later. Go on up."

She did not like leaving him, but there was no choice. She went up to Marie, in the attic, and saw that she was all right, and then to her own bedroom. The boy had been there the night before, but tonight Elizabeth had had his cot moved into her room. She undressed slowly, and said her prayers slowly, praying in addition for Stephen, and for the Deepings and Andy, and old Peter. One got used to things—to the fact

163

of their being out there in the mist and snow. She shivered and, sitting on the edge of the bed, poured herself the last drink of the day, and saw that this bottle, too, was nearly empty. The lamp by her bed flickered. The oil was getting low. Something must happen soon—the mist disperse, the road from Nidenhaut be cleared. All the bewilderment and tension and danger would be over, and things would be as they had been before. She found she was beginning to cry, the tears coursing down her hot cheeks, and she put the light out, and climbed into bed.

But she did not sleep. She was worried still about George, and found herself listening for the sound of him coming up to bed. The occasional creakings of the house came into focus; she had long been accustomed to them as a background, but each, now, might be his footstep on the stairs or the landing. Might be, but was not.

She thought of another old and creaking house, more than thirty years away. That summer, with all the cousins staying . . . Solemnity among the grownups, and lectures on extravagance. The terrible news about Uncle Lee, told to her by Cooper first, as he always told her things first, and the realization that that was why the Mulway cousins were staying, and staying so long—that they were orphans, and poor. "Dad's taken a beating in the stock market, too," Cooper had explained, "but nothing like the one Uncle Lee took. They don't know about it, Mandy—they've been told he's ill. So we must be nice to them, but we mustn't let them know, get suspicious even. You see that?"

She had seen that. "Are you going to tell Clyde?" she had asked. Cooper had shaken his head. "I don't know. I'm not sure he could keep it a secret." A warm feeling: Clyde was a year older than she was, but she was the one Cooper trusted, always had done. Though Clyde was nice, too, even if he talked too much and laughed too much.

And the cousins were nice: Hilda, her own age, Catharine,

164

a few months younger than Cooper, but so shy and innocent, and Charlie, who was only six. It had been a wonderful summer altogether—such fun and, despite the stock market and what had happened to Uncle Lee, so full of happiness. There probably were squabbles from time to time—there had to be with Cooper and Clyde both around—but she could not remember them. Only bright mornings going down to the sea, golden afternoons in the long grass of the orchard . . . and on the few wet days, the house creaking to six pairs of feet. Sardines and hide-and-seek, and that game that Cooper had thought up with all the complicated rules—something like chess, something like cops-and-robbers—playing it through all the rooms and corridors of the house. In all her life, she had never known such a feeling of belonging as she did that summer, a sense of giving and sharing and loving.

And all gone, dispersed, faded like an old photograph to the point where it doesn't mean anything any more. Cooper killed somewhere over Berlin. Clyde dying in the hospital in North Africa. Catharine in that other hospital, in Vermont, and unlikely to come out even though she might live another thirty years. Hilda just through with her third divorce and remarried. And little Charlie the broker, making the money his father lost, desperate and successful and twenty pounds overweight, with three overweight children and an underweight wife. And herself, of course.

A board creaked again, and again there was silence after it. She looked at her watch, squinting at the tiny luminous fingers. Past eleven. He would not be coming up now before two. She might as well go to sleep.

And sleep still evaded her. She drifted back, in reverie, to that good time and, though wakeful, was happy. The time on the boat . . . the time on the beach . . . the picnic among the sand dunes . . . even old Caesar dying, because there had been the time of burying him, and crying, and yet feeling that it was right for him to die, an old dog, and be buried in the orchard, with the wooden cross the boys had made, and the inscription Cooper had written: "Caesar—aged Twelve—mostly a Bulldog."

It was ten minutes after twelve when she looked at her watch again. Douglas would have gone to bed. She got out, felt for her slippers, and found her wrap hanging from the door. She did not bother to light the lamp, but made her way blindly to the landing. The glow of light from below directed her to the stairs. It was dark, but she could manage, using the banister to guide her. She made as little noise as possible so as not to disturb the others. There was a lamp lit in the hall, and light came from the half-open door to the bar. She pushed it right open, and went in.

George was looking out of the window; the curtains had been drawn back. He turned around quickly, hearing her. His eyes were cold, his mouth working, and she thought he was going to be angry with her.

She said, "I just . . ."

She did not know what to say. He stared at her for a moment, then said, "I didn't know it was you, Mandy." His voice was mild, and she saw his face relax. "Couldn't you sleep, lovey?"

"Not very well."

"You don't want to let this business get you down." He came across the room, and put his arm around her waist. "Don't forget you're the girl we all depend on. Anyway, now that you're down, we'll have a drink."

He had drunk a great deal. His voice was just faintly slurred which was unusual for him. She said, "I'm not sure that I should."

He released her, and went behind the bar.

"What will it be? Brandy? Gin?"

"Just a little gin, then." She watched him pour it, and another whisky for himself. "I'm drinking too much, George."

166

"We all are," he said. "We all are. Perhaps we ought to get out of this business. What do you think? Remember that chap who wanted me to do crop-spraying? I might take him up on that. Parsons? I've got his address somewhere. Operating from Bournemouth, wasn't he? We could get a cottage in the New Forest . . . beautiful country. And drink beer. No one can drink too much beer. What do you think about that, Mandy?"

"It might be fun."

"I could do it all right. Piece of cake, after a Lancaster. And a *useful* job—you know what I mean? Dig for Victory— two blades of grass growing where one grew before—that sort of thing."

"Yes," she agreed. "You could do it."

"And a bit of spraying in foreign parts, so we don't get too bloody insular. That's the trouble with the English—too bloody insular. A few months in South America, maybe. You would come along with me, of course. I'm not going anywhere without you, Mandy. You know that."

She said, "Do you need me, George?"

"Need you?" He stared at her. "Of course I need you. You know I do. Don't you?"

Not now, she thought of saying—not here, in the small hours, being lonely, and drunk, and confused and miserable. There is a different kind of needing, a belonging. As it was with Cooper and me, and even Clyde, and the cousins. And you don't need me like that; it's a long time since anyone did.

She smiled, and said, "Yes, I know." He was still looking at her. "One says silly things in the middle of the night."

His gaze left her, and went into the distance. "Get out to the Far East, perhaps. It's pretty big stuff in those parts. I've always wanted to see India. Flew us out there in forty-five, and back the same week. One of those bloody silly things they used to do."

He was happy, talking. In the five years since there really had been Parsons—a small excitable man with bulging eyes

167

behind horn-rimmed spectacles, and what he himself kept on referring to as "vision"—this theme had cropped up at intervals, when George was tired, depressed, overworked. He had been flattered even then by the notion that he could, well into his forties, go back to flying. As the years passed, the idea had taken on an elaborate, dreamlike quality. She listened, and nodded, and drank the gin he had poured her. It was something that he could live in the future still, even a dream future.

He looked at the time once, and said, "You should be getting back to bed, Mandy. Another long day ahead." But when she maintained that she was fine, and not at all tired, he did not press things. He filled her glass again, and his own, and went on talking.

At two o'clock, she reminded him to call Selby. She went to bed, then, hearing them talking quietly on the stairs. George came up soon afterward. He got into bed, and was soon asleep. For a while, she lay awake. Caesar, she thought . . . the way the kitten used to play with him, jumping on his back, putting its small head in his slobbering mouth. But which kitten? Not Franklin. Joey. Who had died, an old cat, in forty-seven, in the year Lois was born . . . And it was not sad then, because she had not seen him for so many years, had almost forgotten him. And because there was so much to live for.

For all her lateness in getting to sleep, she awoke at the usual time, and did not feel particularly tired. She found the matches, and lit the lamp. George was sleeping, hunched on one side, his face relaxed and peaceful. She had her drink, found wrap and slippers, went to the bathroom, washed face and hands and brushed her hair quickly, and went downstairs. Douglas heard her coming, and came out of the bar. She asked him, "Is everything all right?"

"Fine. I had a very quiet watch."

She nodded. "You can go to bed now. Marie will be down in a minute."

He stretched himself. "It doesn't really seem worth while."

"I'll be making a cup of tea."

"Good. Then I'll stay up."

He came with her to the kitchen, and they chatted while she put the kettle on, and started preparations for breakfast. He was, in his quiet manner, a pleasant young man—rather serious, callow, perhaps, in the English way, but good-natured, she thought, and with more of a sense of humor than one would think. He told her some things, stories from his life as a lawyer, that were really droll. One, a complicated story about a divorce, with agents bursting into the wrong bedrooms, brought her genuinely to laughter. She said then, "That girl ought to be down by now. Probably she's dozed off. I'll just go up and call her. Can you make the tea when the kettle boils, Douglas?"

He said, "Making tea is the beginning and end of my cooking. I pride myself on it."

She would have gone right up to the attic, but from the foot of the narrow stairs she saw that the lamp was burning up there. So she stood at the bottom, and called quietly, "Marie. Are you coming?"

Marie said, "Madame . . . Can you help me?"

She sighed. More of Marie's helplessness. Her foot on the stairs, she said, "What's gone wrong now?"

"The lamp. It does not burn properly."

Everything she touched she maltreated. She had very likely succeeded in getting the wick burning unevenly. But there was no reason why she should not have brought the lamp downstairs. And the light that diffused through her open door looked clear and steady. A shadow . . . She had a feeling of constraint and awkwardness, reminding her of the other girl, the Austrian, and how she had stumbled on her with her

Italian boy friend in the room. That could not be the case now. But the shadow on the wall just inside the room . . . unmoving, though Marie, as she could hear, was moving about. It was not her shadow. Then whose?

I am being silly, she thought. A trick of the light—was it the shadow of a person or of something else—a coat, perhaps, a chair. . . . ? Her eyes were not very good, and the light was not bright. It was ridiculous not to go up and see what was happening.

Marie said, "Will you come, madame?"

And her hackles rose.

She said, "In a minute, Marie. I've got something to do."

George woke at her touch. She whispered, "Marie . . . It may not be anything, but I'm worried. Do you think . . ."

He sat up, snapping out of sleep easily, as he always did. He said, "The gun?"

"Douglas has it downstairs."

"Get it. Bring him up."

When they returned, George was at the foot of the stairs leading to the attic, motionless, looking up. Marie's door was still partly open, light flooding out. The shadow had gone from the wall. George motioned to them for silence and, leaning toward Mandy, said softly, "Call her down."

She called, "Marie. Bring the lamp down and we'll fix it in the kitchen. Hurry, girl. We're late this morning."

There was no reply. She called again, "Marie! I want you down here right away. No nonsense."

Silence answered her. She looked at George. He reached out his hand, took the gun from Douglas, and began climbing the stairs. His face was grim and she saw his eye twitch. Douglas, after a moment's hesitation, followed him, and she went after them. The stairs groaned under their feet. She waited for some sound from above—reproach, outcry, she did not know what. But none came.

170

George kicked the door open and went in, the gun tucked beneath his right arm and his finger inside the trigger guard. Now, fearfully, she expected the gun's explosion, and its hideous aftermath. But there was no shot. Instead George's footsteps quickened, running across the room.

It was empty. The window was open, and George was there, looking down. The cold blast of the outside air made her shiver, but she followed Douglas and stood beside her husband. It was very dark, and the mist was as thick as ever. The snow on the ground was a dim white blur, showing nothing.

And forty feet below.

10

Leaning out, Douglas said, "My God! She must have killed herself."

"She? Or they?" George turned away from the balustrade. "I wonder."

Mandy had turned, too, and was hurrying toward the door. George called, "Where are you going?"

"Only to see if she's all right."

George went after her, and caught her arm. He said, "Don't be a fool, Mandy. You're probably meant to do just that."

She stared at him. "But we can't . . ."

"There are four of them out there, five if we count the boy. A couple of them may be injured, but we don't know about that. You're staying in the house. Go and wake Selby, and get him up. He and Douglas and I will go and have a look at things. With the gun."

"But she may be badly hurt!"

"Yes. And it might be better if she were dead. Go and wake Selby."

172

When she had gone, George closed the windows. There was a hook-and-eye catch which he put on. Going out, he locked the door from the outside, and did the same for the other room, which had been Peter's. He put the keys in his pocket, and motioned Douglas to go down the narrow stairs ahead of him.

Selby met them on the first-floor landing, buttoning up his trousers. He had a white exhausted look; he had had much less sleep than the others the previous night, Douglas remembered, and the graveyard watch on this one. And physically a person with more febrility than stamina, he would have thought.

Selby said, his rather high-pitched voice sharp, "Well? They've got Marie? How did they get at her? I'm pretty sure no one went up during my watch."

Douglas said, "Nor during mine."

"I'm guessing," George said, "but Peter was a mountain climber in his young days. I think maybe he came up the side of the house, and in at the window. She had left the catch off." He exhaled heavily. "A pretty careless girl, in some ways."

Douglas said, "In his young days . . . but now? How old is he—getting on for seventy?"

"Sixty-four," George said. "He was born the day Queen Victoria died. He was a bit proud of that."

Douglas thought of Peter, his white hair and his slight rheumatic limp. "Even so . . ."

"It's possible," Selby said, "if you don't much care what happens to you. Or whoever's in charge of you doesn't care. Mandy says she jumped from her balcony. I suppose both of them did. Same thing applies."

George said, "I reckon we ought to go outside and see. If one of them broke a leg . . ."

"That would be a help," Selby said. "We haven't had a chance to look one of them over properly, except at the beginning. And then we didn't know what we'd got hold of."

Them, Douglas thought. The enemy. And it was true, of course. But what kind of enemy? He asked, "What had we got hold of?"

"I don't know," Selby said. "I'm beginning to get some ideas. The first thing is to go and see what we can find out there."

It was very dark still, and bitterly cold. Elizabeth had got up by now, and she and Mandy stood by the door—George had instructed them to bar it after they had gone, and only open up again on clear recognition. Douglas carried a torch and George had the gun. They were to stick close together, on either side of Selby. He led the way up the slope from the front door, and to the right around the side of the house. The snow had drifted to a depth of several feet; there was a brittle crust but it was fairly soft beneath the surface.

"Here," George said.

Douglas shone the beam of the torch. There was no doubt that they had found the place. A hole in the snow, and a second a little distance off—a hole made by a heavy body, presumably a falling body. There were tracks around them, confused and uninformative. Douglas flashed the torch in different directions. It revealed nothing but the snow and the mist.

George said, "No point in looking further. We might as well go back into the warm."

"They may not have gone far," Douglas said. "If one of them were hurt, for instance."

"Not badly enough to stop him or her walking away," Selby said. "Or being carried. Either way, we're not likely to find them in the dark."

They went back in silence. Mandy peered through the glass when they rang the bell, and admitted them. She said, "Was she hurt?"

174

George shook his head. "We don't know. She didn't stay to tell us. I'll lock up, Mandy. Can you rustle us up a cup of coffee?"

"None left. Only tea."

"Right, tea it is." He pressed her arm affectionately. "But make it quick, love. And get some breakfast on—we're all hungry."

Elizabeth had gone to get Stephen up, and had said she would awaken Jane and Diana. The three men, when they had got rid of their outdoor clothes, went through to the kitchen, and joined Mandy, who was preparing breakfast. She made them tea, and they sat around the table drinking it.

Douglas said, "It would have been a good piece of climbing by a young man. And why go all the way up there? Why not break in on one of the lower floors?"

George said, "Whoever was on guard might have heard him. Up there he was pretty safe. He probably guessed there was a chance Marie had not fastened her window properly— he knew how careless she was—but if she had, he could have broken into his own room without making much noise."

"And the plan of action?" Selby asked.

"He gets Marie, presumably while she's asleep. Converts her, or infects her, or whatever it is. Then if they can get Mandy up there, they have her as well. It's the right time, isn't it? One or two people stirring, the rest in bed. Marie and Mandy come downstairs to Douglas, Peter a little way behind them so that he's not noticed. Till it's too late. After that . . . open the door, I suppose, and let the others in. All over in half an hour."

Selby nodded. "It sounds reasonable."

"Too bloody reasonable altogether," George said. "It only went wrong because Mandy had a hunch."

Mandy turned from the stove. "It was something about her

voice. Her speech . . . not slurred exactly, but kind of slow. Slower than she usually spoke."

"That's one of the things," Selby said. "Or seems to be. Remember Andy, and Ruth. Reflexes just a little bit slower, I would guess." He rubbed his hands together restlessly. "My God, I'd like to get hold of one of them, to examine at leisure."

"Would it help?" Douglas asked. "I mean, we know they're dangerous."

"We might find out the particular ways in which they are dangerous. How they infect others. How vulnerable they are to physical stimuli. We might find out quite a lot of things."

George stirred his tea again, and drank it. "Any more in the pot, Mandy?" He turned back to Selby. "Not much chance of that, I should think. They're pretty good at staying out of reach."

Selby said, "It might be possible. There's this urge to infect—a kind of hunger, almost. They will take chances for that: look at old Peter. We might be able to do something with it. Set a trap."

Douglas asked, "In the house?"

George said positively, "Not in the house. Something might go wrong."

Selby nodded. "Outside would be better."

"Set a trap?" George said. "With one of us? How? You can't just stick someone out there."

"It needs thinking about."

Douglas had a picture of himself in the role . . . in the snow, the cold shapeless gray all around, and shapes emerging from it . . . fear prickled for a moment down his spine. He felt relief when George said, "You couldn't do anything with the mist as thick as it is. You wouldn't know where you were."

"Something in that, I suppose. But it might clear."

176

"The sensible thing," George said, "is to hang on where we are. We're learning all the time."

"And losing," Selby said. "If we had a specimen . . ."

Mandy brought the teapot over to them. "Specimen?" she asked. "How can you talk like that? Marie, Peter, little Andy . . ."

No one answered her. Selby said, "We need to give it thought." He stood up from the table. "One thing we can do is bar the other windows in the house. I doubt if they will try to get in during the day, but we can't rule out the possibility."

The voices started about an hour later. Mandy was the first to hear them. The kitchen window was barred, but she had opened it to clear the cooking smells. She called up the stairs excitedly, and they left their work on the other windows and came down to see what was happening. She said fearfully, "They were calling—through the kitchen window."

"Who?" George asked.

Selby said, "Calling what?"

"Marie first. And then I heard Ruth's voice. And Leonard's. They were asking me to come out."

They looked at each other, and headed for the kitchen. There was no sound, apart from the clock ticking. She might have been imagining things, Douglas thought. Then, while they stood listening, the voice came from somewhere outside. Ruth's voice.

"Mandy. Come out, Mandy. We won't hurt you. There's nothing to be afraid of, Mandy. Come out."

Selby moved quickly and quietly, taking the steps over to the window, and mounting them. He stared out, his head just above the level of the window ledge.

"See anything?" George asked.

"I don't think so. No." He called out, "Ruth, you come in

177

here. Come in the house, so that we can talk properly. We'll open the front door for you."

There was a pause, and the voice said again, "Come out." Its tone was neither threatening nor cajoling, merely flat. Others joined with it—Leonard's recognizably, and then a jumble of voices. "Come out. Come out. Come out."

"The mist is still thick," Selby said. "And they're staying out of range." He got down from the steps, closing the window first. They could still hear the voices, but only faintly. "God knows what they're trying to do—not to communicate, that's certain."

Elizabeth came in from the hall. She said, "What's happening? Steve said he thought he heard his mother's voice."

Selby said, "He did. Trying to get Mandy to go outside. They may try it on him, too. Make sure he pays no attention."

She nodded. "I'll see to that."

George said, "I don't get it. They couldn't really have expected her to do as they said. Unless . . . I suppose it could be just to get on our nerves?"

"Could be." Selby shrugged. The voices still came to them, thin and distant. "Obviously, there's no point in trying to talk to them."

Mandy asked, "Are you sure there isn't?"

For answer, Selby went back to the window and reopened it. The voices were a jumble, but some words stood out: "Come . . . come out . . . out . . . come out, Mandy . . . out . . . out . . ."

Elizabeth said, "Why Mandy?"

"Probably because they expect her to be in the kitchen." He closed the window once more, shutting off much of the noise. "I think we ought to get back to fixing those windows."

They nailed lengths of wood across all the windows in the upper part of the chalet. The planks ran out before the end,
178

and they had to break up wooden boxes for the last few small windows—the result was far from neat but looked effective. For Douglas, the work was more depressing than reassuring: they were reinforcing a prison from the inside. The gray mist still cut off the sun, and with wood nailed in front of the glass, the rooms were very dark. From time to time they heard the far-off outcry of the voices; they came and went in a weird periodicity. He was glad when they hammered the last nails in the slats across the frosted glass of the first-floor bathroom, and George said, "I reckon that will do."

Selby asked, "What about the ground-floor front?"

"No more wood. In any case, there's always someone on watch down there. I think a small noggin is indicated after all those exertions. Bring the hammer and nails down, Douglas, will you?"

It was a relief to be in a place where the windows let in all the light, even this meager mist-filtered light. Douglas glanced at his watch. Half past eleven. The work had taken longer than he had thought. While George fiddled about behind the bar, he went through to the salon. He had only seen Jane for a few minutes that morning, and was, he realized, looking forward to seeing her again. She was sitting in the armchair by the fire with a book—the same leather-bound book she had had the previous evening. It was this, unexpectedly, which gave him pause, reminding him of the confidences they had exchanged then, and that they had not been alone together since.

The pause was only momentary. He went across the room, aware of being glad that he had found her by herself. They were all thrown together, made closer and more human to each other, by the danger outside, but the alliance of shared privacies was a different and more compelling one. For himself, the weakness of wanting where he was not wanted. For

179

her, the ennui of ceasing to want altogether. And, for both of them, loneliness.

She looked up as he approached, and he said, smiling, "We've barred every part of the house except this. It should be secure enough now."

He had not, of course, intended to touch on their earlier conversation again; it was enough that it had taken place, that there had been an act of understanding, of recognition. But he was unprepared for her reaction to him; it showed confusion, uneasiness—distaste even. She said, "Yes. I heard all the hammering."

It was a minimum response, and plainly meant as such. She accompanied it with a faint, polite smile, and returned at once to her book. He stood in front of her, feeling a fool. After a moment, he said, "George is opening the bar. Do you feel like a drink?"

"No." She shook her head. "I don't think so, thank you." She looked up again briefly. "Don't let me stop you, though."

The dismissal had been underlined. He felt annoyance and resentment, chiefly that she should, as he suspected, have thought him crass enough to be capable of reopening a topic she might want to remain closed. He had an impulse, in view of her present behavior, to do exactly that—to tell her that it was her self-centeredness, her withdrawal from other people, that made life seem pointless to her. He resisted it, but continued to stand there, partly because of uncertainty, partly through perverseness. Then he heard the different sound and said, involuntarily, "What was that?"

She looked up again. "What?"

"Listen." He hurried across to the double French windows that gave access to the veranda, and opened them. "Now!"

She put her book down and came to stand beside him. He saw that the indifference had gone, that she looked excited, but he was too excited himself to feel any satisfaction because of that. She said, "An airplane! And fairly close."

"Helicopter." He called out, "George, Selby!" The mist out there swirled, as though rocked by the uneven rhythm of the engine note. He said happily, "That's a pretty good noise to hear, isn't it?"

They came in from the bar, carrying their glasses. They both looked pleased; George was grinning broadly. They stepped out onto the veranda, and Douglas followed them. The helicopter was very close, not more than a couple of hundred feet away, Douglas guessed.

Selby said, "Isn't he taking something of a chance, in this soup?"

"Must be thinning," George said. "He'll be skimming the top of it." He stared up into the mist. "Somebody up there likes me. And I like him. I really, really do."

"He can't come down," Selby objected, "and we certainly can't jump that high. It doesn't leave us a great deal better off."

"They're doing a recce," George said. "I suppose they've had a forecast for mist clearing, and they're maybe a bit worried about us. We've been cut off for over four days, after all." He grinned again. "Even if they can't get to us, it's nice to know they're thinking of us."

Selby stared out. "I think perhaps it is clearing slightly. Not much. But it's looking a fraction brighter."

"Yes," George said, "it is."

By the time lunch was ready, there was no doubt that the mist was thinner. Visibility was up to fifty or sixty feet, and there was a distinct brightening in the quarter where the sun would now be. The helicopter had long gone, but the day still had a cheering aspect. Mandy had contrived to turn flour and water, salt beef, tinned vegetables and various dried herbs into a rich dumpling stew, and George served a Dole Pinot Noir with it, heavy, satisfying, almost black. He was very happy, and kept the glasses filled.

Eventually, Selby objected. "We're going to be fit for nothing this afternoon, unless we go a bit easier."

"What do we need to be fit for?" George said. "We've done all the bolting and barring."

"We were going to make a sortie to get hold of one of them. Or lay a trap, or something."

"No point in that," George said. "The mist's clearing. As soon as it's lifted, we'll have the chopper back. They'll get us out of here, and then you can hunt your specimen at your leisure. Nothing in it."

Elizabeth said, "Has anyone heard any voices since the helicopter was over? I haven't."

"They've cleared off out of the way, I reckon," George said. "Probably scared the hell out of them."

Selby said doubtfully, "I wonder."

"Anyway, the thing to do is sit tight." George filled his own glass to the brimming point. "Sit tight and wait. Time's on our side."

11

Relief displayed was, as a matter of elementary logic, a measure of prior tension. George, Selby realized now, had been under a greater strain than had appeared: hence this euphoria. Mandy brought tea into the salon after lunch, and George suggested brandies. None of the others accepted, but he poured a large measure for himself. His face was somewhat flushed from the drink he had already taken, but otherwise he looked all right. He would have a good capacity for alcohol, and probably not show much up to the point of passing out.

With the slightly intoxicated relief came other things. He got on to the subject of Selby's children, and the possibility that they might be anxious about their parents. Selby shrugged.

"I shouldn't think they'll have been told anything. They're both at pretty sensible schools. We got cards off to them the day before things closed in on us. And we can telephone to them as soon as we get to Nidenhaut."

George stared at him. "And, after all, it isn't as though they see much of you, is it? How old are they, anyway?"

"Cassie's eleven. Mike's eight."

"Eight? And how long has the poor little sod been away at boarding school?"

"Since September."

"Christ! It doesn't bear thinking of."

Selby said mildly, "We had a good look at the school before he went there. In fact, we ruled out my old place because we thought it a little on the spartan side. This one is pretty comfortable. Pleasant, too, and with nice people. He's settled in well. He enjoyed coming home for Christmas, but he was cheerful enough about going back afterwards."

"You were sent away at eight, too, I suppose?"

"Yes."

"And enjoyed it?"

"I remember crying a bit, the first few nights. After that I enjoyed it."

"Because you had it to go through, it's O.K. for him, too. That's it, isn't it?"

"It's not exactly the way I would put it."

"Shove him through the mill, and he's all right for life. Prep school and public school. Who gives a damn what happens to him, as long as he's stamped in the right mold?"

Selby said, "There are a number of ways in which early life can be tough. You know that as well as anyone."

"I wasn't packed away at the age of eight. I can imagine what my ma would have said if anyone had tried that one on."

"Different people see things differently. Variety is supposed to be a spice, isn't it?"

George said disgustedly, "Variety! Where's the variety in a set of carbon copies?"

"Well, between species, then." He smiled at him easily. "Your species and mine."

184

He had made the remark out of idle curiosity, which was satisfied by the deepening of the color in George's face. An unkindness, he admitted, but there had been provocation. And if you put on protective mimicry, it was not a good idea to shout anti-slogans to the tribal cries. The man's sense of fitness should prevent it. But could not, of course. A man might deny class, creed, country, but the chip on the shoulder was something he carried for life.

He went on, willing to placate now. "Actually, I am opposed to chucking kids indiscriminately into schools. There are some children who never should be sent away, and a lot of schools that no child should ever be entrusted to. And in a different kind of society, values would be different. One has to do the best with what one has. I'm a rule-of-thumb man, not an idealist."

Which was true, he thought, and reasonably honest. It was pleasant to ameliorate, in one's small way, the human lot, but not a burning concern. To that extent his work was peripheral to his life, not central. What was central, he wondered? Elizabeth? Or good living—or self-esteem? The question, he decided, was a dull one, and he dropped it.

George said, "I'm opposed to the whole thing. The British are the only nation in the world that go in for it. Because they're too bloody idle to take the trouble to look after their own kids."

He had recovered himself, but he was talking loudly.

"There may be something," Selby said blandly, "in what you say."

Shortly after, George broke off, on the excuse of seeing to the furnace. He was, plainly, still angry with Selby, and probably with himself also. No, Selby thought, despite the provocation he had been wrong to let himself be drawn. One owed a duty to the weaker brethren, for one's own peace of mind if nothing else. He went to the bookcase, but found little of interest. He was leafing through a work, in French, on ophthalmology, and speculating as to how it had come to be here, when the door from the dining room opened. He turned, and saw Diana.

"Well," he said, "I thought you were all busy playing Monopoly."

"I've been wiped out. I was looking for someone to talk to."

And where was the book, he asked himself, one thousandth part as attractive as a girl, pretty and young and setting herself out to please? He said warmly, "Go no further. You've found him."

She smiled and went to the French windows. "It's looking so much brighter," she said. "The sun's almost shining. Can't we go outside?"

Selby stood beside her, and inhaled her scent with pleasure.

"I don't see why not. As far as the veranda, at any rate. But we'd better put something a little warmer on first. I would reckon that it's colder than you think out there."

They got their coats and went through to the veranda. It was cold, but less raw than it had been. They leaned against the balustrade, their arms not quite touching, and looked out. There was still not much to see: the snow in front of the house, the heap of stacked logs, and the outhouses beyond them. Seventy-five feet, perhaps. And patchy—mist swirled in, clouded across the open space before them, slowly dispersed. Too tricky to risk a helicopter in, especially in this kind of country. But clearing. There was a pearly gleam all around them, as though they were in the center of some huge frosted egg.

Diana said, "It's good to be outside. I hate being shut up in a house for too long."

"Yes," Selby said. "I'm with you in that."

"Or, worse still, in a flat. I rather hate flats. Do you live in a flat, Selby?"

186

He nodded. "A gloomy place, off the Cromwell Road. But we do have a little place in Kent we can repair to at the week's end."

"Kent? Lovely! What part?"

"Near the Sussex border. Not far from Hawkhurst."

"Yes, gorgeous! Especially in the spring."

She spoke with enthusiasm, and the right small touch of wistfulness. And at this point, obviously, it would be reasonable to say that she must come down with them some weekend. No, my little one, he thought, the plans I have for you do not embrace weekends at the cottage, with or without Elizabeth in the offing. In the country, maybe, but a different part of the country. Suffolk, perhaps. There was that charming pub on the river; and flat landscapes, he felt, tended to bring out the liveliness in a girl.

"Pleasant enough," he agreed. He waved his arm toward the point where the sun's disk, for a moment, almost showed through. "If I were of a religious turn of mind, I think heliolatry would be my pigeon."

She stared at him, laughing. "Heli-what?"

"Sun worship. Did you see the sign outside that chalet, on the way up to Nidenhaut?"

"No. What sign?"

"In French, and carved in a great chunk of wood. It said, give or take the nuances of my translation. 'The sun is the fatherland—to follow the one is to serve the other.' "

"What does that mean?"

He grinned. "I'm not sure. I like the sound of it, though."

She dropped unexpectedly into earnestness. The blue eyes looked at him solemnly.

"Do you take anything seriously, Selby?"

"Lots of things."

"What?"

"The small things. I leave the big ones to people with more

profound minds and more elevated natures. Why, do you take life seriously?"

She said mournfully, "I'm afraid not. I try to, from time to time."

"Don't try. The beauty of life is this, that each should act in conformity with his nature and his business."

"Who said that? Shakespeare?"

"No, though he might well have done. An ex-member of my profession used the quotation to wind up a very sensible book he wrote, but I've forgotten where it came from."

There was a pause while she thought about it.

"Yes, I suppose it is sensible. Except that one doesn't always know what one's nature is meant to be. Or one's business." She gave him a quick look. "People have mad moments."

She was referring, possibly, to the night before last, and the interrupted kiss. Interrupted, he remembered with a small inward shiver of distaste, for him, not for her. It had not been mentioned between them since. He wondered whether to tell her about the face, here in daylight with the mists thinning all around them, but decided against it. He was against connecting kisses with unpleasantness.

"Nothing wrong with mad moments," he said, "time and place being appropriate."

She made a restless movement, which brought their arms into contact, and stood back, her gloved hands on the rail.

"So cooped up. How long before we get away, do you think?"

"Tomorrow, probably."

"Do you really think so?"

"You'll be back behind your typewriter in less than forty-eight hours."

"No, I'm not looking forward to *that*."

"Cast your eye further ahead. Those walks through the

park, counting the crocuses. And just a few more months before you start queuing for the Proms. After all . . ."

"Look!"

She was staring at the mist. Selby looked in the same direction, but saw nothing.

"What was it?"

"I thought I saw something move. It looked . . ."

"What did it look like?"

"Andy."

"It could be." He listened. "No voices. They're keeping quiet at present. They may be scouting around, though. What was he doing?"

"I don't think he was doing anything. Standing still."

"No one else?"

"Not that I saw." She shivered. "I had a nightmare last night, about all this."

"It is nightmarish. But nearly over."

"I was at home," she said, "in the flat, alone at night. Sylvia was out, and I was doing some mending. And the door opened and Ruth Deeping came in. I wasn't frightened at first, because all I remembered was the first part of the holiday, and I thought how nice it was that she had found my address and come to see me. It was still all right when Leonard came in. I asked them to sit down and said I would make some tea. But when I went through to the kitchen, the boy was there, Andy, lying dead on that table with the boxes round him, and I remembered, and wanted to run away, but the only way out was through the room the other two were in . . ." She gave a small laugh. "How silly these things are when you think of them the next day."

"Yes."

He spoke absently. Out there, at the limit of visibility—was there something, or was it merely imagination, sparked off by what Diana had seen, or thought she had seen? The mist billowed closer, and whatever it was had gone. In any case, what would it matter if one did see them, any of them? There was nothing one could do about it, and at a distance they were not a danger.

"I used to have nightmares," she said, "when I was a little girl. Or the same one, over and over again. It was an old man, and I couldn't scream, and I tried to run, but my feet wouldn't move. Lots of people have one something like that, don't they?"

Selby nodded. "Where was your old man?"

"In a garden. With a wall round it."

"Mine was in a wood. I suppose he would be even worse by the time he got round to you. Twenty years older."

"What makes people have them?"

"Fear, I think. And suggestibility. And parents warning children about dangers they can't begin to comprehend." He looked at her. "Are you cold? Do you want to go inside?"

She shook her head. "Not really. I'd rather stay out." She put a hand on his arm. "It will be over soon, won't it?"

"Very soon." She was not much more than a child still, with a child's helplessness. He had a feeling of protectiveness toward her, untouched by desire. "The mist will have cleared by evening. They'll probably send the helicopter back up here then. We'll very likely be in Nidenhaut tonight, dancing at Putzi's."

"It would be fun."

Her hand rested on his arm. He put his own hand over it, and patted it. The mist came in suddenly with a bite of cold, mocking his hopeful words. Her hand moved, and gripped his. In a moment, the mist was all around them, a cloud which made it impossible to see more than a foot or two ahead; the girl herself was a wraith, even though their hands were linked.

He said, "I think we'd better go in, you know."

She did not reply, but abruptly moved toward him. Her face swam forward out of the gray, tilted up, not provocative

190

but fearful. He kissed her, and felt her body shiver through the thick coat she was wearing. She said quietly, "I'm afraid."

"Don't be." He kissed her again, gently. "Only a cloud. Look, it's thinning."

It thinned very rapidly, ugly gray turning back to pearl. One could see as far as before, possibly farther. He released her, except for a hand on her shoulder pressing her around to look out. At the snow, and the boy who stood there, motionless, gazing up at them.

"Andy!"

It was an exclamation of shock, and horror. But there was nothing horrible about him, Selby thought. He looked cold, and his face and bare hands had a bluish look. Like Kay, in the Snow Queen's palace. And was there something there, too, that one could touch—a fragment of ice in the heart to be melted, a happy ending as in all the best fairy stories?

He was thirty or forty feet from the veranda. Selby leaned over, and called softly, "Andy, come on up, old chap."

Hesitantly, almost reluctantly, the boy took a step forward. His eyes remained fixed on Selby. Diana, her voice hushed, said, "Do you think . . .?"

"Quiet," he told her. "Don't frighten him." He spoke to the boy again: "Come and talk, Andy. You'll be all right with us."

The boy did not move. Selby went on talking quietly, telling him to come to the house, and he stayed there, watching, seemingly listening. Selby felt a growing confidence. Perhaps they were not as united as they had appeared—an observational error. Or perhaps, incredibly, it was some kind of sickness, that had run its course in the boy and now was wearing off. Whether that was true or not, if he could only get the boy, examine him . . . He had said he wanted a specimen. One stood there, alone, almost within reach.

He whispered to Diana, "Don't make any disturbance. I'm going to try to get him."

191

"Is it safe?"

He did not answer her, but moved away toward the steps, which, at the far end of the veranda, led down to the ground. He walked slowly, his hand guided by the balustrade, his attention on the boy. From time to time, he called softly to him. He was afraid that at any moment the boy would take fright and run away, but he still stood there. Selby came to the steps, and carefully walked down.

He advanced across the churned-up snow with growing confidence. The boy showed no sign of coming to him, but no sign of retreating either. Twenty feet. He said, "You look as though you could do with a good hot dinner, Andy boy." Fifteen. "And a bit of a warm by the fire." Ten. "I don't think . . ."

The boy's head moved slightly; he was looking not at Selby but at something behind him. Selby turned slowly, concerned, even in this momentary apprehension, about not scaring the boy. He saw Diana first. She had followed him down the steps and stood at their foot—with some thought of helping him, presumably, but he cursed her under his breath for her stupidity. Then he saw the figures, moving around the side of the house toward her, and cried out to her, careless of anything else but the need to warn her, "Diana! Get back! Right away."

He saw her turn, as he began to run toward her. She screamed, and then they were on her. Deeping and Peter picked her up, ineffectively struggling, and carried her back through the gap between the chalet and the outhouses. He ran after them, his feet slipping on the frozen snow. He thought he was closing the distance between them, but their figures were becoming less distinct. Cloud was coming in again, the sky darkening. They went around the corner of the house, and he tried to run faster. He turned the corner, and a figure smashed into him out of the mist, throwing him sideways into the snow.

There was only one figure, disappearing, as he scrambled to his feet. He ran after it, but the fall had winded him and there was a stitch of pain in his side. It was a long time since he had tried sprinting. He came to the next corner, and had to lean against the wall. There was nothing and no one to be seen—only the fog. After a moment, he straightened up and limped on. He heard voices, and recognized George's. With that he realized his own danger, the danger of any one of them isolated and outside the protection of the house.

He called, "Wait—I'm coming," and the effort made pain stab through him. But he broke into a feeble trot all the same, rounded the last corner, and was directly under the balcony. There were voices up there, the creak of boards as people moved about. He said again, "I'm coming. Stay there."

They were all on the veranda, watching him as he climbed the steps. All that were left. He felt sick, and exhausted, and ashamed of himself.

George said, "What was all the noise about? And Diana? Where's Diana?"

"They've got her." He looked at Jane. "It was my fault."

12

Jane could not believe it, could not accept his words and what they meant. The Deepings, yes, and the two servants, but not Diana. The idea was monstrous and impossible. She remembered her at Christmas, at their parents' home, a little drunk with champagne, urging her, "You're turning into a terrible stick-in-the-mud, Jane. You want to get away, have a change. Go to Switzerland, or something. If you want company, you can take me. I can scrounge the time off, and I'm not proud." It just could not have happened. But she saw Selby, powdered with snow down one side, clutching his chest with his hand, and saw him wretchedly looking at her.

George said, "What happened?" His voice was peremptory. "Why did you leave the house?"

He told them, fleshing the fact out with words. When he had finished, George said, "You bloody fool."

Selby nodded wearily. "I know. But there's no point in go-

194

ing into that now. You've got the gun? We'd better go and see if we can find her."

The mist pressed close to the house; the other end of the veranda was only just visible. She saw George look around. He shook his head, almost imperceptibly, but he said, "Yes, we'll do that. Are you fit yourself? Come on, Douglas." He turned to the women. "Get inside and bolt the door. If there's any trouble, break one of the windows and yell for us."

Jane said, "I'll come with you."

"No." He looked at her grimly. "You'd be a hindrance, not a help."

"I want to."

His voice turned harsh. "Wanting's got nothing to do with it. Get inside. All of you."

Elizabeth had stayed close to the door with Stephen. She moved inside, and Mandy and Jane followed her. Mandy bolted the door, and Stephen said, "Is it all right now? Can we go on playing Monopoly?"

"Not just yet," Elizabeth said. "Perhaps later." She looked over his head at Mandy. She was as calm as ever in appearance, but her voice had not been quite steady. "I think it might be a good idea if we made some tea, don't you?"

Mandy said, "Yes. I'll put the kettle on."

"We'll come with you."

They all went into the kitchen. It was very quiet; the clock ticking, the dull roar of the stove, nothing else. There should have been reassurance, Jane thought, in the sight and sound of ordinary things, of Mandy going about the everyday business of filling a kettle and putting it on to boil. But it was the world pressing in from outside of which she was most conscious, the grayness and coldness into which Diana had been snatched. And into which the men had gone. If anything happened to them . . .

The sound, distant, but unmistakable, shocked her.

Stephen said, "Is Uncle George shooting at somebody? At them?"

At them, she thought with horror. His mother, his father, Andy . . . His child's mind had taken a leap of adaptation where she could not follow, from which she recoiled. Diana —was she to fear her, too, and hate her? But perhaps it was not adaptation, but evasion, an ability to dissociate name from person, new fear from old affection. There were refuges for a child where the adult could not go. She looked at the boy, not knowing whether to shudder or be glad.

Elizabeth said, "To frighten them away, I should think."

They were waiting for another shot; there was tenseness, even behind Elizabeth's serenity. A silence of expectancy had fallen on them; Jane found hands and teeth involuntarily clenching and, when she had willed their relaxation, clenching again. She started when Mandy dragged the steps noisily across the floor, climbed them, and brought a bottle out from behind a jar of sugar. Mandy looked at the other two women; she wore an odd withdrawn expression.

"I thought I would have a little drink," she said, "while the kettle boils. Would you like one?" She smiled slightly at their negatives, and poured into a small glass. It was transparent liquid: presumably gin. In a flat voice, she went on, "The nights are all right, but one has to get through the days."

The remark had a lunatic irrelevance which under other circumstances might have seemed funny, but was not funny now. Elizabeth said, "The kettle's boiling. I'll make it, shall I?"

One needed something to do, Jane realized—take a drink, even if it meant revealing a vice and a hiding place—make the tea—anything.

She heard her own voice asking, "Are there any biscuits left?"

196

"No," Mandy said regretfully. "Some scones in the larder that I made this morning, though."

"I'll get them."

The larder was only a step from the kitchen, but she found herself hurrying back. They drank their tea and ate scones in a silence which Jane hated but could not bring herself to break. She was close to the screaming point when the doorbell rang. Elizabeth said quietly, "Thank God." In weird unison they got up and went out together to the hall.

The relief of the men being back was so great that there was only a minor pang in realizing that Diana was not with them. George said to her, "I'm sorry, Jane. No trace of her."

Elizabeth said, "The shot?"

Douglas said, "George caught a glimpse of"—he glanced at Stephen, who was listening—"someone. I don't think he hit him."

Elizabeth said, "We've just made some tea. Go and sit down, and I'll bring it through."

Jane helped her in taking tea and scones to the salon; Mandy seemed content to let them do this. When they came in, George was making up the fire with logs. Selby stood near the window, looking out. He seemed stunned still. Jane took a cup of tea over to him.

He said, "I'm sorry."

"You couldn't have known she would follow you. If she had stayed where you left her, near the door, she would have been all right."

He shook his head. "What I did was stupid."

She had spoken to comfort him, but she needed comfort herself. She said, "She was struggling with them. She might have got away, mightn't she?"

"We called for her. There was no reply."

"She might have run away from the house. In the mist, and frightened, she might not have known where she was head-

197

ing." He stirred his tea in silence. "She might be hiding out somewhere, waiting for the mist to clear."

"Yes." He did not look at her. "It could have happened that way."

George said, "There are one or two things we've got to get straight." His voice commanded their attention. "As, for instance, that we take no chances at all now. We don't go anywhere, even in the house, by ourselves. I'll make an exception about going to the lavatory, but even there we'll have a couple of us opening the door to make sure it's empty and the window is properly closed and barred."

Elizabeth said, "But we're all right inside the house, surely."

"The one thing we can't afford to do is underestimate what we're up against." His glance flicked across the room. "That's what Selby did. He saw the boy, and thought he could grab him—that they were being careless. But what they were doing was what he had talked about doing earlier: setting a trap. They probably expected to get him—rush him when he was far enough from the house for them to be able to cut him off. Then Diana decided to follow him, and she was an easier target. So they took her instead."

"One at a time," Elizabeth said. "It's been like that all along, hasn't it?"

"There were four of them," George said, "leaving out Andy. The two men grabbed her and got her away. I suppose one of the others knocked Selby over as he came round the corner. One at a time is all they can manage."

Jane said, "What happens?" She steadied her voice. "What do you think happens?"

"We don't know," George said. He stared at her, almost brutally. "Does it matter? They take them over."

"They?"

In a dull voice, Selby said, "I've been thinking about that."

He paused, and George said, "Well?"

"It's not a disease, not in any sense of the term we can envisage. The same goes for hysteria. There's too much purposive action, cold intelligence. As for Marie's mountain devils, even if I believed in them, I couldn't believe in them acting this way. They work together, co-operate, in a way that neither sick human beings, nor hysterical human beings, nor even devils could manage."

"They plan things," George said. "We can do that, too. Don't forget you were trying to think up a scheme for getting hold of one of them. It might have worked."

"There's a difference," Selby said. "Remember what bait they put out. Andy. Could we have put Stephen out in that way? And his parents are amongst them. If there were anything of Ruth left in the figure that resembles Ruth, do you think she would have allowed them to do it?"

"No," Elizabeth said. "You're right about that. What are you saying, Selby—that they're zombies, something like that?"

"Zombies were supposed to be automata, weren't they? And automata couldn't have carried out that last exercise."

Douglas said, "Going back a bit—you said devils couldn't work together as they have been doing. Why?" He added hastily, "I'm not suggesting they are possessed by devils."

Selby said wearily, "The diabolical is divisive, not co-operative, or so religion tells us. Every man for himself, and the weakest goes to the wall."

"Religion may not be right."

"It's maintained its views for a very long time." He turned away, and stared out of the window, where the mist seemed to be thinning again. When he turned back, he said, "The point is that we have different ways to account for abnormalities in function and behavior, but every one is based, to some extent, on experience. One discovers new diseases, new forms of hysteria, but always, to some extent, they obey the old laws.

199

You can't use familiar terms to describe the unprecedented. Say they're possessed by devils, if you like, but it doesn't mean anything—not in any helpful way. I wouldn't recommend relying on a crucifix nailed against the door, or a sprig of garlic."

Elizabeth said, "I think garlic was for werewolves. Or was it vampires?"

"Familiar terms tell us nothing," Selby said. "Nothing."

"So all you're saying," George said, "is that we don't understand what's going on. Fair enough, but it doesn't advance us much, does it?"

Selby shook his head. "No, that's not all I'm saying."

"Then what?"

"Men have been recording the abnormalities of themselves and their fellows since they learned how to scratch signs on papyrus. I don't know of anything that's anything like what's been happening here. That's why I called it unprecedented. We're faced with something that seems to use human intelligences, but is not human. If it had existed before on the earth, men would have encountered it."

Elizabeth said, "Intelligence doesn't arise out of nothing. Are you saying that snow and ice have somehow acquired consciousness? Or what? The devils would be easier to accept than that."

"No," Selby said, "intelligence doesn't arise out of nothing. It has antecedents." He nodded toward the window. "That has antecedents. But not on this planet."

There was a silence, before George said derisively, "Men from Mars?"

"From God knows where. And not men. An intelligence that can use men."

Douglas said, "Do you think, as an explanation, that's any more probable than the others you've rejected?"

Selby said, "Yes, I do. If modern astronomers are to be believed, stars possessing planetary systems run into hundreds
200

of thousands, possibly millions. It's an overwhelming probability that some of those planets—perhaps most of them—have produced life. Not necessarily anything like the life we know. We might not even recognize it as life when we saw it."

Douglas said, "Then how—"

"I don't know. Steve." He went to the boy, and spoke to him quietly, earnestly. "Tell me again what happened at the beginning—when the sledge ran into the snowbank and tipped over."

He creased his forehead, trying to remember. "We fell out. At least, Andy fell out. I managed to hang on. And then I began pulling the sledge back up the hill for another run. I called to him to help, but he didn't."

"Why?"

"He said he'd found something."

"Did he say what?"

"No, but I saw it. At least, I guessed it was it. A blue ball."

"How big?"

"Not very big."

"As big as a football?"

"No. A lot smaller."

"A tennis ball?"

"Perhaps. And it gleamed."

"The sun was shining on it?"

"No. I don't know. The gleam—it looked as though it came from inside."

"And Andy touched it?"

"I suppose so. He was bending over it. That's when he fell down."

"But when you came and picked him up, it had gone—vanished?"

"Yes. I looked, but it wasn't there."

George broke in. "What's all this supposed to mean, anyway? A blue tennis ball that disappears—are you telling us that's what's responsible for everything?"

Selby said, "Parasitic forms of life are common enough. We know of thousands of them, both plant and animal. What about parasitic intelligence? It hasn't happened here, but it might have done elsewhere. A spore of intelligence. Waiting to be absorbed, and then homing on the brain like the liver fluke homes on the sheep's liver."

"Can you have pure intelligence?" Douglas asked. "Doesn't intelligence depend on there being a brain in the first place?"

"It does in terms of our present knowledge," Selby said. "But the whole point is that our present knowledge isn't adequate to cover what's been taking place. If the facts don't fit, then you need a new hypothesis. And we can't explain things any longer as derangements of individuals. One fact we have to face is that they are a group, serving a group purpose, working in a harmony closer than any group of human beings could work. That presupposes something behind them, or in them, that's both intelligent and alien."

"Coming out of a blue tennis ball?" George asked.

His tone was derisive, but he was uneasy, Jane saw. For her own part she did not know whether to take what Selby was saying seriously or not. It did not seem to her to matter very much. No explanation of what it was all about could help Diana. With a swift agony of remembrance, she insisted to herself that what she had suggested to Selby was true: she had got away from them, escaped across the snow—was hiding somewhere, scared and cold but unharmed. At least she had been wearing a thick coat.

Selby said, "The color is unimportant, I should think, though blue is a common effect of the action of certain forms of energy in the atmosphere. It gleamed from the inside, Steve said. That sounds a bit like energy, too. We can't guess what kind. As to the ball—a sphere is the most economical three-dimensional shape that exists."

Douglas asked, "How do you think it got here?"

"There was a chap called Arrhenius who suggested that life came to the earth from some other planet in the first place, in spores propelled by light rays."

"Can light rays propel anything?" Douglas asked.

"Yes. A very small effect, but it exists. And this would have no mass worth talking of if my guess about it is right. More or less pure energy."

Douglas said, "These things float through space, down through the atmosphere, and lie there, waiting for someone to pick them up—is that what you're suggesting? Well, wouldn't the same sort of thing have happened before, if so? You said unprecedented."

"We're talking of astronomical time," Selby said, "astronomical distances. It takes light over four years to get here from the nearest star, and being propelled by light is a very far thing from traveling at the speed of light. Our galaxy is a hundred thousand light years across. That thing could have been traveling since before the earth came out of the sun." He shrugged. "This may not have been the way it happened. I'm simply pointing out that it could."

George said, "It all sounds very interesting." His tone was heavily sarcastic. "I don't know that it helps much, though."

"Perhaps not," Selby said, "except that, in my view, 'Know thy enemy' comes pretty close to 'Know thyself,' as a precept. If this thing is an intelligence, and alien, then there is one thing it must know—that there can be no question of toleration between it and us. We have to wipe it out, if we are not going to be assimilated by it. It knows that the rest of us in the house have been alerted, and it knows that there is only a limited time before we will be in a position to alert others. That helicopter this morning must have thrown a scare in it. And that, I imagine, is why the tempo of attack is quickening. It must have us under control, before people come in from the outside."

Elizabeth said, "If this is true, what about Andy?"

"What about him?"

"Well, the coma—and then rushing away from the house. If he had been taken over, why did he not just go up to his mother? She wouldn't have guessed."

"Perhaps the first contact was more difficult than later ones. There would be some initial confusion probably. The prime feature in any intelligence is the ability to learn. I think we have to assume that this one has learned a lot in the last few days."

George said, "As far as I can see, the answer is still that we take no chances. If we stay barricaded in the house, we should be all right. And when the mist clears . . ." He walked to the window, and looked out. "It doesn't look quite as thick out there as it did."

Jane followed him to the window. Her eyes strained against the veils of mist. Diana was there somewhere; the thought hurt her, as no thought had done for many years.

Selby said, "And we must expect trouble. That has to be faced, too."

13

Mandy had not listened very closely to the things Selby had been saying. They sounded impressive and clever, and perhaps it was all important, but what she was most conscious of was that the glow was fading again, and with this awareness came the beginning of need. As a lover might think of the face, the smile, of the beloved, she saw the shelf in her mind's eye, and the bottle on the shelf. It was, she remembered, half empty, though she had only filled it again that morning. Was she drinking too much? But she was nowhere near being drunk, and the glow was fading, and, after all, these were special circumstances—the others all knew that.

Though it was not fear she felt, but loneliness. Even though they were standing within a few feet of her, sitting in a chair with a foot stretched out, no more than an inch or two from her own, they seemed very far away. Their voices came from a long way off—George's, too. She registered at one point that he was angry with Selby, but the anger was at a vast distance, like thunder over the hills, in summer, when the cousins were staying at the house . . . Caesar had been frightened of thunder, and had always run to hide in the cubbyhole under the stairs, and Hilda had laughed about it, and she and Clyde had joined her in poking fun at him, until Cooper had come along and said how cruel it was, and made them see things in a different way: the poor dog shivering there, afraid of something he did not understand, and seeing those who should love him laughing at him. And she had known that, although he was talking to all of them, he was talking most of all to her—it was her he was disappointed in. And had thrown herself down in the warm dark, hugging the shivering dog, and pressing her face against his neck so that no one should see her tears.

She turned, when there was a pause in the conversation, to slip quietly away. George asked her, "Where are you going, Mandy?"

"Just to the kitchen."

"I suppose that's all right. But leave the door open, and the moment you see anything suspicious, yell out."

She nodded, and left the room, but he came after her and caught her up in the hall. He said, "Are you all right, lovey?"

He put his hand on her arm, but still she did not feel that he touched her. She said, "Yes. I'm quite all right, George."

"Remember. Don't go down to the basement by yourself." He frowned. "I think we'll close the stair door, and slip the catch on, anyway."

The door at the top of the stairs to the basement was normally fastened back against the wall. George swung it to, and fastened the hook. The outside, exposed now, carried a layer of dust; Marie was really terribly slovenly if one did not watch her closely . . .

She said, "I'll get a duster for that."

206

The dusters were in the right-hand drawer of the kitchen table. She went there first, and took one out. Straightening up and turning away, she glimpsed the shelf, and it suddenly had a shattering reality—the shelf, with a chip showing the old darker green under the new paint, the squat shape of the sugar jar and the vanilla pod, black against white. Bright sharp surfaces in a drab and misty world. The bottle was only partly hidden by the jar; she had not bothered to push it right behind it. And the steps were there, as she had left them. She climbed up, and got it down, and poured herself a small tot, and then a larger one.

She had had one sip, and was pausing in contemplation of a second, when George came into the kitchen.

He said, "I was a bit worried, in case . . ." He saw the glass in her hand. "Well, I don't think that's a bad idea, at all. What one needs, on a day like this. I'll get a glass and have a little snifter with you."

His voice was cheerful or rather, she thought, cheery. It was kind of him, but then, he was a kind person; she had always known that. She poured gin into the glass he held, and her hand shook slightly. Mandy, she chided herself, you did that on purpose. It really is naughty of you.

George said, "Cheers." He did not, she knew, care for the taste of gin by itself, but he drank it with every sign of appreciation. "Warmer now," he said. He put an arm affectionately on her shoulder, but it did not really make him seem any nearer. "Mandy," he said, "when all this is over . . ."

She held her glass in both hands, and waited for him to go on. She could not feel interested in what he was going to say, and that was wrong, too. She smiled, trying to look at him as though it mattered, anything mattered.

"We're going to get away," he told her. "Cancel the bookings for the rest of the season. There aren't all that many, and the Buffet de la Gare will take them. We'll have a proper holiday. Take the bus and wander through Italy a bit. Stay where we like, as long as we like. A few weeks in Siena. You always said you'd like to go back there and spend longer. We'll have the spring in Italy—it's the best of the year."

He was looking at her, hopeful of a response, and she knew it was important not to let him down. She said, "That sounds lovely, George."

"And we might get across to Venice. You've only been there in the summer; it's a different place when you don't have to hold your nose whenever you step into a gondola. And San Marino. We've never really seen Italy the way it should be seen, taking our time, not rushing anything."

She said again, "It sounds lovely."

But what it really sounded like was something out of a radio play, in the old days, before television, when there were plays on the radio, and one listened while one's eyes watched other things—knitting, the clock on the wall, the kitten playing with its tail, or the faces of other people in the room. So that one's attention was never wholly caught, the problems and promises never quite real.

George said, "You really would like it?"

He was watching her. She smiled. "I really would."

He looked relieved, and that pleased her. He said, "Are you coming in now to join the others?"

"Why, no," she said. "I'm going to dust that door, and after that I'm coming back in here to start things for supper." He looked uncertain. "Now, don't you worry, George. You can see I'm all right here, and the door will be open, and everything."

"Is there anything I can do?"

"No, not a thing. You go back there and keep them cheered up. I'll call if anything happens."

They went to the hall together, and George went on through to the voices in the salon. Mandy dusted the outside of the door, carefully, taking her time. She could hear them talking
208

and, once, George laughing. She felt again the sense of great loneliness, but knew that if she went in there nothing would happen, except that their voices would be louder, and they would expect her to listen, and perhaps reply to them. She finished the dusting, and went back to the kitchen. She could hardly hear them at all now, and that was better. She poured herself a drink, and thought about supper.

Food was getting to be a difficulty. Apart from cans of corned beef, potatoes were the only things left in fairly good supply. Stuffed potatoes were probably the answer. She could manage an egg each, from the dwindling supply of those that had been put down in water glass, and with chopped ham and onion, and grated cheese on top, they should be quite nice. And to go with them? Well, there were three cans of spinach left. And a soup beforehand, though the stock was getting a bit thin by this time. Things were becoming thin all around. Ah well, she decided, tomorrow could take care of itself.

She had another drink before she went to the larder to get the potatoes she needed; luckily Peter had brought a sack up the day before. While she picked out nice big long ones, she thought of Peter, and Marie, and how different it was not to have them around. She wondered what they were doing outside, what it was like to be changed as they had been. Something Selby had said came vaguely to mind—about them doing things together. Then perhaps they were friendly to each other, because people could not do things together without being a bit friendly. That time when she had fallen out with Clyde, and not spoken to him for two days, and then Cooper had got them all working together, building a dam across the river, and in no time at all everything had been different.

She took the potatoes to the sink, and scrubbed them carefully, and cut them in half. She was scooping out the center of one of them, when she heard the voice. The window was open, but the wood was still nailed across it; she had had to put the lamp on so that she could see what she was doing. The voice came from outside the window. Ruth Deeping's voice.

It said, "Come out, Mandy. Come with us."

The voice was not loud, the tone neither hectoring nor wheedling, merely reasonable. And friendly. She lifted her head and looked up at the window. Between the rough slats she saw the grayness of the mist, nothing else. The window was well above ground level, of course—six or seven feet above.

"Come with us, Mandy."

She had said she would call if anything happened, and she supposed she ought to tell the others—tell George, anyway—about this. But the voice was quiet, and not dangerous. How could it be dangerous? And it asked nothing; neither response nor even attention. It was strange, but the fact that it asked nothing made it seem closer than those other voices. Scooping the pulp out of the potatoes, she thought about that. There was more to it than asking nothing. It gave her something: a feeling of being wanted.

"Come out, Mandy. Come out."

She had left the bottle on the table; there seemed no point any longer in putting it up on the shelf. Her glass was empty, and she filled it. She let her tongue play with the spirit before she drank, feeling the taste buds tingle. As she did so, she caught sight of herself in the mirror on the wall behind the lamp, and felt like laughing. She went closer, and examined herself. That square, rather puggy face, the skin coarsened and marked with the tiny red lines of broken capillaries, the brows which had always—except, at his insistence, during the time of her marriage to John—been too bushy, the eyes, vacantly and fuzzily staring at her: where in those was the girl that Cooper or Clyde would have known?

"Come with us, Mandy. Come with us."

And where, for that matter, was the mother that Lois and Annette and Johnny knew, in the house on the Parkway, with its split levels and lawns kept green by sprinklers even after so hot a summer, on that bright fall morning, crisp and smelling of leaves and smoke? None of them would know me, she thought, and saw the face crumple, the eyes of the stranger in front of her blur with meaningless tears.

"Mandy. Mandy. Come out, Mandy."

"I can't come out," she said.

There was a pause, and the voice said, "Yes, you can. There's nothing to stop you. Come out, Mandy. Come with us."

She took her glass with her back to the sink, and went on with the potatoes. That had been wrong: thinking of the children. In one's prayers at night one thought about them, but during the day it was wrong. Unfair to them, unfair to George. One made a choice, a decision, and one must abide by it or be lost. As one grew older and lonely, she supposed, there were bound to be memories, but one must choose the memories that were permitted. Of Caesar, and the boys, and the cousins. There was nothing wrong with that.

"Come out, Mandy," the voice said. "You will be happy with us."

The time they went for a picnic, on bicycles, and little Charlie got lost. They had hunted for him, with growing anxiousness, for what seemed hours. Anxiousness and fear—there had been a child murdered a month before that, talked about obliquely but in tones of horror by the grownups, with mystification and excitement by the children. Behind each bush there was a body, or a killer. And in the end they had found him sleeping in the grass by the river, like Portly in *The Wind in the Willows*. They had scolded him and laughed at him until he began to cry, and after that the girls had fussed him and Catharine had made him a daisy chain. Fear and loss could end in happiness—at least they could then.

"Come with us, Mandy," the voice said. "We want you to come with us."

She had wanted to ask Charlie: had he heard the music, the Piper at the Gates of Dawn? Because it was her favorite book, and that was the favorite part in it. She had got him to herself at one point, but of course the question seemed silly when it came to that, and she could not frame it. What if she put it to him now, to the jowling face with the executive spectacles and the hair that was just beginning to be thin—what answer would there be? She shook her head. Bewilderment, and thinking her crazy, were the only responses there could be. It would be too terrible if he said yes.

"Come out, Mandy. You think it's cold out here, but it isn't."

She said involuntarily, "It's not cold I mind, but being lonely."

"But there's no more loneliness, for any of us. We are all together. Come with us, Mandy. You won't be lonely once you're with us."

She heard footsteps in the hall, and a moment or two later George came in, followed by Elizabeth and Jane. He said, "Did I hear something?"

Mandy smiled. "Only me, talking to myself."

"The girls want to lend a hand," George said.

She shook her head. "No need for that. I can manage fine."

"Look," Elizabeth said, "it's ridiculous that you should do all the work. We're in this together."

"I'm really all right. I promise you."

"All the same, we're going to help."

She looked at George in appeal; he would see, surely, that she wanted to be by herself, and persuade them to go away. But the appeal went disregarded.

He said, "I'll leave you all to it, then. And another pot of tea wouldn't go amiss, I reckon."

Elizabeth nodded. "Will be done."

Left with the two women, Mandy felt herself on edge. It was not only because of their presence, though it was an irritant to have them near her, doing things she could have done herself and, above all, talking. The talk meant nothing, communicated nothing. But there was something else that troubled her, and which she did not grasp at first. The voice. If the voice came again, they would tell the others about it; even if they did not do that, they would be sharing it, and she did not want it shared. It had spoken to her, not to them.

She said, "I honestly don't need any help. I really am better by myself."

"I'll tell you what," Elizabeth said. "You go and rest, and leave things to us."

"No, I'm not tired."

"We're being selfish, as a matter of fact," Elizabeth said. "We need something to do, don't we, Jane?"

Jane said, "Yes. It helps."

Her voice was subdued; she was worrying about her sister still. Mandy wanted to tell her, There's nothing to worry about, everything will be fine. But she could tell that it wouldn't help to say that, wouldn't help at all.

"The mist is starting to clear again," Elizabeth said. "Perhaps this time it will lift properly." When the others did not say anything, she went on, "We'll be free tomorrow, if not tonight."

Free, Mandy thought—what does being free mean? A child is not free, because it lives in an adult world: the holidays always end in school. And the adult? One let oneself into a cage with the first choice one made, and then into another cage inside the first, and a third inside the second. Like boxes, one within the other, and each door snapping to as one went in—whether one went gladly and clear-eyed or fumblingly and reluctant, the lock was as unbreakable, the way back barred. And because the cages were inside each other, each new one

213

pressed more closely, until, presumably, in the very last one it was no longer possible to put one's arms out, no longer possible to breathe.

In a cool, considering voice, Elizabeth said, "It's not a thing I usually do, but I think when we get clear of this I am going to get drunk. On champagne. I haven't been drunk on champagne since I was a bridesmaid at my sister's wedding."

There had been no sound from outside, and Mandy realized suddenly that there was not going to be. Not while the others were here. She felt at once glad and impatient. They had not gone away. They were outside, waiting until she should be alone again.

The tea was made and there was nothing more that needed doing at the moment. She went with them to the salon, and stayed there, drinking tea and listening to them talk. The mist outside really seemed to be lifting. One could see quite a long way, and once Elizabeth said she glimpsed, for a moment, the pale gold of the sun. This made them all optimistic and cheerful, even Jane. She still thought, probably, that Diana might come back. But why should she, Mandy thought? Come back for what?"

She moved to slip out, and George said, "What is it, Mandy?"

"Nothing. Just something I've remembered needs doing in the kitchen. It won't take me long."

"I can help," Elizabeth said.

"No. It's very little."

Watching her, George said, "All right, lovey. Shout if you want us."

She smiled, and nodded. He was thinking that it was the drink she wanted, and protecting her. He was a good man. She had been lucky in having George. She went into the kitchen and stood near the window. She could see the bottle on the table, but it was not important. She said quietly, "I'm here."

At first there was no answer, and she thought they had gone away. Then Ruth's voice said, "Come out, Mandy. Come with us. There will be no loneliness then."

"And will one forget things? Properly forget them?"

"Yes. Everything that needs to be forgotten."

She stayed a moment longer. She was hesitant still, but she realized there was no room for delay. George might come to see how she was.

She went into the hall, and stopped. Going to the front door meant passing the open door of the salon. They would hear her, perhaps, or even see her. She went to the door to the basement stairs instead and, careful to make no noise, undid the catch. She pulled it back, and walked down quietly, and quietly along the passage to the door to the outside.

The bolt was not easy to draw, but she managed it. She went out, and saw that it was quite true: the mist was clearing, turning to haze and radiance. She paused, wondering which way to go. The voice had been on the other side of the house, but she did not want to go around there, where it was dark. She wanted to go toward the brightness. And it did not matter, anyway. They would find her.

She walked down the slope of snow. It occurred to her that they would see her if they looked out of the salon window, but that did not seem to matter, either. Perhaps they would call her back, but she knew she would not go.

Ruth's voice called to her. "Mandy."

She turned around, and saw them coming toward her—Marie and Peter, Ruth and Leonard and Andy. And Diana. There was no menace there. There was an end to memory, an end to loneliness. She looked past them at the house; she had come so far that it was hazy in the mist.

Poor George, she thought, and went to meet them.

14

Once during the afternoon, following a passing reference by Selby to the United States, Douglas thought of Caroline. His reaction surprised him. He felt neither the sick lurch of depressive anxiety, nor the rarer but equally familiar false euphoria at being rid of her. It was not so much that he thought of her more objectively; simply that she seemed less real. Reality was narrowed down to the sharp point of here and now, himself and those with him. He tried, as a tentative exercise, to hold her in his mind, see her with greater clarity, but she would not come alive, and he abandoned the attempt. He was concerned for Jane. He wished there was something he could do or say, but of course there was nothing.

At least she, along with the rest of them, had been somewhat cheered by the improvement in the weather. She was clinging to the hope of Diana being alive out there, and uncontaminated by the others. He was glad that she was able to do that, but dreaded the reaction that might come when the slim hope had to be abandoned. As it must. There was no doubt in his mind—any more than there was in the minds of George and Selby—that Diana had been taken over.

George interrupted something Selby was saying about the difference between the central and the sympathetic nervous systems to excuse himself—he wanted to see how Mandy was getting on. He was obviously worried about her; unduly, Douglas thought. She had seemed remote and absent-minded all day, but there was a fairly simple explanation for that. She had probably been on the bottle for some time, and the strain of events was making her hit it hard. She would be all right when the strain was lifted—they all would.

But George called, and his voice had urgency in it. Selby ran for the kitchen, the others following him. George met them in the hall, his face tight.

"She's gone."

Selby said, "The window . . ."

"Still barred."

"No one's come in through the front door," Selby said, "or gone out through it. I've had that part of the hall in view all along."

Elizabeth said, "Perhaps she's in the basement."

They all looked at the door, and saw that the catch was off. George reached it in a couple of large strides, and pulled it open. He was calling, "Mandy!" as he went down the stairs, his voice echoing.

The open door faced them at the end of the passage. They crowded through it and gazed out at the sweep of snow, the retreating mist horizon. Nothing. George plunged forward, but Selby grabbed him and held him with surprising strength.

"Don't be a fool."

"I've got to get her," George said, "before—"

"You can't go out there alone. And we need to get clothes on. And the gun." He hesitated. "The bolts have been drawn from the inside, George."

George stared at the bottom of the door. He said, "Yes. She went out, didn't she?" He looked at the two men. "Let's go and get that gun."

The men were pulling coats on in the hall when Elizabeth, from the salon, called, "Wait! I think . . ." In a different voice, she said, "Come here a minute."

She was at the window when they went in, and silently drew their attention to what she had seen. Visibility was more than a hundred feet, perhaps a hundred and fifty. There were shapes out there, at the very edge of vision, figures that moved. A dart of the late afternoon sun shone through and illumined one, then two of them. Marie, and Leonard Deeping. And the little figure would be Andy. Douglas tried to count—with the child, was it six or seven? Six, at least.

Jane, beside him, gave a small cry of horror. He put his hand out, and took hers. She was trembling.

"At the end," she said. "It is . . ."

It was Diana. The group was moving forward, on a path that took them obliquely across the front of the house, and as they advanced they became more recognizable. Old Peter, Ruth—and a somewhat shorter figure between them, trudging through the snow in a gray woolen frock and flowered apron. Mandy.

He said inadequately, not knowing whether he was addressing Jane or George, "I'm sorry."

In a choked voice, Jane said, "I knew it really, of course. I tried not to, but . . ."

George said, "She went out to them, didn't she? Why? What made her do that?"

"They don't mind our seeing them," Selby said. "But I notice they keep out of gunshot range." He turned to George.

218

"You see there's no point in going out, don't you? She's with them. Whatever happened, there's no compulsion about her being with them now."

George was staring out where the figures were disappearing into the mist to the east. He said, "I knew there was something wrong. I could tell. But I didn't know what. I ought to have done something. I ought not to have let her be alone."

"None of us must be from now on," Selby said. "We don't know how they got her out there. Perhaps they are learning to play on—well, human needs, weaknesses. I don't see how they can do that if we stay together, though."

Elizabeth said, "The basement door . . ."

"Yes, we left it open, didn't we?" He nodded toward the window. "It seems safe enough at the moment, but you can come down with me, all the same."

Their footsteps retreating through the hall clattered as though in an empty house. That was silly, of course. There were still five of them here, and the boy. Stephen was looking out of the window in the direction where the figures had been, though there was nothing to be seen now but mist and snow.

George said explosively, "I need a drink."

He went off to the bar. Douglas said to Jane, "A drink would probably do you good, too."

She shook her head. "No." She bent down toward the boy. "Steve, shall we carry on with that game of Battleships?"

Stephen turned slowly from the window. "Yes."

Douglas was about to ask if he could join in with them, when he caught her eye. There was appeal in it, an appeal to be left alone with her misery. Or alone except for the boy, who could not hurt her with sympathy; would help, in fact, by needing to be helped. They went into the dining room, and Douglas remained standing by the window.

He felt a small chill of fear. They had gone—the Graingers, George, Jane, and the boy—and he stood here by himself. It was a temporary desertion: it would not be long before they were back. But he had a picture of what it must be like to be the last left of this diminishing band, abandoned, and waiting for God knows what. He shivered involuntarily, and went to join George in the bar.

A strange woman's voice was speaking French, and as Douglas came into the bar he saw that George had the transistor radio switched on, and was listening to it. A brandy and a whisky bottle were standing on the counter, and glasses stood upside down on a cloth. George gestured toward them, an indication to Douglas to help himself. He poured a fairly stiff measure of whisky, and topped it up from the siphon. While he was drinking, the door opened to admit Selby. There was a pause in the broadcast, and then a man's voice announced something in German. George switched the set off.

"Weather forecast," he said. "Help yourself, Selby."

Selby reached for the whisky bottle.

"Good or bad?" he asked.

George, before he replied, poured brandy into his own glass, and tipped in the remains of a bottle of ginger ale. Douglas had a swift depressing vision of snowstorms, being cut off for days more, with the threat growing around them.

"Good," George said. He drank with an appreciative smack of the lips. "Couldn't be better, in fact. A little cloud, but nothing below ten thousand feet—three thousand five hundred meters in their version. Well above our level, anyway."

"That is good," Selby said. "Bloody good. So by tomorrow morning . . ."

"There should be nothing to prevent a sodding great armada of choppers dropping in on us. Though one will do. One will do very well."

220

Douglas asked, "Where's Elizabeth?"

"A good question," Selby said approvingly. "She's with Jane and the boy. And everything is locked and bolted belowstairs. We're ready to stand siege."

"They outnumber us now," Douglas said. "Does that mean that they'll attack us?"

George shook his head. "I doubt it. Only two men. And we have the gun."

Selby said, "Unless they think we would be reluctant to do anything to hurt our . . ." He hesitated. "To hurt people we know. Or creatures looking like them."

George said grimly, "If they do, they'll find they've made a mistake. My best friend bought it over Cologne—he got blown into the bomb bay and was jamming up the release. I had to get him out because, quite apart from anything else, I wasn't sure one of the bombs might not have gone on time fuse. I got him clear, all right. Piece by piece. And the bombs."

"He wasn't walking about," Selby said, "looking at you."

"Mandy's dead," George said. "That's something else I learned around then—to accept death when it happens." He lifted his glass, and drained it. "There's no point in whining about death. Whatever's still using Mandy's body, I'd give it both barrels on sight, and without hesitation."

There was no doubting the iron of his determination. After a pause, Selby said, "No, I don't think it will come to a mass attack. The balance of physical strength is fairly even—Elizabeth and Jane are both stronger, I should think, than any of the women out there—and, as you say, we have the gun. But it will come to something. The pressure is on, and even if they haven't got the benefit of a weather forecast, they must realize there's a good chance that we shan't be cut off for much longer. If they don't clear things up tonight, they probably never will. And the stakes are high."

"We'll all sleep in the salon," George said. "We can drag some mattresses down from the bedrooms. And two on watch all the time."

Douglas looked out of the window. The day was fading rapidly; the haze was golden, low down in the west. He could see quite clearly the easy slope where, a few short days ago, he had been learning to ski. It was difficult to accept; the nightmare seemed to have been going on forever. One more night. That was difficult to accept, too. The patch of gold was shrinking, and suddenly went, leaving gray. The sun would be behind Grammont. Only one more night, but it was going to be a long one.

Selby finished his drink, and helped himself to more.

"We shouldn't put too high a slosh on, either, I suppose. Ought to keep our heads clear."

"You're the doctor," George said, "but to hell with that for a prescription. I intend to get tanked up."

He spoke with a bitter, almost feverish mirth. Had time turned back for him, Douglas wondered. Did he see this as the old days come again, the days of drinking and death? Or was there something else to it—a fear of the horror of living death? Did he need to drink to blot out the memory of Mandy, walking away from him across the snow?

Selby said, "If it does come to a fight . . ."

"Well?" George asked.

"We'd better all make sure we avoid any prolonged physical contact."

Douglas said, "What do you mean by prolonged?"

"I wish I knew. I'm pretty sure it is a contact thing—adsorption to nerve endings, something like that. Mandy . . ." He looked at George. "We don't know why Mandy went out there, but it couldn't have been because they had taken her over at a distance. If that had happened, she wouldn't have gone out and left the door open. She would have let them in. And all the other cases were clearly contact. But not *immedi-*

222

ate contact. Diana was struggling, trying to get free of the two who had hold of her. They need some period of physical mastery. Perhaps a minute or two, perhaps half an hour."

George drank again, and once more refilled his glass.

"In Mandy's case," he said, "it was nothing like half an hour."

"It's probably quicker where someone submits willingly. This is something we don't know much about, and aren't likely to, except if it happens to us. But we'd better be careful to avoid clinches as far as possible."

"Don't forget the gun."

"Yes," Selby said. "Two barrels—and you're in the middle of a melee by the time you reload. I think we ought to break up the furniture to some extent, and equip ourselves with clubs."

"Go ahead," George said. He thought about this, and laughed. "Christ, yes! I don't know what clause it comes under, but there must be something in the insurance policy to cover damage caused in resisting a Martian invasion."

They brought mattresses down while there was still some light, and arranged them in the salon. They left lamps burning on the landings and in some of the bedrooms, partly to mislead the enemy and partly so that there would not be the feeling of darkness above them as well as all around. Selby said something about laying on a mobile patrol of the upper floors, to be on the safe side, but the idea fizzled out. No one was keen on doing anything which would involve splitting their small forces.

Elizabeth and Jane, with Stephen helping them, cooked the supper which Mandy had prepared. They brought the table and chairs through into the salon, to be more central for keeping an eye and ear on things. George, accompanied by Selby, went down to the basement to bring some wine up, and at the same time to check that all was in order down there.

When they came up, they fastened the door again at the top of the stairs.

George was carrying a wicker basket full of bottles.

Douglas said, "You look as though you've brought the whole cellar."

"Half a dozen Dole," George said, "and half a dozen Johannisberg for those who like it white. The Johannisberg should have been put outside for chilling, but we decided not to be too pompous."

He had drunk a great deal already and so, despite his warning earlier, had Selby. But there was no question of either of them being at all intoxicated, and Douglas noticed, during supper, that they did not take very much wine. He drank more himself, having confined himself to a couple of drinks earlier on. The Johannisberg was very good. And the stuffed potatoes were good, too. Everyone ate well, which was heartening. Whatever apprehensions there might be about the night which they had now entered, it had not robbed them of appetite.

The women cleared the table, which the men put back in the dining room, and they settled down. Elizabeth suggested putting on the radio, pointing out that it scarcely mattered now if the battery ran down, but George opposed this.

"Too likely to blanket sounds."

Selby said, "I agree. We want to be sure of hearing things."

"Mustn't we talk?" Elizabeth asked.

"I don't see why not," Selby said. "As long as no one talks fascinatingly enough to get our complete attention."

It was a cozy scene, Douglas thought. The settee had been brought up in front of the fire, and Jane and Elizabeth were sitting on it, with Stephen between them. The three men were in armchairs, two on one side, one on the other. A good supply of logs had been brought in, and the fire crackled warmly. There were two lamps lit here, and light from other lamps showed through the open doors that led to the dining room, the bar, and the hall. At their backs, the heavy curtains were drawn against the dark. They had their glasses of wine from supper, and they sat together chatting like members of a family, or like old friends who were comfortable with one another. The only discrepant note was provided by the shotgun, resting against the pinewood wall, a few inches from George's right hand.

By consent, they did not talk of recent events, and avoided reference to those who had been lost. Conversation was light, and anecdotal. Selby told a few medical stories, and George some R.A.F. ones, including a rambling and hilarious account of two days spent in a rubber dinghy on the North Sea, in the company of an air gunner who had gone off his head with religious mania. Would all this, Douglas wondered, reduce itself eventually to such dimensions—be a story told around a fire, and a comic one at that?

It was in the tailing away of their laughter that Jane said, "Listen."

"What?"

"I thought I heard a sound."

Alert, Selby said, "Which direction?"

"Somewhere outside, I think."

They watched and listened, while Selby walked quietly across the room, and pulled the corner of the curtain to one side. He peered out for a moment, then twitched it back.

"Nothing. It's pretty dark out there, of course. Though it should be brighter soon. There's a moonglow in the east." He clicked his tongue exultantly. "I could see the shoulder of the mountain! That means the mist has gone."

George got up and went across to look. Coming away, he said, "Dark, but clear. We'll be all right in the morning."

Douglas saw in their faces the reflection of the surge of happiness and relief he felt himself. Only a matter of hours.

Stephen said, "We'll be taken on the helicopter, won't we? Just to Nidenhaut, or all the way down?"

Elizabeth said briskly, "Wait and see. But one thing we do

need to do is to get you off to bed. Come on. We'll give you enough of a wash in the kitchen."

"Leave the door open," Selby said.

"Don't worry."

She took the boy away with her; they heard her go, and heard the distant sound of their voices as she attended to his toilet.

George said, "One never quite believes weather forecasts, but the Swiss are . . ."

He broke off. There was no doubt about the sound this time, nor of the direction. It came from below, and outside— a hammering, and the tinkle of breaking glass. They looked at each other, and Douglas felt his chest constrict.

Selby said quietly, "This is it. Trying to break in. Do you think the planks will hold?"

"I'm taking no chances," George said. He picked up the gun, and glanced at Selby, who nodded. "Let's go."

Douglas followed them. The constriction was fear, but one could go forward, defying it. Halfway down the stairs to the basement, he realized that Jane was following, too. He half-turned, and told her, "Stay upstairs."

Selby was some way ahead with the light, and she was only a silhouette against the lamplight coming through the doorway above her.

"No. I'm coming."

Her tone did not brook argument, and there was no time for it, anyway. And he was glad of her behind him. They came down the stairs and across the passage. The light showed that the others had gone through into the room that had held the boxes. They followed them and saw them staring at the window. It had been broken from the outside; glass was strewn on the floor inside. But the planks were in position, and there was no sign or sound of anyone out there.

"I suppose I could give it a barrel, anyway," George said. "As a warning."

226

"I shouldn't bother. I . . ."

The crash of glass again, but it was difficult at first to tell where the sound came from. Then, the heavy rapid creak of boards over their heads. They began to run for the stairs, Selby first, the lamp swinging as he ran. They were in the passage when they heard Elizabeth scream. Almost at the same time, there was the slam of a door, and Douglas saw the oblong of light above them blotted out.

15

Even in his combined rage and panic, Selby had the sense to thrust the lamp behind him for someone else to grasp. It was taken from him, and he flung himself up the stairs and against the door at the top. It gave slightly against his weight, but did not open. He drew back, and charged it again, with no better result. His left shoulder felt numb from the impact. He swung around, and hit it with his other side. The door seemed to shift for a moment, but that was all.

He could hear the boy crying, but there was no sound from Elizabeth. The thought of what might be happening to her maddened him, and he slammed himself at the door. Behind him on the stairs, George was saying something which at first he did not take in. In the end, he found himself plucked back by the bigger man.

"Get back," George said. "I've got at least four stone more than you to put into it."

228

The thud of George's onslaught was followed almost at once by a tremendous crash, and Selby had the wild hope that the door had broken. But no light showed, and the crash, he realized was of something falling, not breaking, something massive. George smashed his body forward again and then, turning, called down, "The gun!"

He was wheezing from his efforts. Douglas had the gun, and he handed it up the stairs to him. George held it under his arm, and fired it. The sound was like a blow almost, a hammer against the ears in this narrow space. There was the sharp, choking smell of gunpowder. But, even when George threw himself at it for the third time, the door held.

"Light!"

Jane reached up with the light. They could see that the shot had torn a ragged hole in the wood of the door, about an inch across, but there was more wood behind that, pitted and scarred but substantially intact. George rammed the butt of the gun against the hole, but nothing moved. He said wearily, "It's no good."

Selby pulled at him, trying to get past. "Let me have a go!"

George gave way to him, and he thrust and heaved at the door, but it did not give at all now. Behind him, George said, "It's the hall dresser. They've pulled it over and it's wedged against the door. A year's heaving wouldn't shift it. It weighs a ton."

He tried once more, but he knew George was right. There was no shifting it from this side. From this side . . . He abandoned the effort abruptly, and tried to push his way downstairs, past George. But George gripped and held him.

"What are you up to, Selby?"

Selby struggled with him, but he felt weak and bruised, helpless against the other's greater strength. He said, conscious of the feebleness, the absurdity, of the remark, "Let me go!"

"Go where?" George asked. "Out of the back door, and up the steps to the veranda? The way they got in? You damn fool, you'd be completely at their mercy."

He could see it was probably true, but he was not prepared to be sensible. He could still hear the boy crying, somewhere upstairs. In horror and misery, he found himself speculating: was the boy watching, held by one of them, perhaps, while the others overwhelmed her—a grotesque and hideous mass rape, of the soul rather than the body? He strained violently against George's grasp.

"I'm going . . ."

"Listen," George said. "Listen. I know how you feel, but there's nothing you can do for her. Nothing. You've got to think of yourself now."

"Why?"

"And of us. And of a couple of billion people outside. Don't you see? *They've almost won.*"

The words, and the grim conviction with which they were spoken, shook him into acquiescence. He relaxed, and let George shepherd him downstairs. They stood together in the passage, George's hand still firm on his arm. He saw all their faces in the lamplight, saw how little their fear was concealed, and wondered what his own face showed. Elizabeth, he thought in agony. Oh God, let her not be hurt.

"They expected to split us," George said, "and we fell for it. A disturbance at one of the basement windows—the boy could do that easily—and some of us at least would go down to investigate. Then a quick breakthrough into the salon, the door to the stairs slammed, and the dresser dragged across to make sure of it. Whoever was left up there would be no match for them."

"If we'd all come down . . ." Douglas said.

"They would still have had possession of the house. They've got us trapped down here. They can keep us here until the
230

chopper's come in, and they've got hold of the crew. That's if they don't manage to finish us off first."

"How?" Douglas said. "We can't get at them, but they can't get at us, either."

"Can't they? They only have to pull the dresser away, when they're ready. Nothing easier."

Jane said, "What can we do?"

"Think before we act, for a start," George said. "We haven't been doing too well at that."

He was talking sense, Selby realized. He tried not to think of Elizabeth, but the visualization swamped him with agony. His body shuddered uncontrollably.

Douglas said, "If they did manage to—well, do for us, surely they wouldn't get far? Two billion—taking over the human race, that is. You weren't really serious about that, were you?"

Talking would take his mind off its compulsive self-torture. Selby said, "He was serious. And they could do it. Particularly with a helicopter at their disposal. They could seed themselves throughout the Valais, as a start. In isolated places, waiting for a child unaccompanied, perhaps. And the child going home to its brothers and sisters, its mother . . . Even after people began to realize what was happening, there wouldn't be much they could do about it. They would cause chaos before they had taken over even a substantial minority. And chaos would serve their ends." He stared at the lamp, which was beginning to smoke. "Once they're clear of this place I can't see any way in which they can be stopped."

"So they mustn't get clear," George said.

Elizabeth was a pain that crushed and ground at him. He said, "I wish I knew how we could stop them. Nine of them, against four of us. Two of them are children, I know, but it doesn't help very much." He stared at the gun which George was holding. "Have you got any cartridges for that?"

"One," George said. "In the barrel I didn't fire just then. The rest are upstairs."

"Yes," Selby said, "I thought so."

"We've got to think," George said, "and think slowly and carefully. One more mistake might be the last."

Jane said, "Will they give us time to think?"

"They're not pressed for time," George said. "They've got us down here, and it won't be light for another eight hours. And the moves they've made so far have been pretty well spaced out. We've got time to think. But we'd better make good use of it."

True, all true, Selby thought. One desperately needed to think. But his thought was of Elizabeth; his mind rocked with wretchedness.

After a time, he knew it must be over for her, and his pain became the less acute though still searing ache of loss. And anger. He had a cold determination to cleanse and avenge and destroy. It had been his mother, dying of cancer when he was seventeen, who had been the reason for his choosing medicine as a career. He had felt something like this at that time. But this was filthier than a cancer, rousing a more bitter, more personal hatred. And cold. It was essential to think clearly unemotionally.

Douglas was elaborating an idea for luring some of them down and cutting them off from the rest, splitting the forces of the enemy in much the way that their own had been. The idea sounded weak, impracticable.

Selby said, careless of seeming rude, "Look, there are two ways of coping. One is to finish them off in some way. The other is to make sure they don't strike up contact with the outside world before we do. That involves surviving the rest of the night, of course."

"Well, yes," Douglas said, "but if we were to . . ."

George said, "I've been thinking about that—about finish-

232

ing them off. We haven't got much, but we've got the *mazout*."

Douglas and Jane showed incomprehension.

Selby said, "A fire? Would it work?"

"It might. I can't think of anything else that would."

Jane said, *"Mazout?"*

"The oil," George said, "for the central heating. Fifteen hundred liters of it, on my last reading." He looked at Selby, ignoring the others. "Make a pretty little blaze."

"Where's the tank?" Selby asked.

"In that little lumber room, to the right of the basement door."

The thought excited him. "She'd go up with quite a bang."

"The whole chalet would. A real bonfire."

"You mean, we start a fire down here?" Douglas asked. "And then what? Just clear out, and wait for help." The prospect seemed to relieve him. "As long as help does come tomorrow."

Selby said, "However quickly it caught, they would have a chance of getting out, wouldn't they? The windows at the front aren't barred, and there's the front door."

"If they were upstairs, they might stand a chance," George said, "but if they were down here . . ."

"How do we get them down?"

"They'll come eventually. They'll have to come. They daren't take a chance on leaving us until morning. An hour or so before the light, I would reckon."

"Wait till they do, you mean?" Selby said. He thought about this, and did not like what he saw. "A bit chancy, isn't it?"

"Only one of us needs to wait. Have a trail laid of oily rags. The tank's on the far side from the stairs. Set it off when they're all down here."

"And the rest of us?"

"Get out well in advance. Get away from the house. If anything did go wrong, they would need to be away from here—

chance they might be able to warn whoever comes in from outside."

That made sense, Selby thought. It all made sense. But it was going to take a lot of nerve on the part of the man who stayed behind. He would have to wait, possibly for a couple of hours, for them to come, time his little job of arson to perfection, and contrive to make his getaway. If possible. The odds did not look too good.

He said briskly, "It might work. I can't think of anything else that would. You know the local terrain, George, so I reckon you ought to lead the main party."

George looked at him. His face, in the lamplight, was unsmiling.

"You three are going," he said. "I stay. I reckon I have a right to put a match to my own bloody house."

Selby thought of George, listening in the darkness, waiting. It was not a question of heroics. Each man had his own fears, and circumstances disabled them in different degrees, and in different ways. He was trying to find an argument to force this home painlessly, when Douglas said, "We draw lots. The three of us. That's the simplest thing, surely."

Selby's eyes crossed George's, a fleeting recognition by both of them that this, at least, was out of the question. They might have misgivings about each other, but neither was prepared to leave a job like this to the third.

George said, rather loudly, "Let's get it straight. I'm in charge here. We need you, Douglas, to look after Jane. And we need Selby to convince anyone who flies in about the kind of trouble we've got upstairs. They'll believe a medico where they would say you or I was round the bend."

Douglas said, "I see the argument for sending Selby off. There's no argument against us two drawing for who stays."

He spoke with the stubbornness that a weak man sees in himself as strength; and therefore clings to. It was absurd,
234

Selby knew, to think of hurting people's feelings at a time like this, but obstinacy of this kind—in both Douglas and George —was something that could not be ignored. Something, too, that could ruin everything.

He said to George, "Have you got the dice on you?"

Douglas said, in an incredulous tone: "Dice?"

A faint smile twisted the edge of George's mouth. He had taken the point. They could eliminate Douglas, an unskilled player, fairly easily, and then settle it between them. He said, "Always carry them." He brought the dice in their small leather case from an inside pocket. "No pot, though. I'll go and recce for something."

Douglas said, "This is damn silly. It would be a lot quicker to draw lots."

"Less fun, though," Selby said. "And we're not pressed for time. We shall hear them if they start shifting that sideboard."

"I think it's ridiculous."

But, having made his protest, he was, Selby thought, not unhappy. The odds were very much against his winning. He had a means of escape with honor.

George, returning, said, "I've found this." It was a weather-beaten blue plastic mug. "Not very wonderful, but it'll do." He broke the dice from their case. "Aces up, kings towards."

It was George who won the right to start, with a king against two knaves. He threw, and passed to Selby.

"Two pairs."

There were aces and tens, with a nine. Selby took the nine out, and tossed it open. It showed a queen. He slid the mug to Douglas.

"Full house. Queens on tens."

Douglas took the pot, looked under it, hesitated and, with a wry grin, brought the dice out. He left the two aces, and threw the remaining three. He passed the pot to George, without looking under it.

"Four aces," he said.

George lifted the pot. The dice were ace, ten, nine. He said briefly, "Bad luck," rattled, and threw. Having looked, he passed it to Selby. His gaze was fixed, unwavering.

"Full house. Jacks on nines."

It was not there. Selby knew that with utter certainty. Another pre-emptive false call, as on the occasion when they had been dicing for the smaller, less frightening stakes of the night watch. George would have his escape with honor, too.

He lifted the pot. There was nothing there at all—at least, nothing but a pair of nines.

"Well," he said, "that settles it."

"No!"

He looked up and saw George staring at him, and realized that he had permitted himself to smile, and that George had seen it and known the conclusion he had reached about his play. He cursed himself for a fool, and said mildly, "Got to stick by the rules, George. We all agreed to the conditions."

"First life," George said. He was smiling, also, but with anger. "Two to go."

"We didn't say three lives."

"We didn't need to. We always play three lives, except when it's been agreed to the contrary. Fair enough, Douglas?"

And Douglas, of course, had to agree. He nodded.

"Yes, I would think so."

Selby said, "Two lives. How about that?"

George nodded, satisfied. "Right. You're away."

With a life in hand, Selby was in a position to make the running. He called three queens to Douglas, with knaves, nines and a ten under the pot. Douglas threw the ten for a full house, but looked under the pot and made the call without conviction. George took the top off, and showed an ace.

"That leaves us then, Selby," he said. He rattled, threw, and looked. "Well, I can't afford a lot, can I? Pair of aces."

236

Selby took them, threw a third ace, was given a full house, hesitated, and accepted it. There were two tens under the pot. He threw them, and called the fourth ace. George lifted the pot, and showed knave and nine.

"Putting us level," he said. "You're away."

Selby threw, and looked at what he had got. A broken straight. He hesitated, realized that his hesitation had been marked, and said, "Nothing."

George reached for the pot. "I'll take nothing." He threw, glanced under very quickly, and pushed the pot back to Selby. He was smiling and watchful.

"Three," he said softly. "Three kings."

A pre-emptive call again. Nothing there, probably, but a pair of queens. Which would mean throwing two more queens, an unlikely proposition and one which George could scarcely accept. Taking the call would give him the easy way out, which his unguarded smile had accused George of taking. No, he thought with a quick surge of rage, and lifted the pot off the dice.

There were three kings there.

George picked up the dice, and put them carefully away in their case. His smile this time was triumphant.

"Bad luck, Selby," he said. "You can't win 'em all."

16

Before they left, they helped George to prepare for the fire. There were three cans of kerosene, and they used these to soak the wood of the wall near the oil tank. The oil tank itself George punctured by driving a spike in; oil gushed out onto the floor and the debris of wood and cardboard and bits of cloth which they had stacked around the base. Then the hole was roughly plugged with the end of a rope of cloth which they had made out of torn strips tied together. Some oil still oozed out, but not much. Their only means of illumination was the kerosene lamp, and they had to be careful to keep the flame away from the parts that had been primed for burning.

"Not very elegant," George said, "but I reckon it'll do. O.K., off you go now. I should get as far away as you can. And keep moving. It's a cold night."

Selby said, "Are you sure you're all right?"

"I'll feel better when you're off the premises. No point in cluttering the place up."

They wished him luck, and he drew the bolts for them quietly and watched them slip out. The overhang from the veranda gave them cover for the first few yards; then there was the short distance to the outhouses, overlooked only by an attic window at the top of the house. Selby, when they had crossed and were in the shadow of the first outhouse, looked back and up at the window. There was no sign of a watcher.

The half-moon shone through bars of high cloud, ribbed gray and silver. There was enough light for them to see their way, not enough to make them visible at any distance from the house, which, as they trudged on, faded into the snow-scape, its presence marked only by two dim rectangles which were lamplit windows. It was bitterly cold, though fortunately without wind. They were dressed for an evening around the fire, and the chill struck hard at them. They had found an old raincoat which they had insisted on Jane wearing over her frock, but there had been nothing for the two men. Selby looked at his watch. Not midnight yet. A long night still ahead. They would certainly need to keep moving.

Jane stumbled, and Douglas caught her arm to help her. He asked, "Are you all right?"

Although they were well out of normal earshot, they spoke in whispers. She said, "Yes. Damn. Shoe full of snow, though."

Douglas said, "If we'd stayed longer in the house . . . we'd have been warm at least."

"Warm," Selby said, "and possibly trapped. They could . . ."

He broke off, as the enormousness of it sank into his mind. They could have been trapped very easily. A barrier of some kind against the basement door to keep them from getting out that way. And warm . . . What if the enemy had thought of a fire, too? Easy enough to start, even without the oil tank, since the whole of the top part was in their hands. These wooden chalets went up like tinderboxes. They could watch

239

the house burn, and then wait for the helicopter to come in. There was nothing strange about the sight of people standing around the shell of a burned-out house in the mountains. It must happen several times a year in Switzerland.

"I'm glad we're out of it," Jane said. "Anything rather than being there, knowing they were above us."

Selby said, "Look, I've thought of something."

"What?"

"Our job is to make sure we contact people from outside before anyone else can—just in case George's scheme goes wrong. We're heading for Nidenhaut. But the helicopter came up from the valley, and it came in from the west. It would be dropping down by the chalet before we could have a hope of attracting attention."

They stopped and stood in the snow. Jane drew the raincoat closer around herself, shivering.

"You think we ought to go the other way?"

"I think we ought to split up," Selby said. He was talking to Douglas. "You take Jane on toward Nidenhaut, in case they get through by road. I'll go west."

"Do you think it's wise—splitting up?"

"I think it's essential. We should have realized that before."

They seemed doubtful, but he cut short their hesitations. It made no sense to stand and argue in this cold. He walked away from them, taking a course to the west and downhill, as though he were making sure of giving the house itself a wide berth.

When they were out of sight, he took a bearing on the distant lights and began the upward climb. Although it was so cold, he found himself sweating from the exertion. He came up well to the east of the house, and retraced the course they had taken to the rear of the outhouses. Checking the attic window again, he felt fear and, with it, irresolution. There were probably a dozen ways in which the scheme could go

240

wrong, even with both of them. Which would mean them both finished off, and everything depending on Douglas and Jane being able to attract the attention of rescuers before the creatures at the house did.

The window was empty as before, but he took a step back into the shadows. When one looked at it that way, it was absurd for him to go back. He should do as he had said he would—head westward away from the house, station himself where he would be able to wave to the helicopter as it came up from Montreux. That was the course that made sense. George—George was expendable, as they all were.

The fear, which had raised his doubts, resolved them. He wanted most desperately to turn away, and it was that which made turning away impossible. He looked up once more, quickly, at the house, and ran across the powdery snow.

He found the window which had been broken earlier, and hitched himself up. The door at the far side of the room was framed by lamplight. Keeping his voice low but pitched as far as possible, he called, "George." There was no immediate reply. He called again, "George!"

Letting him in, George said, "What the bloody hell's the idea of this? Have you gone mad?"

Selby said, "It's quite simple. You can't do this on your own. No one could. The odds against are ridiculous."

"On getting out? Maybe. But I can take that lot with me."

"You can't even do that. If they come at you from both sides—you're trapped and they're not. You've got no retreat. They have."

"Do you think two makes much difference?"

"Enough. If one of us is outside, covering the veranda with the gun, and the other ready to fire things . . ."

"A gun with one cartridge," George said bitterly.

"They don't know that. One shot will throw them back, at least long enough for us to start the fire and get out. That means two more of us to try and get hold of that helicopter before they do. Which is what counts."

"Yes." George paused. "What about the other two?"

"Stationed on the Nidenhaut road. They won't come back."

"That's something, anyway." He grinned suddenly, cheerfully, like a boy. "I'll admit I wasn't exactly enjoying my own company."

"Anything happened up above?"

"No. Not a damn thing. That's what was beginning to get on my nerves."

Selby said, "It's occurred to me that they might have the same idea." George looked at him blankly. "Fire, I mean. But I don't think they'll do it without trying something else first."

"Any ideas about that?"

"No. But I think we should have the door open, and one of us on duty there with the shotgun. The other on the alert for the stairs, and ready to start the fire."

"Makes sense." He offered the gun to Selby. "You take this, then."

"It would work better the other way round."

His stare was distrustful. "Why?"

"Two reasons. One is that I'm not used to the gun. The other is that when that second barrel has been fired, it may need to be used as a club. And you can put a lot more weight behind it than I can."

"Leaving you the fire job."

"Yes. I qualified for my Scout badge in a sogging wet April day in the New Forest. Arson is one of my few major talents."

George considered this. "O.K. But if I call you out, come at the double. Right?"

Selby nodded. "Right."

Time passed slowly, and he felt, as George had done, the crawl of uncertainty against his nerve endings. Though it was nothing like so bad, he reminded himself, as it must have been for a man waiting by himself. He could hear the rhythm of George's breathing, an occasional cough. From time to time they spoke to each other, but the great comfort lay in knowing the other man to be there. Communication between human beings might have its illusions, but there was no doubt of the stark reality of its absence.

In his reflections he removed himself as far as possible from this place and time, because to be trapped in the present would be to think of Elizabeth, and thinking of her could serve no purpose. He reviewed again the cases he would soon be dealing with—if things went right—at the Clinic. The Minchin girl's naevus, the craggy arrogant nose that Gordon Moncrieff wanted fined down and straightened, the breasts that Helen Enderby, a widow and anxious for reimmersion in matrimony, agonized over in front of her dressing-table mirror. He planned his campaigns against them in meticulous detail.

Three o'clock. George shifted, breathing out heavily. He would be cold, stationed near the open door. Here, farther up the passage, it was not so bad. Selby had the lamp with him, but they had put it out when they started this watch. He felt in his pocket for the matches. For a moment of terrible apprehension they were not there; and then he found them.

A sound. He looked at his watch again. Ten past four. The heavy dragging of wood, from the direction of the top of the stairs. There was a low whistle from where George was, showing that he had heard it, too, and then he heard George move quietly. He opened the door, and Selby saw him for a moment, silhouetted against the dim outside light. He opened the box of matches a little way, touched the matches reassuringly with his fingertips. The door was pulled to, with George outside. He felt frightened, and dreadfully alone.

More dragging and then, unmistakably, the door being opened at the top of the stairs. Some light came obliquely to

243

him. He pressed himself against the wall. Footsteps. A voice. He wanted to cry out. Elizabeth.

"Selby?" she said. "Are you there, Selby? I want to talk to you."

Her voice, and yet not her voice. The inflection, the exact timbre, but not her. A hint of dragging, of deliberateness.

"Come up here, Selby," the voice said. And then, with grotesque obscenity. "Come on, darling."

Whatever it was that used her voice, he hated it as he had never hated anything in his life before. He could have torn the flesh that had been hers to get at the creature that inhabited it and betrayed it. If he had had the shotgun, he did not think he would have been able to prevent himself running forward and firing it.

Another voice. Diana. "Jane? It's me, Jane. It's Diana."

And Mandy, calling to George. Selby listened and waited. There was a pause, and another voice which made his hair stand on end. The first victim, the boy Andy, speaking in a child's treble but with the assurance, the authority, of an adult.

"They may have gone out."

"It would be cold for them." Deeping. "Can they stand these extremes of temperature?"

Andy. "For a time. And they would be afraid. I think they have gone outside."

"We should be careful."

Peter, the voice still German accented. Each one individual, and yet, horrifyingly, stamped with a common identity, an absolute unity of purpose.

Andy. "Yes. But much depends on this. We must risk losses. Follow me down."

He could trace their passage down by the movement of the light, but they were still hidden from him by the angle of the passage. If they came straight for the door . . . But he could hear them moving about near the foot of the stairs: they were searching the rooms there first. Although his nerves were screaming out for action, he managed to hold himself immobile. It had to be left till the last possible moment. He saw the light brighten as it came his way. Only then did he light the match and, bending down, put it to the oily trail.

It began to gutter out, without catching, and he dropped it and fumbled hastily for another.

Deeping's voice. "What was that?"

Now it caught, burning up and flaring toward the drum. Flames suddenly leapt high, so quickly that he was afraid the explosion would come while he stood there. He ran for the door, as a babble of voices was raised behind him, slammed it and turned the key on the outside. There was no sign of George. He raced for the steps that led up onto the veranda. He had reached the top and was running toward the French windows and the salon when the house seemed to explode beneath him.

To his right, a great surge of flame crackled against the side of the house. He called to George, and heard him answer from inside. "You can clear off now! All under control."

A shot was fired, deafeningly, as he reached the hall, and he saw George standing at the top of the stairs, the gun pointed down.

Selby shouted, "Close the door on them! We can't waste time."

The dresser, still on its side, had been pushed away to the right of the doorway. Selby began heaving on it as George slammed the door closed. He could not shift it. Then George threw his weight against it and, with a protesting screech of wood against wood, it began to move. While they were still forcing it across, the door strained against the flimsy catch. But the catch held, and a moment later the dresser was in place, locked against it. They relaxed, panting.

The top panel of the door heaved again under pressure, but the bottom half was anchored by the dresser. In the distance Selby could hear the crackle of flames, and smoke was beginning to drift across the hall from the salon. Curls of smoke, also, came through the edges of the door. The top bulged again, and the smoke was clearer.

Now the voices began.

Diana. "Selby! Let me out, Selby. Please, please!"

Ruth, Marie in her broken English, farther off children's voices, pleading, begging for help. And Elizabeth. Selby turned away, in nausea and pain.

"We'd better get out now," he said.

They could see, as they passed the open door, that the other side of the salon was already a furnace. Smoke, pouring into the hall, caught at their throats, choking. By the time George had opened the front doors, Selby was finding some difficulty in breathing. They went out, and the night air pierced the lungs with its sharpness and coldness.

Selby had remembered to get their coats and boots from the hall while George was opening the doors. He handed George's to him, and they put their coats on. Neither would risk yet the temporary defenselessness that putting the boots on would involve. They stood only a few yards from the door of the house and watched the flames, leaping first behind the bar window, billowing across the hall, rising at last, like a ghastly coronet, over the roof of the house.

George said, "I shouldn't have bothered with that shot. You were quite right. The answer was to slam the door on them."

"It doesn't matter."

George shook his head. "It might have done."

Now the flames were everywhere in front of them, and the

air roaring with their unappeasable fury. Heat beat out at them, and they moved back.

"I saw one of them coming up the stairs," George said. He stared at the fountain of fire. "It was Mandy."

17

The cold hemmed them in, an exhalation from the darkness of the night, from the crisp, cruel snow underfoot. Its crust broke beneath their feet, so that each step forward was an effort, eventually an agony. They went on for a very long time, not talking so as to conserve energy, side by side but a foot or two apart. The moon still hung behind the high bars of cloud, throwing barely enough light for them to see their way. The shoulder of the mountain, toward which they were heading, was visible only as a darker sector of the sky.

She said at last, "I've got to rest. For a while, at least."

"No. You must keep moving. You must."

Selby or George would have been peremptory, but even in her coldness and tiredness she was aware of something else in his voice. A concern, a pleading. It touched her as brusqueness, at this stage, could not have done. She forced her body forward. There was no knowing what had become, or might become, of George and Selby. All that was certain was that two of them remained, that neither must desert the other.

He began to talk to her, his voice at times laboring on his breath. He was doing this, she realized, to help to keep her going. He talked chiefly about his family: he had two married sisters, a brother who was a Regular Army officer, at present stationed in Germany. He made them sound like nice people, and he spoke of them as though she would meet them one day. Her mind touched on the implications of that, but quickly returned to its main preoccupation with fatigue, coldness.

She said, "I can't . . . I must rest."

She stood still, shivering, feeling her body swaying toward the ground. He came to her, and caught hold of her. His arms were around her and she relaxed against him. She thought bemusedly that he was stronger than she would have guessed, to be able to support her like this. And his warmth was a comfort. How long a time it was since she had been aware, as she was now, of the goodness of the human body.

After a time, she summoned her will power and said she could go on. They went on as before, but the shoulder of the mountain was much nearer, blotting out a wider arc of sky, looming over them on their left. They were forced farther downhill and came to the point where the ground, on their other side, dropped sharply away. Soon after, they reached the heap of snow and rubble that marked the avalanche, and could go no farther.

She leaned against a wall of snow, and he put his arms around her as he had done before. She opened the old raincoat George had given her and pulled him inside, closer to her. Is it desolation, she wondered, that makes people into lovers: the pressure of coldness and fear and loneliness? But there was more to it than that. An understanding, at least, an admission. She had been afraid, and lonely, and cold of heart, and had not known it. And a reaching out. They rested against each other, and comforted each other.

He got her to walk about, and then they rested, embracing, and stood up and walked again. Time passed in this alternation; slowly, but it passed. They were resting when he said, "What's that?"

"What?"

"Look."

She turned, and saw the glow in the sky. The side of the mountain prevented their seeing exactly what it was, but there was a redness up there, a brightness against which the line of rock stood out.

"The house," she said.

Not needing to discuss it, they retraced their steps. The glow grew stronger, and at last they could see it plainly, see the distant blazing pyre which still had the outlines of the chalet. She thought of Diana, and was glad of her earlier grief. She could feel no sorrow now.

They walked, and rested, and walked, while the slow hours of night went past. The flaming beacon on the hillside subsided into embers that, at last, went out. There was only shadowy moonlight again, a dim dark world in which, utterly weary and bitterly cold, they were aware of themselves and of each other. Nothing else. The voice that called them across the chill wastes was at first unreal, a cry in a dream. But it persisted, and grew stronger.

"Jane! Douglas! Where are you?"

George's voice. It was Douglas who answered. He called, "We're here. Over here."

"Right. I think I've got a bearing. But keep on shouting."

Douglas was calling, "Here . . . this way . . ." She caught his arm.

"Are you sure . . . ?"

"It's George," he said.

His breath warmed her cheek. "Is it?" she said. "Is it?"

He stared at her. She could see his face more clearly. Dawn was sifting into the sky behind them. He said, "My God. I'm not sure. Shall we try to get away?"

"You can. I'm too tired."

He took her in his arms. "Then there's no point."

The figures came toward them across the snow, and she recognized Selby beside George. Just the two of them. It was all right, then. Unless this was another trap, to get them to show themselves, to keep them from hiding. But she no longer cared, except for Douglas. She thought confusedly that if she went toward them and they attacked her, he might be able to get away. She stumbled forward, trying to run, but he came after her. And the figure that might be Selby, only a few yards away, had stopped and was doing something. She stopped herself, and felt Douglas catch hold of her.

Selby stripped off his heavy coat, and came to her with it.

"Here," he said. "You'd better have a turn with this."

She began to laugh and cry in relief. "You're not . . ."

"What?" He took her meaning. "Possessed? You thought they might have got us, too? No. You saw the fire?"

Douglas said, "Yes, we saw it. But we couldn't be sure."

George had taken his coat off, and was putting it on Douglas. He said, "I won't offer my boots, unless one of you happens to take size twelve."

"Is it really all finished?" Douglas asked. "All?"

Selby said, "Yes." He hesitated. "We thought we'd better come for you now, before help arrived. It might be difficult explaining why you two had pushed off on a night like this."

"Explaining?" Douglas said. "You mean . . ."

George said, "We've been working this one out. We four were playing dice after the others had gone to bed. In the dining room. The fire started at the other end of the house—a cigarette end in the bar, perhaps—and had reached the stairs before we could do anything."

Jane said, "You don't think they would believe the truth?"

"Do you?"

She shook her head. "I suppose not."

"A holiday tragedy," Selby said. His voice was dry, spent. "We believe what we are conditioned to believe. And now I think we'd better be getting back. Those who survive don't generally stray far from the ashes."

They were waiting just below the ruins of the house when they heard the sound of the helicopter's engine. The sun had not yet risen here, but the sky was very bright in the east. Noise was magnified suddenly as the helicopter rose up over the spur. They waved their arms, and saw it dip toward them.

Lightning Source UK Ltd.
Milton Keynes UK
UKOW04f1951241114

242094UK00001BA/274/P